Also by Stella Barcelona

DECEIVED
SHADOWS
JIGSAW
CONCIERGE

"*Deceived* brings history to life in a suspenseful, contemporary tale that sends the protagonists on a research trip to a past close to their hearts. Barcelona's debut book brings an excellent author to the fore; the intrigue blends beautifully with the romance." –Heather Graham, New York Times Bestselling Author

"A weaver of words, Ms. Barcelona creates a story that draws you in from page one, keeps you on the edge of your seat, and leaves you wanting more." –InD'Tale Magazine, review of *Deceived*

Shadows is "a smart techno-thriller with a steamy and surprisingly touching love story between two characters who are both torn between duty and desire...a tangled, dangerous and well-plotted escapade." – RT Book Reviews

"Terrifyingly possible, *Shadows* is romantic suspense on steroids – Long and Short Reviews, Review Blog

"An emotional roller coaster of a novel that leaves you breathless. Intelligently written, the plot is both edgy and intense." –RT Book Reviews, review of *Jigsaw*

"A thrilling world of intrigue, terrorism, love, and hate, where her characters come to life in the pages of her book. ... Ms. Barcelona is a master storyteller and readers will be coming back again and again." – InD'Tale Magazine, review of *Jigsaw*

"Exceptional . . . It's a slow burn, it's a multi-layer story, it's a multi-plot story, it's a total and utter plot twist that I really did not see coming." –The Archaeolibrarian, Review Blog, review of *Concierge*

"A well-written, spellbinding book! A++" –Between My Bookendz, Amazon Review of *Concierge*

Shadows, RONE Awards Winner – "Best Suspense Thriller Novel 2016" –InD'Tale Magazine

IMAGINE

Stella Barcelona

Taylor -
Happy reading -
Stella Barcelona

To my mother, Melva Barcelona.

Thank you for encouraging me to read.

Chapter One

Thursday, November 1
New Orleans, Louisiana

Even at 2 a.m., Frenchmen Street remained crowded with Halloween revelers. As she and Ace stepped out of a nightclub, leaving between a band's sets, Leo noticed a red and yellow pedicab a block away. The driver sat on the bicycle seat, his forearms draped over the bike's handles, his gaze scanning left to right.

Pointing, Leo said, "Hey. Look. Pedicab. Should we grab it?"

"Sounds good to me," Ace said, moving closer to the curb to make room for a group of faux vampires.

Leo lifted her arm and waved at the driver. Ace did the same, as a jazz combo's tune drifted from a bar across the street. When the pedicab driver pulled up to the sidewalk, his gaze lingered on her. "Nice. *The Matrix*. A classic. You're Trinity, right?"

"Absolutely. Ace, this man gets a big tip!" Leo had been excited when she'd found the skin-tight, black jumpsuit with leather accents–the same kind worn by the female heroine of *The Matrix*, a computer programmer and hacker with kick-ass fighting skills. Going all out, she had cut her brown hair and tinted it black. Dark sunglasses and high-heeled boots completed the outfit. The costume had turned out great, but for the boots. Her feet were killing her, and she should've known better. No serious badass would go into the world expecting battles while wearing five-inch stilettos.

Facing the driver, Leo pointed to Ace, at her side. With a smile and a headshake, she said, "Let me introduce you to a lame version of Neo. Or, the person who used to be Neo. He took off his sunglasses hours ago."

"Couldn't see the band," Ace said. "I told you that."

Despite his lack of enthusiasm for the sunglasses, or her theme for their costumes somewhat imitating their lives, Ace's transformation to Neo had been easy. A close-fitting sport coat on top of a dress shirt, slacks, and wrap-around sunglasses—all black—had transformed him into the character played by Keanu Reeves in the movie trilogy. At six feet one, with broad shoulders and lean muscles, Ace was a natural as Neo. A natural, but only when the sunglasses hid his eyes, which most definitely weren't Reeves' chocolate brown. Ace's were cobalt blue, with a darker rim.

Their costumes would have been better with leather trench coats, but the sticky warmth of the seventy-three-degree night made coats a bad idea. Visible Glocks would have been a great addition as well, but using weapons for costume props was against the rules of their employer, Black Raven Private Security Contractors. Agents Sylvia Leon, known to friends as Leo, and Adam Evans, known to friends as Ace, were off duty and visiting New Orleans for two nights. The security company's rules provided that off-duty agents were to keep weapons, if carried, concealed.

The driver returned his gaze to Ace, cocked his head, and studied him. "I've met Keanu Reeves. He was here filming. Nice guy. Your height's right. Body type works—"

"Glad you think so."

Missing Ace's sarcasm, the driver continued. "Cheekbones work. You've got his serious look going. He rocked that in *John Wick*. But your hair's too light. It threw me."

"Would you dye your hair for a Halloween costume?" Ace asked.

"To be Neo next to her as Trinity?" The driver flashed a smile, as Leo eyed him with fresh interest. Big brown eyes. Dark brown, wavy hair. He looked like he was in his twenties, which made him somewhere around her age. His Tulane Law School t-shirt and exercise shorts revealed plenty of muscles to power a pedicab. "I'd have done anything."

"Awwww. So nice!"

"Don't let her appearance fool you," Ace said. "She's not nearly as hot as she looks."

Leo jabbed an elbow into Ace's ribs, fast and with enough force to be felt. "You have no idea."

The sideways look that Ace gave her held an amused gleam. He arched an eyebrow. "So defensive. Why?"

Ignoring Ace, she gave the pedicab driver one hundred percent of her attention. "I'll return to New Orleans for Halloween next year. You and I have a date."

Poised on the bicycle seat with his arms resting over the handlebars, the driver's grin faded slightly. He did a slight nod in Ace's direction. "Wouldn't want to piss off your boyfriend."

"He's not my boyfriend." The correction came automatically. "We're just friends."

"And sometimes barely that," Ace said.

Leo lifted her arm for another elbow jab into Ace's ribs. He grabbed her wrist and pulled it down before she could connect. She turned to face him as he let go of her arm. Her high-heels put them almost at eye level.

The pedicab driver was correct—Ace was a master of the sort of deadpan-but-simmering expression that Keanu Reeves had perfected in film. He was doing it now. Not smiling. Not frowning. Just staring at her, thinking. About what, she had no clue. Over the course of their friendship, she'd learned that there were times that he was an easy read, and times that he wasn't.

They'd met two years earlier, on Ace's first day with Black Raven. They'd become instant friends. Over time, that friendship had grown, but they'd never crossed the line that separated friends from something more. For a few reasons. Being more than friends was against explicit rules that governed agent-to-agent interaction.

More importantly, neither had been inclined. Yet there were times when she allowed her mind to wander, when she thought about him in ways that had nothing to do with being friends.

Like now.

They stood so close, their chests were almost touching. He smelled fresh. Reminiscent of the ocean? Perhaps. Definitely outdoors. Pine. '*Not cologne,*' he'd told her once, with a low chuckle. '*Just soap.*'

The pedicab driver cleared his throat. She glanced the driver's way. His gaze was bouncing from her to Ace. "Where to? Late night, holiday rate's a buck fifty a minute. From here, I'll go as far west as

Julia Street. North to Claiborne Avenue. To most places in the Bywater. Anything else, you're on your own."

"Jasmine's. On Rampart Street," Leo answered.

"Waldorf Astoria," Ace said, at the same time.

She faced Ace again. Notes from a saxophone spilled from open doors, indicating that break time had ended for the band in the club they'd just left. "Are you really ready to go back to the hotel?"

"You're not tired?" he asked.

"Not at all, and it's my trip, my way, on your dollar. That was our bet, Patriots-fan."

"No need for the thousandth reminder."

A little more than thirty-six hours earlier, he'd flown into New Orleans from Atlanta. He'd been at Last Resort, Black Raven's training facility. She'd flown into New Orleans from Denver, where she'd been working at corporate headquarters with Black Raven's cyber-division, on the endless projects that kept the security company running with state-of-the-art efficiency.

Two nights in New Orleans for Halloween, at his expense, was Ace's debt for losing a bet they'd made on the Super Bowl in February. He'd picked the Patriots. She'd chosen the Eagles. Since they'd arrived in New Orleans, a day and a half earlier, she'd rubbed his losing pick in his face each time it was time to pay for anything.

In a fast, unexpected move, he reached out and took off her sunglasses. "Hey—"

"There. Better. Tired of wondering what you're thinking." As he slipped her glasses into the pocket of his sport coat, he glanced into her eyes. "Has this trip to New Orleans been everything you wanted it to be?"

Swift, sudden emotion yanked at her heart. Ace knew more about her than just about anyone, so he knew that New Orleans had been her father's favorite city. Knew that, as a young girl, she'd visited the city with her dad multiple times. And Ace had remembered that she'd been longing to return to New Orleans, but hadn't been able to make herself do it, because her sentimental feelings for the city were tied up with her feelings for her father. Aside from a hurried, touch-and-go helicopter landing on the levee of the Mississippi River for Black Raven's Hutchenson job, she hadn't returned since her father's death. Not that she and Ace had ever dwelt for long on her feelings for her father or his tragic death. She didn't do emotional subjects well, if at all.

She swallowed, pushing through the sadness. "It's been great."

He used his index finger to push her hair off her forehead, away from her eyes. Taming her thick, wavy hair into Trinity's sleek hairstyle hadn't worked so well, even with hairspray and gel. He smoothed the hair down, with tenderness. That was a new thing. She wondered if he was even conscious of it. They'd both drank a bit of alcohol. Maybe he was feeling the effects.

Alcohol or not, the resulting tingling caused by his lingering touch reminded her that she needed to work a little harder on the 'just friends' angle.

"It's okay to feel something," he said.

"You know my theory about feelings."

He gave her a half smile. "Yep. Sure do."

They just get in the damn way.

Thankfully, the band in the jazz club that they'd just left shifted from their slower warm up to a rousing rendition of "When the Saints Go Marching In," distracting her from his question and the unusual lingering tenderness of his touch. There was no way she could be anything but happy while hearing that song. "Guess I'm just not ready for the night to end."

He gave her a nod. A slight shrug. "Then we'll head to Jasmine's."

"We don't have to. Do you really want to go back to the hotel?"

"Hey," the driver said, with a snap of his fingers. "Trinity. Neo. Another guy's hailing me across the street. Should I move on, or are you two going to make up your minds?"

Ace glanced at the driver. "Put us on the meter as of ten minutes ago, while we figure this out."

The driver glanced at his watch. "Fine by me."

Ace placed his hand on her elbow, guiding her towards the pedicab's bench seat. "You decide. I'm good for whatever."

"It's just that it's still early," she said.

"That's the tequila talking."

"Nope. It's all me, and you had some too, you know."

"Don't remind me. I should've never let you talk me into that."

She stepped off the sidewalk and into the pedicab. As pedicabs went, this one was large. A red vinyl bench seat provided plenty of cushion. Leo sat down, sighing as her feet started throbbing in earnest. They'd been out for hours. They'd walked from bar to bar. They'd stood. She'd danced. She'd had a couple of margaritas. When she got tired of the sugar in the frozen drink, she'd switched to plain tequila. She'd only had a few shots of it though, and she'd had plenty more water. She felt perfectly sober. At least sober enough to feel sharp jabs of pain travelling from her toes, along her arches, and all the way to her calves. "Hell, hell, hell!"

"What?" The cab creaked as Ace got in, stretching his legs as much as he could. Lifting his right arm, he extended it on the seat behind her. There was almost enough leg room for Ace to look comfortable. An overhead canopy gave a feeling of coziness.

"Stupid boots. My feet are killing me. You win. Hotel."

To the driver's back, Ace directed, "Waldorf Astoria."

The driver stood on his pedals and eased the pedicab into forward motion. Over his shoulder, he said, "By the way, it's called The Roosevelt."

Leo laughed as she unzipped her boots. "I've told him that about eighty times. He's just trying to get a rise out of me, and I'm not biting."

She winced, trying to rub sharp pain out of her arches. When she looked up again, they were on Esplanade Avenue. With the Frenchmen Street music clubs behind them, the night grew quieter. Gas lanterns flickered in the doorways of the historic mansions, homes, and condos that lined either side of the street, while most of the interior lights were off. Traffic was light. A couple on the sidewalk lingered in the glow of a streetlight, facing each other. The pedicab glided smoothly through a blanket of fog at street level. Misty swirls lifted into the oaks that lined the median, rising to meet the twisted, gnarled tree limbs.

Leo glanced at Ace. “Beautiful, right?”

“Yeah.” But he wasn’t looking at their surroundings. He was looking at her. Deep in her brain warning signals started clanging, but the noise was easy to ignore because there was something serious in his eyes. Something intense. Something that caught her attention more than the view, making her wonder whether he too felt the pull of attraction between them.

That thing that she couldn’t name compelled her to lean in closer. “Thank you. Best Halloween ever.”

Because he was taller, she was looking up at him. He lifted his hand, cupping her cheek for a second before tracing his index finger along her jawline. He hesitated, as though he was making sure she wanted what he wanted, then shifted in the seat and leaned in closer. She could have pulled away, but she couldn’t resist.

Instead of breaking the moment with a snarky quip or by turning her head, she gave herself permission to ignore all the reasons why they shouldn’t kiss, deciding for the next few minutes to be free. To be, for once in her life, someone who believed in wishes, dreams, and happy endings. Someone who went with desire’s whim.

She raised her face to his. The tips of their noses touched first. He pressed his forehead against hers, caressing her with his gaze until their lips met in the sort of lingering touch that was never intended for the friend zone. The velvety feel of his lips, both hard and soft at the same time, jolted her, bringing her entire being alive with the realization that he was the only person she’d ever want. If she ever allowed herself to want.

As he wrapped his arms around her and held her close, she closed her arms around his neck. By the time the pedicab turned from Esplanade Avenue into the French Quarter, they had shifted into an open-mouthed kiss borne of a sudden lust that was so deep, there was no hope of satisfying it. She lost all sense of place, time, and caring about the fact that friends didn't kiss like this.

Breathing heavily, he pulled away slightly. He cradled the back of her head with one of his hands, and lifted his other hand to her cheek, rubbing his thumb along her cheekbone as he looked into her eyes.

Though there were times when he was impossible to read, this wasn't one of them. The gentle touch of his thumb along her cheek, the tender, yet intent look in his eyes, told her that she was something he'd been coveting, that nothing he was doing was accidental. Then he bent his forehead to hers again, with his lips meeting hers. She nibbled on his lower lip, hearing herself sigh as they pulled each other even closer.

As the intensity of their kiss ramped up again, becoming a connection that was more than a joining of lips and tongues, he grabbed her hips and lifted her onto his lap. Time passed, and she shifted, turning so that their bodies melded, because kissing suddenly wasn't enough. With her legs straddling him, she ran her hands along his back, grabbing fistfuls of his jacket and shirt. Deepening their kiss, holding her tight, he moved forward in the seat, using both hands on her hips to press her into him. She folded her legs at her ankles, with the heels of her feet at his lower back. His low groan met her sigh, and still, their kiss continued as though neither had any intention of ever ending it. Where their hips were joined, she felt the hard length of him. *Yes*. That's what she wanted, and if she pressed harder, and moved her hips, just the right way...

"Hey. Trinity. Neo. We're here." The pedicab driver's voice sounded like it was coming from a mile away, but it had the repercussive effect of an earthquake.

Reality crashed around her, carrying the first faint pulse of regret. She unwrapped her arms from Ace's neck, glancing at the hotel's top-hatted bellman, who stood at the red-carpeted entrance.

Using both hands on Ace's shoulders to push herself off of him, she lifted her hips off his lap. As she slid onto the seat, and away from him, she faced forward and tried not to think about his erection and the fact that she'd been grinding herself onto it. As heat from an unwelcomed blush burned her cheeks, neck, and chest, the tingling at her core told her that if they'd gone at it for just another few seconds...she'd have had an orgasm in the middle of the street, for the world to see.

Holy shit!

Her mind exploded with chaotic aftershock. There was only one reason for what had happened.

I lost my freaking mind. And so did he.

As each breath carried her further into reality, the driver met her gaze. He gave her a look that seemed slightly disappointed. "For the record, I didn't fall for that line about you two just being friends."

The driver's words jolted her. *Friends*. That was all they were. Right? She glanced at Ace, who was leaning forward slightly, gripping the bench seat with both hands, as though stunned. His shirt was untucked. Yeah, she'd done that, pulling herself closer to him. His hair was mussed. She'd done that, too. When he looked at her, she saw that his eyes remained a portal to everything that had inspired their kiss. Desire. Hunger. Lust.

For a brief second, she was torn. If she was reading him correctly, he wanted more. Yes, she did, too. If they went there, though, they'd never get back to where they belonged. With words intended as much for herself as for him, she said, "Snap out of it."

He sat straighter and squared his shoulders. "Yeah. Right." He paused, as though reflecting on their kiss, then added, "Wow. Huh?"

While her body waged a war with reason, the driver's voice grounded her. "Fare is thirty-seven fifty."

As a little more of their reality crept into her mind, she watched Ace give a curt nod. Ace said, "Got it," for the benefit of the driver, yet he didn't break eye contact with her.

"What were we thinking?" she asked.

He straightened his jacket and ran his hands through his hair. With a shrug, he said, "Should seem obvious. We wanted to kiss."

"Seriously?" She punched his arm. "Is that all you have to say?"

"Give me some time." With a serious look in his eyes, his gaze searched hers. "I'll come up with more."

That he seemed so comfortable with what had happened jolted her into realizing she was going to have to be the one to use logic, reasoning, and willpower. She grabbed her boots and exited on the sidewalk side, as Ace stepped out of the pedicab on the street side. She stepped onto the hotel's red carpet in bare feet. By the time she made it up the stairs, through the revolving doorway, and five steps into the lobby, Ace had paid the driver and was at her side, walking in stride next to her.

"Wait," he said.

"Not a chance."

"Where are you going so fast?"

"Should seem obvious." She let sarcasm flood her comments, as she used his words. "My room. Alone. You're going to yours. Or wherever you want to go for a reality check, which we both really need."

"But we should—"

"Shake off whatever just happened. That's what we should do."

Because it wasn't just a kiss. It was way more than that. And I know you know that.

"At least look at me." He faced her as she pressed the elevator button five times. She glanced his way. A smirk of a smile played at his lips. "That was a great kiss. Might be the best ever. Don't act like it's the end of the world."

Come on, elevator. Hurry up.

Finding it hard to look at him, she looked away. Yet the shiny bronze doors were as good as a mirror. She met his gaze. "Friends don't kiss like that. As co-workers we can't. It's against the rules—"

His smirk became a full-fledged grin. "Yeah. At Black Raven, in case you haven't noticed, that sort of rule gets broken sometimes."

"Not by me. When co-agents break rules, especially elite agents like us who are subject to being placed on the same high-risk jobs, it gets complicated, and there are consequences," she turned from him and faced the elevator doors again. His smile faded as he stared at her reflection. “Ones I don’t feel like dealing with, and I suspect that you don’t either. Not now. Not ever.”

The elevator dinged.

Thank you, God.

As the doors opened, she said, “My elevator. Get your own.”

“Are you serious?”

“Deadly.” Stepping into the elevator, she turned to face him, relieved when he didn’t cross the threshold. “We’re not doing that again. As a matter of fact, I’m going to pretend that it never happened. If you value our friendship, you will too.”

Chapter Two

Saturday, December 1
Port of Macau, Ling Wen Enterprises Shipyard

A burst of chilly wind rushed over the port's gray, choppy water. He buttoned his all-weather coat. Ceremonial flags that had been raised for the ship's christening snapped with the breeze. Dark clouds, steadily building, hinted at the hell that he'd planned for the cruise ship's maiden voyage. As carefully as the ship had been constructed, he'd designed a plan to profit from destroying her.

A crane lifted a harnessed, oversized bottle of champagne off the dock, towards the ship. Every inch of the four-hundred-and-forty-foot luxury cruise ship, from state-of-the-art air filtration systems to the casino's Baccarat crystal chandeliers, had been designed to provide an unforgettable experience while guests played high-stakes games of chance. Freshly unveiled for public viewing, the vessel's graceful curves and lines paid homage to fine maritime design and craftsmanship.

Inhaling the salty tang of ocean air, he accepted a flute of champagne from a tuxedo-clad waiter as his gaze scanned the crowd. Shipyard workers were beaming with pride at their creation. Executives of Imagine Casinos Worldwide, smug that they'd produced what would be hailed as the crown jewel of gambling-themed, luxury cruise liners, were answering questions from the press. Casino guests from the land-based Imagine Casino of Macau, several of whom would be aboard for the ship's first cruise, smiled with excitement at having an exclusive preview. No one seemed bothered by the gloom of the ship's christening day, and they damn well didn't know of his plans.

With a slow arc, the crane operator swung the giant bottle into position. Lingering cries of hovering seagulls resonated, as the din of conversations among the hundred or so onlookers quieted into whispers. According to maritime lore, if luck would run in the ship's favor, the bottle of champagne, made of thick, gold-colored glass, would shatter against the ship on the first attempt.

From behind him, someone asked, "Is that a bottle of Armand de Brignac?"

"Looks to be the same thing the waiters are serving," the man on his left answered, in Mandarin. "Brut Gold, Ace of Spades."

"That bottle is huge. Nebuchadnezzar-sized?"

"Got to be. Can't believe Theodore Baru is smashing that against a ship."

"Only the best for Baru. Five thousand Hong Kong Dollars says the bottle doesn't break on the first hit," the man on his left said in English. "Any takers?"

He was tempted, but didn't bite. He had a lot more than five thousand dollars riding on the ship's future, and he'd left none of it to chance. He'd conceived of the plan and, due to the scope, hired one of the best criminal masterminds. A key player in the underworld of Chinese triads, his second-in-command was known as an executioner, a man who could not only execute complex transactions seamlessly, but also had no problem executing people as needed.

"I'll take the bet," a woman on his right said. "Want to raise it to ten thousand?"

"You're on."

Once the oversized champagne bottle was high above the bow, the crane operator paused. A Christian minister and a Buddhist monk rose to their feet on a podium that had been assembled for the occasion. The monk stepped to the microphone first. Onlookers bowed their heads, while the monk said a prayer in Mandarin.

Instead of praying, he kept his attention on the champagne bottle, now high above the ship's glistening bow. Nestled in a harness with three chains that were affixed to the crane, the bottle gently swayed until it became still. When the monk was through, the minister moved forward and lifted his arms to the sky. In English, the minister prayed, "Almighty God, benevolent Lord of all the oceans and waterways..."

He tuned out the prayer, confident his plan wouldn't be thwarted by God-like intervention. Like the prayers, the champagne was an offering intended to assure safe passage for the vessel and all who travelled aboard her. Which wasn't going to happen. No matter what religions they practiced. Or whether the bottle broke on the first drop.

"...and may God bless this ship, which we christen today, with the name Imagine."

When the minister lowered his arms, the crane operator released the two chains that held the harness. The final chain, a safeguard in case the bottle didn't shatter, remained affixed to the neck. It freely spooled out as the bottle careened downward, smashed against the ship's bow, and shattered with a loud pop. Shards of glass flew as fifteen liters of fine champagne foamed and sprayed into the air, over the bow's glistening handrails, and onto the anchor.

Amidst a round of applause, he bit back a twinge of disappointment and reminded himself that he wasn't superstitious. Since a young age, he'd worked hard at designing his reality, which he and his hired gun were doing by planning details with precision—from takeover of the ship, to roundup of passengers, money transfers, destruction of all evidence, and escape.

As a chorus of toasts erupted, the crowd lifted their glasses of champagne. "To Imagine."

"Imagine."

"May she sail fast and safe."

He turned to the woman on his right, who was now ten thousand dollars richer because the bottle had broken on the first drop. They clinked glasses. She smiled, and said, "Imagine."

He nodded. Yes, he'd imagined it. He'd not only imagined it, he'd planned it. As he sipped the cold, bubbly liquid, he smiled, confident in his plans. Oddly, he felt no remorse over the mass murder that would take place in twenty-two days, when his wild, twisted dreams would become a reality. Imagine's inaugural voyage would end with the ship resting on the ocean floor. He'd be wealthy beyond his wildest dreams. Best, no one would ever know that he was the mastermind behind the worst naval disaster in modern times.

Chapter Three

Tuesday, December 18

Denver, Colorado

Due to flight delays out of Saudi Arabia, Ace arrived at Black Raven's corporate headquarters a few minutes late for a job briefing that was supposed to start at two o'clock. After handing his duffel bag to the agent who manned the front desk in the expansive lobby, he jogged up the stairs to the third floor and entered the briefing room where Zeus Hernandez, a partner in the company, stood at a podium.

Against the right wall, a petite woman sat at a table that faced the audience and the podium. Her attention was focused on her laptop screen. Ragno was the head of Black Raven's cyber and intelligence division, and legendary for having her fingers firmly on the pulse of the company's most complex jobs. Her multi-tasking skills were famous, and Ace had no doubt that she was working on multiple projects while waiting for the presentation to begin. Her presence underscored the importance of thc job that was the subject of the briefing.

Behind Zeus, a white projection wall had the flickering, pinpoint light of a remote-controlled cursor. Zeus, who had dark hair, dark eyes, and was taller than most, looked up from his iPad. He gave Ace a barely perceptible nod.

As the heavy door clicked shut behind Ace, conversations ebbed. Twenty-five or so agents were seated in leather chairs at four rows of crescent-shaped tables that faced the front of the room. Ace recognized field agents and cyber-support agents, who often worked in tandem with each other. The interactive nature of their work ensured that field agents had access to data of all sorts, as needed. Several gave him a nod. From the far end of the first row, Leo shot him an over-the-shoulder glance. Their eyes locked.

Her slight smile was casual, yet his heartbeat accelerated. The quickening was slight and subtle, but unmistakable. He'd last seen her in person as their Halloween night came to a screeching halt with the aftershock from their kiss. Now, even from across the room, she looked better than she had in Ace's memory. Her hair, chin-length and choppy, had returned to its normal chestnut color from the raven-black she'd used for her costume. The lighter color made the gold in her hazel eyes more apparent.

"Now that Evans has arrived," Zeus said, as Ace settled into the nearest available chair in the back row, "we'll get started."

The lights in the room dimmed slightly for the presentation, while on the front wall, between Zeus and Ragno, an image of a cruise ship appeared. The vessel had bold, elegant lines, with six decks above the water line. The image shifted, and a video started, presenting a 3-D tour that began with a close-up of an enormous, gold-colored bottle of champagne exploding as it smashed against the ship's bow.

"Cool," someone said.

"Waste of good bubbly," someone replied, as the video shifted to an expansive casino, with glittering chandeliers and a sea of gaming tables.

"Is that the job site?" another asked, a hopeful tone in his voice as the image shifted to the interior of the ship, focusing on a theater where plush chairs faced a stage with Christmas trees. A subtitle identified the room as the Calliope Theater.

"Hope my room has a balcony," came another voice.

"You'll be in steerage," Leo said, joining in the chatter.

As he watched the video, Ace wondered what Leo's role would be on the job. Leo, a rarity among the agents, had cyber skills that rivaled the best programmers and analysts in the cyber division, but she also had field skills that qualified her for the most elite teams, on the highest risk jobs. Sometimes she worked from Denver, while on other jobs she worked in the field.

"You will have two days of prep work here," Zeus said, as the video tour of the ship stopped in the boat's expansive engine room. "Then a twelve-agent field team will depart for Macau."

"Where's that?" Wade Kamin, sitting in the first row next to Leo, asked the question that Ace knew was designed to get a rise out of Zeus.

A few agents chuckled. Someone tossed a balled-up piece of paper at Kamin. He caught it as it bounced off his head and tossed it back.

"Nebraska," Zeus answered, without cracking a smile.

"Lame one, Kamin," someone else called.

"Aw, come on. That was funny," Kamin said. "Sort of."

"The field team will be undercover on a three-day gambling cruise, on the inaugural voyage for this ship, which was christened on the first of December." Zeus gestured with a slight flick of his head to the wall, where the scroll of print at the bottom of the image indicated they were looking at The Compass Rose Bar, an upper deck lounge with low seating areas and large windows that overlooked the ship's expansive stern. "Ship's name is *Imagine*."

"Wait. Are you saying that this cruise ship operates out of Nebraska?" Agent Dean Marks asked. The young field agent, whose comment brought a solid round of laughter and chuckles, sat on Ace's left.

Marks sounded so honestly confused, all heads in the room turned towards him, then ricocheted back to Zeus. Evan Ragno glanced up from her computer, then focused on Zeus to see his reaction.

Someone asked, an incredulous tone in his voice, "Is the kid serious?"

As Ace studied Zeus for any sign of humor, he chuckled. There was a slight softening at Zeus' lips as he focused on Marks, but then his habitual neutral face, closer to a scowl than a smile, returned.

Too bad.

A smile from Zeus in response to his joke would have earned Marks five hundred dollars from the other field agents in the room. Getting Zeus to actually laugh during a briefing would have earned any agent a thousand dollars.

The longstanding smile wager amongst field agents had been won a few times. The laugh wager, never. When it became obvious that Zeus wasn't going to crack a smile, all laughter in the room faded.

"In four days, on the twenty second, the ship will depart out of Macau, which is an administrative region of China, near Hong Kong," Zeus continued. "Let me be clear. This job is on a ship that will be flying the flag of the People's Republic of China, and it will be travelling in the South China Sea. For those of you who are geopolitically challenged, that means we'll be operating within the jurisdiction of a Communist regime."

Zeus' glance from agent to agent underscored the seriousness of his words. "We are undertaking this job at the request of a longstanding client. At this time, Black Raven does not have a license to operate in China. My partners and I are willing to assume the risks presented by a job that is not sanctioned by the Chinese government because this is a very lucrative job for a powerful client. More about the client and the job objective later. Stills?"

Paul Stills, on Ace's right, straightened in his chair. "Yes, sir."

"You're first in command of the field agents."

"Evans?"

"Yes, sir," Ace said.

"You're second."

Zeus held Ace's gaze for a second. When interviewing Ace, a little over two years earlier, the man had been blunt. '*Your final mission as a Marine, and the resulting fallout from it, is a drawback. Deserved or not, reputations have a way of coming back to bite, and clients who are paying Black Raven's fees have a way of hearing about them. So, it's going to be a while before you're first in command. You may have to swallow your pride for a few years. We're hiring you because you're better than good. The world is getting more violent. Criminals are getting more creative. Black Raven needs you. You will not only make a great agent, your accomplishments with the Marines tell me that you're partner quality. Not many agents are, by the way.'*

After two years of swallowing his pride, Ace was getting tired of it. He rolled his shoulders to shake off his frustration and gave Zeus a nod. Zeus' gaze drifted from Ace. "Kamin, you're third in command. Leo?"

"Yes, sir."

"You're in the field on this one. We're not expecting complications, but that doesn't mean a glitch or two won't arise. My team's preliminary troubleshooting suggests that communications could get tricky. If that happens, your expertise will be required on site."

From Ace's seat, he saw Leo in profile. She gave Zeus a casual nod, yet Ace knew her well enough to know she was thrilled. She loved fieldwork. Given his own aversion to working in an office, Ace didn't blame her.

That someone of Zeus' stature within the company called Leo by her nickname, and not her full last name, Leon, wasn't lost on Ace. Most agents went by their full last names for official business, but Leo wasn't like most agents. She'd been a teenage software designing prodigy. By the time she'd graduated from college, she had multiple software patents for designs that facilitated data assimilation and cross-network communications. She had caught Black Raven's attention at a time when the company was expending considerable effort to meet the technology-driven demands of its clients.

The company had courted her throughout her college years, and she'd accepted Black Raven's employment offer at the tender age of twenty-one with her own demands. One of which was the opportunity to do fieldwork, in addition to the technology systems work for which she was being hired. After rigorous field training, she'd earned universal respect in the Black Raven ranks when she'd stared down danger, at Zeus' side, on the Jigsaw job. The complexity of her fieldwork on the recent Hutchenson job, where the company had busted a human trafficking ring, had also elevated her stature.

"In the next few minutes, you will each receive a dossier with job fundamentals. It's a working document. Notes you make within will be dated, timed, and are visible to all team members. Marks?"

While Zeus continued with individual assignments, Ace pulled his laptop out of his backpack and logged into his work assignment folder. Keyboard clicks filled the room, as other agents did the same. The dossier wasn't there yet. In the upper right corner of Ace's screen, an instant messaging dialogue box appeared, with a message from Leo. He opened it.

"You look like hell."

He glanced her way. Her attention was focused forward, bouncing between the front of the room and on her laptop screen. Bright light from the screen framed her firm jawline. He replied, *"Nice to see you, too. You wouldn't look so great if you'd been flying commercial air for twenty-four hours. Due to delays, the last leg was coach, and crowded."*

She replied, *"From the looks of this job, we'll be working late. Hungry?"*

"Starving."

"How about Luigi's? If I throw that out to the team, I know they'll go for it. Maybe we'll even catch a glimpse of the game when we break. Want to bet? I'll take the Chargers by 7."

"Yep. I'll take that bet. Luigi's sounds great. You know what I want."

The idea of food from his favorite Italian restaurant in Denver and a glimpse of a football game, even while working, made his world almost perfect. Almost, save for the persistent feeling that he was missing something, which he could now trace back to their kiss.

By the time he'd awakened the day after Halloween, she'd been on a flight out of New Orleans. Her text had said that she'd been called to headquarters on an emergency job assignment. Given her reaction to their kiss, and her aversion to talking about personal things, he had assumed the emergency nature of her job assignment was a classic avoidance move on her part.

Since then, their assignments had taken them in different directions. She'd been at headquarters in Denver, working out kinks in software, most notably a facial recognition system that integrated databases from around the world. He'd been on security details jobs that had taken him from Spain, to England, and Saudi Arabia. Between England and Saudi Arabia, he'd taken time off at his home in La Jolla, California, hoping that a few days of surfing would help clear his head of the thoughts about Leo that their kiss had awakened.

Not a shot.

He wished he didn't feel anything odd when he looked at her, but...so much for that. Truth was, he'd looked forward to seeing her for more days than he cared to count. He also wished he was able to forget about their kiss. Especially because, as she'd requested, it had not been the subject of a conversation. Not that he hadn't tried, in a roundabout way. She'd shut him down, each time, so he had dropped it, each time.

He'd been around enough—and with her in particular—to know when a person needed space. Yet her silence on the issue, amidst the friendly banter of their usual emails, texts, video chats and telephone calls had, for some inexplicable reason, made him dwell on their kiss even more. He hoped the memory of it was as vivid in her mind as it was in his.

Damn well hope it's torturing her, like it's doing to me.

As the document appeared in Ace's work folder, Zeus continued, "And you should all have the dossier now. We had some final tweaking on our end. After you've opened it, follow the prompts to open a dialogue box where you can make notes. We're using a new live word system. Everyone's area of expertise will be reflected as we go through the data. For example, Evans is the job's schematics expert. Kamin is the job's engineering expert. The interactive nature of the document will allow everyone to know each other's thoughts as we proceed."

Ace opened the document and saw the names of the other agents materializing in the right-hand margin. He followed the prompts, and his name appeared, in yellow.

"Ragno," Zeus said. "Ready?"

"Yes. Good afternoon, Agents." Ragno's crisp, matter-of-fact voice filled the room. Looking over her laptop screen, she gave the agents an all-encompassing glance with denim-blue eyes, while she typed a few final clicks on her keyboard.

Several agents answered Ragno with *'good afternoon,'* while others nodded. The woman was a mystery. Ace assumed that her name was manufactured, but no one had confirmed that. Most agents didn't know the details of Ragno's tragic history. Even Ace didn't know all the facts, because everyone in the company, her close friends like Leo included, guarded her privacy. He did know that for years, post-traumatic agoraphobia had reduced Ragno's entire world to her apartment at corporate headquarters and her home office. Now, she was able to freely travel through the various floors of the high-rise headquarters building. She was better, but not healed. To his knowledge, the pretty, petite woman with ash-blonde hair and delicate features never left headquarters.

On his screen, an instant message dialogue box appeared from Ragno, revealing what her last few clicks on the keyboard had been. He opened it. "*Leo being in the field on this one is a lucky break for us. Having her in China will make it easier to keep your secret until Christmas. BTW-What's the pup's name? I need to call her something.*"

Leo's home was an apartment that was next door to Ragno. As he'd landed in Denver, he'd received a text from Ragno, with an image of the puppy that was to be Leo's Christmas gift from him. It had taken some planning on Ace's part, but the puppy had arrived in Denver earlier that morning, via a flight from California. Ace's youngest sister had been in charge of the puppy's transport and delivery to Ragno. The text had signaled the puppy's safe arrival, and had been accompanied with a photo of the black and white, thick-haired puppy snoozing atop a plush blanket. Ragno was happy to be the dog's ongoing second mom, for times when Leo worked in the field.

He thought about the name issue for a second, then sent his reply. "*Let's stick with breeder's name for now. Noelle.*"

From the front of the room, Ragno glanced at the computer screen, but gave no indication that she saw his reply. Addressing the agents, she said, "*Imagine* is a luxury vessel designed to provide the world's wealthiest gamblers with an unforgettable experience. The ship is owned by Imagine Casinos Worldwide, which is owned by Theodore Baru. Here he is, for those who aren't familiar with him."

A photo of Baru appeared on the wall next to the image of the ship. Bald, with light blue eyes, and round, wire-rimmed glasses, he was in his mid-sixties. He was slim and wore an expensive-looking suit that was a little too shiny for Ace's liking.

"Baru will be aboard his ship for the cruise, which boasts the newest casino in his empire of luxury resort properties in Las Vegas, Macau, and Nassau," Ragno continued. "The ship's maiden voyage will host a private tournament for seventy-five of the world's wealthiest gamblers, including one of the top five wealthiest men in the world, Ling Wen, of Hong Kong, where the corporate home of Ling Wen Enterprises is based. As part of our due diligence for the job, you will become familiar with every guest who will be aboard the ship."

"Baru is not our client," Zeus said. "Nor are the guests. Assuming everything goes smoothly, Baru and the guests will never know that

Black Raven is aboard the ship. Well-placed financial incentives have ensured that the in-field team has a variety of undercover positions, designed for optimal spreading around the ship, appropriate visas for entry into the country, and other details that fall into my team's responsibilities."

Zeus didn't have to be more explicit. In that context, Ace knew that financial incentives meant bribes, though the company didn't typically admit engaging in the practice of payola.

"Our client is the Howard Underwriting Group," Zeus continued. "HUG for short. Some of you have worked on HUG jobs in the past. You know that the underwriting group provides K & R coverage for wealthy individuals and upper echelon businesses."

Another panel of light opened behind Zeus. Text appeared, with the headline *'Kidnap & Ransom Coverage.'* Underneath, policy language provided bullet points of K & R insurance coverage.

"For those of you who haven't worked on HUG's files, K & R clauses mean what they say in plain English. A policyholder buys the coverage, and if he or she is ever kidnapped and has to pay ransom to secure their freedom, the insurer will reimburse the policyholder. Each policy has customized requirements about ransom negotiation, payment protocols, and other details, but we won't worry about those now. What makes HUG policies special and worthy of hiring Black Raven, at enormous expense, is the considerable accumulative value of the HUG policies and the wealth of HUG's clients who are insured by those policies."

As Zeus paused, Ragno continued. "Current cyber-chatter has businesses that protect the upper-echelon wealthy—HUG and Black Raven included—on a category red alert this holiday season. There has been a proliferation of terrorist groups, worldwide, that are waging a war against wealth. Trends in violence indicate that, among extremists, wealth is becoming equated with greed. Extremists are now taking aim at the rich."

Slides appeared on the wall behind Zeus, with headlines of mass shootings, targeted bombings, and high-profile kidnappings that had occurred in the past few months. A bombing inside an auction of priceless antiques in Manhattan, New York; ten people, dead. A sniper-style, mass shooting at a ritzy ski resort in Cortina D'Ampezzo, Italy; fifteen, dead. The kidnapping of the LeMoine family, of the diamond cartel, from their home in Dubai, United Arab Emirates; negotiations for their release currently underway.

As the newsfeed continued with headlines of other high-profile kidnappings, Ragno said, "Occurrences such as these have made K & R insurance a hot commodity. Because only a handful of insurance companies write K & R insurance, a disproportionate number of the world's billionaires are HUG clients. Of the one hundred and fifty passengers on Baru's gambling-tournament cruise, forty-three have K&R insurance provided by HUG."

"Baru caters to the wealthiest of the wealthy," Zeus said. "If the worst happens, and K & R coverage is triggered for all HUG clients aboard *Imagine*, liability will be in the billions. Aside from worrying about K & R coverage, HUG's life insurance policies for the guests aboard *Imagine* also present an enormous potential liability. Black Raven will be aboard the ship to ensure that the inaugural cruise is free of any mishap that would activate any HUG coverage."

"Field agents, I'll be in charge of your Denver-based cyber and intelligence support. The cyber agents who are currently in the room with you will be on my team," Ragno said. "We'll call in other agents as needed."

"I'll be in Denver for the duration. I'll lead trouble-shooting should the need arise," Zeus said. "As you all know, I'm the lucky guy who gets to deflect the fall-out from governmental agencies if a job goes off kilter."

Zeus looked from agent to agent. "Let's make sure my governmental liaison skills are not needed on this one. I've dealt with a variety of governments over the years, but Communist regimes are tricky and China's the trickiest of them all. If this job goes sideways, you may all end up in a prison for the remainder of your natural lives."

A gleam in his eyes suggested that Zeus was joking. Dead silence in the room indicated most of the agents in the room weren't finding humor in his words.

"Come on, Zeus. Stop scaring them." Ragno's tone had shifted from pure business to something a little gentler. She shook her head and gave the agents a dramatic eye-roll.

Zeus gave a slight smile. A few agents sighed, as though relieved to see that he had actually been trying to be funny. "If I'm scaring them, Ragno, we have big problems looming."

"Agents, of course we won't leave you sitting in a Chinese prison," Ragno said, with an almost motherly tone in her voice. "Well, at least not for the rest of your lives. We'd eventually figure a way to get you out. I promise."

"A condition of our employment is absolute anonymity," Zeus said. "Simply put, HUG does not let its valued and wealthy clients know that it is covering its own ass. Because Black Raven isn't in the business of trusting anyone else, no one on the ship will know of our presence. Not even Quan Security, which is the private security company that has been hired by Baru. Also, the security teams hired by the individual guests will not know that Black Raven is aboard, unless those agents are Black Raven agents. Your legends are in the working document."

Legends were the details of the undercover agent's role on a job where Black Raven's presence was to be undetected. Ace clicked and found his alter ego. He'd be cruising as Zack Abrams.

As Ace read through the details, Zeus continued. "For the next two days, until the field team departs for Macau, we're going to analyze scenarios where things could go wrong and we'll formulate a fix. For now, I'll give you a few minutes to look through the dossier, then we'll move on to more job details."

Shit!

Details of his legend revealed an immediate issue, but not the kind Zeus was trying to troubleshoot. This problem was purely personal.

Zack Abrams was the fiancée of Chloe St. Laurent, an heiress who loved high-stakes gambling. According to legend, Zack was a man who seemed content to manage Chloe's businesses and was frequently seen at her side whenever she appeared in public. Zack and Chloe were to do what fiancées did on a cruise—stay close to each other, act like a couple in love.

Share a room.

Typically, Ace wouldn't have had a problem with this sort of legend. After all, he was a professional. His issue was that the name of the agent who was to be Chloe St. Laurent was Sylvia Leon. Their kiss had created an issue, and sharing a room with her would force them to confront it.

He glanced across the briefing room. His eyes met Leo's, who was looking over her shoulder, at him, with wide eyes and an *oh-fuck* expression that told him she'd just read the exact same thing. The near-panic in her eyes revealed exactly what he'd been hoping for—that she was also having an issue with their kiss. Despite his own initial reaction to the fact that they were sharing a room, he couldn't help but smile in response to her discomfort.

He moved his cursor to their private dialogue box. *"Don't you think we should talk about why the prospect of us sharing a room horrifies you?"* He sent the message, wondering what creative way she'd give to shut down his attempt to bring up what had happened in New Orleans.

Her reply came about ten seconds later. When he read it, he stifled a chuckle. *"I'm not horrified at all. I'd rather share a room with you than some of the others. Kamin and Stills are known to snore, and Ryan's an insomniac. She'd keep me up all night."*

"You're dodging my question."

"Not a dodge. I'm looking forward to catching up with you. Haven't seen you in person in a few weeks. Besides, we talk all the time."

She did have a point. Even when they didn't see each other, they reached out multiple times a day. Their usual text streams, phone calls, emails, and video chats were nonstop, daily occurrences that had continued despite the abrupt ending of that night in New Orleans. They'd skirted around what had happened, while sharing most other aspects of their lives with one another. Sometimes their conversations were work-related, sometimes not. Typically, their interaction was full of complete nonsense. Like their running dialogue of one-letter dietary restrictions. She'd start it with a morning text that said, *'Only eating things that start with a T today.'* He'd answer with a random letter. They'd send photos of their food choices throughout the day.

He typed, "*I mean really talk. Not like the b.s. we usually...*"

Before he could complete his thought, a new message from her said, "*This job looks great. Right? I've never been to Macau. You?*"

Just like that, she'd shut down his attempt. Again. "*The dodge won't work so well when we're face to face, sharing a room. Yep. Job looks great. Nope. I've never been.*"

"OK. You focus on ship schematics. I'll focus on communications. Let's actually earn some of our paychecks."

The dialogue box flashed with an x, indicating that she'd exited their chat. Once again, he'd let her off the hook. He didn't know what he'd say if she ever gave him the opportunity, and that was one big reason why he wasn't forcing the issue.

Yet there was one thing of which he was certain. Over the last few weeks, with all the lingering daytime thoughts that he couldn't shake, and the late-night tossing and turning that had resulted from burning hot yearning, he knew he couldn't forget their kiss. Couldn't wipe any part of it out of his mind. Not her sighs. How'd she felt in his arms.

The taste of her. How she'd locked her legs behind his hips, sighing into his mouth as she pressed into him. Another thing of which he was certain was that he wasn't supposed to have these feelings for his best friend and co-worker. Such feelings could damn well complicate both relationships, if not destroy them. He also knew something else. He wanted more.

Chapter Four

Sunday, December 22
Aboard *Imagine*, in the South China Sea
6:00 p.m.

Conversations ebbed and flowed as gamblers, intent on beating casino odds and each other, crowded around *Imagine*'s gaming tables. The playing pit where Ace and Leo were positioned had blackjack tables, craps tables, and roulette wheels. Among the tables, dealers were arranging chips into towering stacks. Players then dismantled the stacks into bets and continuously counted their chips by re-stacking them. The gambling action resulted in an endless series of soft, but audible, clicks as bets were wagered, won, and lost.

In homage to the season, Frasier firs, dusted with fake snow and decked with lights and ornaments, stood tall in the casino's far corners. But there was nothing Christmas-like happening at the tables, where, now that they were a few hours into the cruise and the tournament was in full force, the players were determined to win.

Leo, in the role of her legend, Chloe St. Laurent, was trying to stake a claim as a contender. Ace, standing beside her as her fiancée, Zack, knew that the role wasn't taking too much acting on her part. In real life, Leo loved games.

To be more accurate, she loved to win, and this was one hell of a game. Around the craps table where Leo now played, more than eight million Hong Kong dollars rode on the hope that the sum of the next roll of the dice wouldn't equal seven. A cool half million of those dollars were wagered by Leo, compliments of HUG.

Leo gave a wholehearted laugh. It was powerful, yet delicate and feminine. Excited. While the other gamblers at the table grew silent, waiting for James Ye of Taiwan, a thirty-two-year-old who'd inherited billions, to throw the dice, her laughter sent shockwaves through his bones. Like gunpowder in a shell, her laughter packed everything about her into a lethal shot that struck his chest with explosive force. Amidst the sea of confusion he'd been trying to navigate ever since the early morning hours after Halloween night, the simple sound of her laughter carried clarity, as instant as it was inexplicable.

It forced him to recognize the feelings he'd had ever since the elevator doors had shut, separating him from her as she stood there looking frustrated, bewildered, and sexy. Even on that night, at The Roosevelt Hotel, it had taken everything he had not to push the elevator doors open, take her in his arms and tell her...

Son of a bitch, but that had been the problem. He'd had no idea what to say then and still was at a loss, because he knew her well enough to know that any words on the subject of feelings and emotions could scare her away, perhaps for good. Except now, his reaction to her mere laughter told him not to deny reality any longer.

Fuck. I'm in love with my best friend.

The realization twisted his gut into knots, because he'd learned the hard way not to fall for female co-workers. He'd done it once before. As a Marine, he'd made the mistake of falling for a medic who did battlefield work.

Kat.

He'd been on his third tour of duty in Afghanistan. They'd gotten serious quickly. They were even planning on getting married. At least they had been until the worst happened. He shook off the bad memories that came every time he thought of Kat's final moments, in his arms, as he carried her away from the bloody hell that marked his final battle as a Marine.

Now, the certainty that he was in love with Leo also made him wonder, in-the-name-of-all-things-with-a-subzero-IQ, how he could've been so blind to it in the two years he'd known her. As the craps table's current shooter, James Ye, finally let the two red dice fly, he also knew that his epiphany damn well needed to be irrelevant to the job.

One dice hit the table's far rim before plopping on the green felt. *Five.* The other pinged off the middle of the low wall and ricocheted across the playing pit. Chips flew as the wayward die hit one tall stack, then another, before rolling to a slow stop. *Three.*

The dealers started moving chips towards the players, and Leo gave another of her trademark laughs. The melodic sound of it mingled with celebratory whoops of the players as tuxedo-clad dealers assembled and pushed payouts towards them.

"Yes!"

"Great roll!"

He'd heard her laugh countless times before. It usually warmed him and often made him chuckle with her. Now, it made him damn well want to hear it for the rest of his life, which made him worry that he was on the cusp of a colossal mistake.

"Wow!" Leo glanced sideways at him. Caramel-colored eyes, with a dark rim of chocolate brown and lightened by golden-bronze flecks, met his. His heart jumped as she smoothed a lock of thick, chestnut-colored hair behind her ear. She shot him a wide grin. "Fantastic! Right?"

Yes. You, Leo. Suddenly, I realize that everything about you is fantastic. What the fuck took me so long?

The casino's chandelier and LED lights enhanced bronze strands that glistened in her hair. Her cheeks were flushed a delicious coral-pink hue. Espresso-colored leather pants hugged her hips. A gold mesh-metal halter exposed her shoulders, draping over her breasts, hugging them in a way that rewired every circuit in Ace's body to want her.

Not what I should feel for a fellow agent. Or my best friend.

They'd departed Macau in two-foot swells. Similar seas were forecasted to continue throughout the duration of the three-day gambling cruise to nowhere. State-of-the-art stabilizers made roll and pitch nonexistent in such relatively flat conditions.

Still, in that moment, as though *Imagine* had hit turbulent seas, Ace had to adjust his stance. A quick glance around the expansive casino revealed glistening chandeliers that hung straight, without swaying. Gamblers played, without interruption. They weren't sailing in rough seas. The problem was him, because as right as it felt to be in love with Leo, it was equally wrong.

As she collected winnings and rearranged chips, Ace stood still, trying to collect his thoughts. With his newfound, irrefutable knowledge that somewhere along the way he'd fallen in love with her, his gut roiled with a familiar, post-traumatic manifestation of turmoil remembered from the worst time in his life.

Shake it off. I'm in control. I'm not in Afghanistan, and Leo isn't Kat. Leo isn't dying on this job. No one is. I'm better than this.

If he let the anxiety simmer for too long, it would snake upwards and choke him from the inside-out. Soon he'd be flashbacking to four years earlier, when he'd been in a hot, dusty town in Afghanistan, where his unit had been ambushed, and everything in the world had gone wrong. He knew the perils of flashbacks, because he'd had way too many.

But I'm better now. Haven't really flashbacked in two years, and I sure won't revisit that bullshit now.

"I'm betting that Ye will hit his point again," Leo whispered her strategy, punctuating it with a dazzling smile and a certain nod. "He's a streak roller. That was only his fourteenth roll. He has a record of thirty-five consecutive rolls in tournament play, with five points scored. Odds are..."

In a breathy, hushed tone that made him want to kiss her, Leo recited statistics that she'd studied on the likelihood that James Ye would roll another eight before rolling a seven.

Pretending to listen, Ace tried to rein in his thoughts.

And damn well couldn't.

He should have seen this coming, but 'should have' were two words that meant that he'd lost opportunities to see what had been damn obvious. Newfound clarity told him there'd been warning signs, well before their pedicab ride and the kiss that was now, with the benefit of hindsight, a sledgehammer hit that should have knocked some sense into him.

"Zack?" Leo's use of his undercover name jolted him.

"Roll with it, Chloe. Bet your gut." Although his words came out flat and unenthusiastic, Ace was overjoyed he'd managed to say anything relevant.

Enthusiasm faded from her eyes. "What's up?"

What was up was he didn't want to be Zack and Chloe right now. He wanted to be Ace and Leo. Alone, but together so they could have another one of those kisses, in memory of what was now the most notable trick-or-treat night of his life. "You're ahead about a million in U.S. dollars." He cleared the hoarseness out of his voice. "Great job."

She tilted her head as she studied him. "You're flushed."

"I'm fine."

"Are you seasick?" Her eyes gleamed with barely suppressed laughter. "You know I'd never let you live that down, right?"

"I don't get seasick."

She eyed him up and down, gave a quick frown of doubt, then moved a little closer to him to make room for a new gambler at the table. Ace gave the tall, barrel-chested man a nod. Wendall Manley, of Germany—head of the Manley Investment Firm, known for taking enormous monetary stakes in companies that showed promise in medical technological advances. "Are you feeling feverish?"

"No, Mom."

With her chips rearranged, she whispered, "Please don't get the flu while we're sharing a room. I'd happily take care of you if you're sick, as long as I'm not breathing your germy air, twenty-four seven."

"All good. No flu." His mind flipped to the reality of sharing a bedroom with her for the cruise. His gaze crawled over her shoulders, to her neck, to the firm line of her jaw. Her skin, perpetually looking as though the August sun had kissed her and left her a delicious and exotic golden color, called to him. As in kiss me. Lick me. Taste me.

As her eyes narrowed with a wordless *then-what-the-fuck-is-wrong-with-you* question, he realized his current mental quantum leap would require some explaining to her. The sooner, the better. "Had the shot."

"It's only sixty-three percent effective this year." A glimmer of playful light entered her eyes, while the dealers pushed chips in Manley's direction. "Oh. I know! You're worried I won't like my Christmas present."

Despite his discomfort, he chuckled. Then his heart started a free fall. "Nah. You're going to love it."

She cocked her head to the side and studied him, as though searching for a clue. "Want to tell me what it is? You know how I feel about surprises."

"Yeah." His heart sank further with their banter. "You love them."

She gave him a quick up and down glance and a gleam of a challenge lit her eyes. "Of the two, I bet my gift to you wins the prize."

"What prize?"

"For the gift that most captures the spirit of Christmas."

"Which is?"

"Magic. Fantasy. Inspiration. Wild wishes coming true. Hell if I know." She turned back to the table with a shrug and reached for her stacks of chips. "I might like presents, but Christmas has never really been my season."

He knew her better than that. As a young girl, Christmas had been her favorite time, because of the things she and her dad would do. Until September 11, 2001, when her father, once a pro football quarterback who played for the New York Giants, had been in World Trade Center's North Tower. She'd run there as soon as she heard about the first plane crashing into the South Tower; she'd left a private class she'd been taking as part of the home-schooling curriculum her mother had designed.

She'd known her father was at the World Trade Center. She just didn't know where, or what floor. He'd broken the news to her earlier that week that he was divorcing her mother. That morning, he was visiting his divorce lawyer there.

When she arrived at the perimeter, officials had to hold her back. Her father had been yet another name in the long list of victims that came out in the ensuing days. Someone in the media had captured photos of police holding Leo as she fought to get past the boundary that marked the safety zone. Stark grief and heart-stopping panic, apparent in her face as she struggled with firemen and NYPD officers trying to hold her back, had been captured in images that had made the rounds of news wires.

Someone in the media had put two and two together. Who she was, and who her father was. The images were haunting. She'd told Ace why her father was there on September 11, and he knew the fact that her dad had been seeing a divorce lawyer visit was yet another reason why Leo wasn't close to her mother. If Christmas reminded her of all that she lost on September 11, 2001, he damn well didn't want to be giving her a gift that would serve as a constant reminder of the season.

Aw. Damn. I made a big mistake with thinking the dog's name should be left as Noelle.

Ace did a quick scan of the noisy, bustling room, where everything appeared normal. Dealers were shuffling cards. Roulette wheels were spinning. Cocktail waitresses, making their way through gaming tables, carried drinks on gleaming silver trays. Piped-in Christmas carols added to the din.

Security personnel outnumbered guests, and Ace could easily spot them. Including Black Raven, three tiers of security were on board. Tier One—personnel provided by Quan Security, a private company licensed in Hong Kong. They wore tuxedos and red bow ties. Quan had been hired by Imagine Casinos Worldwide to protect the ship and guests who'd been invited to play in the vessel's inaugural tournament.

Tier Two—private security hired directly by the invited guests, some of whom didn't venture out in public, even on normal days, without guards. In keeping with the ship's rules for attire, private security carried credentials and wore tuxedos with green bow ties. As happenstance had it, two of Black Raven's longstanding clients were guests in the tournament. Four Black Raven agents—Jacks, McMillan, Andros, and Payne—were in Tier Two security.

Tier Three—Ace and Leo and the other Black Raven agents who were working undercover for HUG. They'd divided their twelve-man team into four-man units. Alpha, Beta, and Omega.

Leo glanced at him again. Her gaze became concerned, and then she turned fully towards him. Her high heels meant she didn't have to tiptoe to whisper in his ear. "Seems like my fiancée would be happier that I'm winning."

"I'm ecstatic." Firmly in role as Zack, Ace planted a soft kiss on Leo's forehead, where a furrow now indicated that she was wondering what was up with him. The kiss was a bit tame, considering that Zack and Chloe were engaged, but a whiff of Leo's sultry, woodsy essence of rose, pushed Ace's libido into overdrive. His body yearned to satisfy what was quickly becoming a deep-rooted, physical need for her.

Bond No.9's signature scent.

Yeah. He knew the name of her perfume. He'd purchased it after picking her up at the San Diego airport, almost a year earlier, when she'd requested they stop at a mall so she could get gifts for his family, who she was meeting for the first time. He'd liked the fragrance, loved the name of it, and thought the gold, star-shaped bottle was cool. Evidently, she liked it enough to wear it ever since.

Last year, they'd both been off from Christmas Eve until New Year's Day. She'd spent the holiday in La Jolla, in his spare bedroom. They'd hung out at his mom's coffee shop. Between the football games they'd watched, he'd taken her on his favorite hikes. Gone kayaking. Taught her to surf, which she took to with amazing ease, considering she'd grown up in Manhattan and had never been on a board before. Then again, she was a rare sort of genius–not only was her brain-power off the charts, she had a natural, graceful athleticism.

Behind her back, Black Raven agents called her a unicorn. After watching the ease with which she went from surfing novice to almost keeping up with him, when he'd been on a board since he was five, he'd agreed with the unicorn assessment. They'd had a great week. As friends. Best of friends. Like no friend he'd ever had before, male or female. But only friends.

Fuck. I was delusional. Until right goddamn now.

"Ling Wen's playing craps," Leo whispered. "Two tables down."

"I'm aware."

Ace had spotted Wen entering the casino with his wife and four personal, Tier Two bodyguards. Wen was one of the top five wealthiest men in the world and the wealthiest man in China. He had an assortment of businesses, including weapons manufacturing and shipbuilding. A high-stakes gambler, he was coveted by casinos.

Imagine had been built in one of Wen's shipyards. His appearance on the ship's inaugural cruise had drawn other noteworthy gamblers to the tournament, making the cruise the hottest place to be in the gambling world.

A young looking sixty-two, with only a bit of gray in his dark hair, Wen had attained celebrity status in Beijing and beyond due to his spearheading of reforms in Chinese law that governed philanthropic giving. The new laws had paved the way for China's wealthy to fund charities. Wen had personally funded a scholarship program that now eased the way for millions to attend college. Wen and his wife, May, were both HUG clients with K & R coverage.

Even without the aura that came from being unimaginably wealthy, Ling and May Wen were an eye-grabbing couple. Ling was conservatively understated in a custom-tailored suit. With a shrewd, focused gaze, he had a way of looking people in the eye that was disarming. That gaze, coupled with his thoughtful smile, created a charisma that was riveting.

May, a bit younger than her husband, wore a deep-v cut, blood red, silky dress that skimmed her slender body. Pursing lipstick-colored lips that matched her dress, she kissed her husband on the lips. Before Ling Wen threw the dice, his dark brown eyes rested briefly on Ace. He gave Ace a slight nod.

"She's beautiful. Right?"

Leo's comment came as dealers announced that Ling Wen's roll resulted in a ten. While gamblers at their table erupted into a celebratory chorus, Ace almost said, *'she's got nothing on you.'*

Instead, he managed to mumble, "Smoking hot."

Leo rolled her eyes, then turned to face the table. Her halter dress was backless, save for leather strings at her neck and waist. It was bad enough to look at the way the mesh hugged her breasts, but it was even worse to see the bare skin of her toned back. She worked out regularly, and it showed. Somewhere along the way, as in right-fucking-now, Ace had apparently developed a sex-oriented thing for every square inch of his best friend. Even her shoulder blades. Her ass, which glided along his hip as she leaned over to push a rack of chips across the table, was also a turn-on.

To the dealer, Leo said, "A hard eight."

Her naturally breathy tone, the equivalent of testosterone fuel enhancer, carried a suggestion that she was talking about something far different than a pair of fours materializing with the roll of dice. He held back a groan.

Ace wasn't the only one who noticed the all-out sexiness in her voice. Across the table, Ace watched Randy Howell, originally of Seattle but now with homes around the world, glance Leo's way. Howell was a forty-nine-year-old tech entrepreneur, whose fortune was subject to success or failure of the businesses in which he chose to invest. He'd gotten an early start in video-gaming innovations. He had a head full of dark hair that was graying slightly at the temples. With his gaze resting on Leo, he pushed a tall stack of chips towards the dealer. His fiancée—Miranda Lake, a willowy blonde, from Iowa—saw where Howell was looking. She frowned. She moved closer to Howell. He gave his fiancée a kiss, even as his gaze slid back to Leo.

While players continued to call their bets, and push tall stacks of chips towards the dealers, Leo whispered, low, so that no one would hear it, "This is a lot of money. Holy crap. Are you seeing what's on this table?"

"Yeah." But he wasn't counting chips. Howell was now staring at Leo—and not just her face. Through square, black-rimmed eyeglasses, Howell's gaze was locked onto Leo's cleavage. Ace had seen most of Leo. In bathing suits. In exercise gear. They'd even changed at the beach, in a car. He knew how perfect her perky breasts were. What he couldn't understand was why her breasts had never been a turn on for him before, because Howell was apparently figuring it out with clothes covering her and without even knowing her. Jealousy surged within Ace as he watched the man lick his lips.

Funny thing was—he wasn't the jealous type. At least he never had been.

Son of a bitch, but this is a day of firsts.

"Going for a walk," he mumbled.

Leo nodded as he turned from the craps table, her attention focused on the action in the playing pit in front of her, as James Ye lifted his hand in preparation to throw the dice once again.

She's working. So am I. Remember that.

As Ace turned, he almost bumped into Black Raven Agent Amy Ryan, who dodged him without spilling any of the cocktails that were crowded onto her silver platter.

"Sorry," he said.

"Not a problem," Ryan answered, with a dazzling smile that didn't quite match the focused look in her eyes. She'd had three years in the Navy. Four years in Black Raven. Specializing in cyber support in fieldwork, Amy Ryan was Leo's backup for the job. This was her first day ever as a cocktail waitress. She didn't normally wear six-inch heels, fishnet stockings, green-velvet micro shorts, and a gold halter that revealed cleavage, but she was doing it well.

He gave Ryan a nod of encouragement, then strode down the center of the casino, past Agent Paul Stills, who was undercover as a casino host. Under the team's hierarchy established by Zeus, Ace was Stills' backup. Stills, like Ace and many Black Raven agents, had prior military experience. The relative qualifications of Ace and Stills made them almost an equal match. Equal—but for the small piece of Ace's history with the Marines that started with an epic ambush and included death, destruction, revenge, heartache, and Ace's long struggle with post-traumatic stress.

Stills glanced at Ace, gave a slight nod, then refocused on the two guests to whom he was speaking. Eighteen of HUG's clients were currently in the casino, and Agent Stills was talking to two of them—the Blackwells, Nina and Todd, from Texas. Their fortune came from land, oil, and shipping. Todd Blackwell's luck at the gaming tables was legendary. He was fifty-five. She was forty-five, with an easy smile. She flashed her smile at Ace as Stills finished their conversation with them and Ace walked by her.

Gamblers were playing to win not only a fortune, but also expensive toys and gambling-world prestige symbolized by an obnoxiously large Baccarat crystal vase depicting the nine muses of Greek mythology. Imagine Casinos was treating the hunk of glass with the lofty symbolism of the Lombardi trophy. The vase was on Ace's left, perched high on a black marble pedestal in the center of the casino, lit by floodlights and spotlights that made the glass glitter with a kaleidoscope of colors.

"Omega. Status?" Stills' voice crackled through the comm system.

As Ace made his way through the crowded casino, Ace touched his watch, turning down the volume slightly. The Black Raven comm system used state-of-the-art, inner ear implants that picked up audio that was inaudible to the human ear. The implants were a combined receiver and transmitter. Gone were the days of having to wear a mic anywhere near the mouth, as the implant transmitted the speaker's voice through facial bone conduction. With buttons on their watches, or voice activation and recognition, agents could manipulate volume, tune out background noise, and change channels to communicate with any of the agents aboard *Imagine*, either individually or en masse.

The voice of Wade Kamin, leader of the four-agent Omega team, came through his earpiece. In the hierarchy of the job, consistent with the roles Zeus had assigned, Kamin was third in command. Undercover as a ship's engineer, he was currently stationed in the radio room. "Omega team is in position."

The financial incentive provided by Zeus' team hadn't resulted in placing all the agents in such important positions, and Ace and Leo were the only agents fortunate enough to be casino guests, with a luxury stateroom. Omega's other agents were disbursed around the ship as a line chef, a bartender, and a shopkeeper; their sleeping quarters were bunks in dorm-style rooms. Kamin, at least, had a private stateroom in the section of the ship that housed the officers and the crew. "Nothing out of the ordinary. Except Marks just sold an emerald valued at almost a quarter of a million U.S. dollars."

Agent Marks, the young agent who'd almost earned a smile from Zeus during the job briefing, was undercover as a salesman in the ship's jewelry store. Ace chuckled, relieved to be thinking about the job rather than the mental black hole into which he'd fallen while standing next to Leo.

"Too bad he won't be around for payday to get the commission," Ace said.

"Who knows? He might sign on permanently."

As Ace stepped out of the casino, onto the wide deck, he inhaled fresh ocean air, relishing the moist, salty tang. The ship's air system, which he'd studied as part of his review, had complex air filtration and ozone injection capabilities designed to keep the air fresh and stimulating. To Ace, the indoor air still felt sterile and fake. It was obviously engineered for more than clean breathing, just as the wordless, fast-paced version of "Jingle Bells" that came from the ship's speakers was designed to maximize the mood to gamble.

He glanced at his watch—1820 hours. Clouds on the horizon captured the last orange light of the sinking sun. He walked across the deck and rested his elbows on the smooth teak railing. Pressing his watch, Ace opened a line of communication with headquarters in Denver.

"Good evening. Status?" Ragno's voice, crisp and efficient, carried clearly across the continents and oceans that separated them.

"Smooth sailing." Training his gaze straight down, on dark water that crested with small waves that foamed and fizzled, he added, "You'd know if it wasn't."

"I sure hope so. For now, though, unless you guys talk to me, you're just a green blip on my radar. From what I can tell, you're the only fish in the sea."

Ace glanced again at the darkening horizon, which was devoid of other vessels. "As expected."

"Correct."

Although the South China Sea was one of the busiest waterways in the world, the cruise's charted course wasn't in major trade pathways. The cruise had no ports of call. It had activities that revolved around the tournament and keeping the gamblers happy, pampered, and titillated so that they gambled more. And when gamblers took a break, there were spa services. En-suite massages. Cocktail parties. Champagne and caviar bars. "Something Leo just said reminds me that we have to give the dog a different name. Definitely not Noelle."

"I was thinking of that. It's best not to tie the Christmas thing so solidly to anything you give Leo."

"Ideas?"

Ragno was silent for a second. "None. Leo will change anything we think of, anyway."

"How is she?"

"Adorable. If I didn't love Leo so much, I'd claim her for my own."

He'd been around Leo long enough to know that while Christmas wasn't her favorite season, she certainly loved thoughtful gestures. He'd planned this gift ever since seeing her interact with the dogs in his neighborhood when she'd visited the prior Christmas. The puppy had been produced by the union of a Cavalier King Charles spaniel and a French poodle owned by two of his California neighbors.

Yeah. The thought that I've put into her Christmas gift is a leading indicator of being in love. Jesus Christ, I've been an idiot.

"There's another reason not to call her Noelle," he said. "By the time we return to Denver for debriefing, I'm thinking Leo will have had enough of Christmas. Baru's got good taste, but the theme's overdone. Christmas trees and holiday music everywhere. Cocktail waitresses are dressed as Santa's elves."

"Tomorrow they'll be reindeer."

Ace chuckled. "Ryan isn't happy about it."

"How's *Chloe* doing?"

With spoken emphasis on Leo's legend's name, Ragno was giving Ace a not-too-subtle reminder of who they were, and that they were on a job. "Ahead by a million."

"That's my girl. Playing to win."

"Yeah. Playing her heart out. Like always."

Despite his off-the-cuff response, his chest tightened. Without regard to her own limitations, Leo never backed down. Tenacity was an admirable trait, one that was greatly valued in a Black Raven agent. As a friend, he liked that about her. Coupled with her ruthless competitive streak, she had a way of keeping him on his toes that he found exhilarating and refreshing. Yet given his personal history with Kat's death, the potential danger that came with his and Leo's line of work, and his newfound knowledge of the depth of his feelings for her, acknowledging Leo's play-all-things-to-win approach to life produced a foreboding that was as dark as the ocean's dark, roiling depths.

Chapter Five

7:10 p.m.

The Oscar de la Renta, off-the-shoulder silk dress, black with silver-metallic embellishments, was more delicate than anything Leo owned, but perfect for the legend of Chloe. It was exactly the type of dress the flashy gambler would have worn for the first night of the cruise. It was also a hell of a lot harder to get into than Leo's favorite attire of jeans, t-shirt, and leather jacket. As she stepped into the dress, Ace, on the other side of the bathroom door, turned off the water in the shower.

Hurry.

The zipper started at the bottom of her butt, where the sheath-like dress was the tightest. It glided easily for a half inch, then stopped midway over her butt. As she tugged, the front fell forward, exposing her chest. Drawing another breath, she readjusted the dress, then reached behind her, pulling the sides together. Tugged again. It moved enough to give her optimism.

He'd laid out his tuxedo on the bed, giving a solid clue that he planned to dress in the bedroom. She'd spent nights with him in close quarters. Most recently, during the past summer, they'd moved his Airstream from California to Georgia, to a parcel of land he'd purchased near Black Raven's training facility.

Now, staying in a room with one king-size bed, soft lighting, champagne on ice on a silver tray, and a vanity that was stocked with candles, condoms, and KY jelly, seemed...awkward. As in I-want-him-to-kiss-me again awkward. Because she did, and she needed to squelch that feeling. Step on it. Make it end. At least not have her butt and boobs showing when he came out of the bathroom.

Sucking in her breath, she tugged again. Pulled.

Nothing. Bathroom door?

She glanced over her shoulder. Still shut.

Thank you, God.

Exhaling, she looked at herself in the mirror. Damp hair. Wild eyes. Boobs spilling out over her strapless bra. Considering the scope of their job, the multifaceted planning, the cadre of weapons and gear that the advance team had stowed in the crawl space beneath where she stood, the fact that a stubborn zipper was an obstacle was laughable.

She twisted the dress around her, so the zipper was in front. She sucked in her belly, which was the only reason she could see why the zipper on the size four dress was stuck, and gave another tug. Could she have really gone from a size four to a six? Dammit.

The answer? Yes.

The leather pants she'd worn earlier had been tight. Come to think of it, in the last couple of weeks, everything had been tighter than normal. Too many days of eating P foods. Her favorite letter, because foods that started with 'P' had the most of what she considered to be comfort foods—pizza, potatoes, and peanut M&M's.

The zipper moved a few inches, then stopped.

She held her breath, while through her audio, she heard Ace, from the bathroom, checking in with Stills, Kamin, and Ragno.

Tuning out their chatter, she focused on the task at hand. *Dammit.* The zipper had moved too far to reposition the dress without unzipping it. She sighed, unzipped it, and moved the dress so the zipper was exactly where it needed to go, firmly over the crest of her butt, right in the middle. She tugged. It stuck again, forcing her to acknowledge that she'd been on an eating binge since Halloween, one that obviously defied the hours of exercise she did each day. As though chocolate would make her forget how he kissed her like a man who hungered only for her.

Ask him for help.

No.

Why not?

He doesn't know how he makes me feel.

All that happened in New Orleans was a tequila-inspired kiss. Nothing more.

She could still remember the day she'd come across a helmet-clad rider on the remote blacktop road that wound its way through foothills as it led to Last Resort, Black Raven's training facility in Georgia. She'd challenged the rider by gunning her bike ahead of his, pulling back, and doing the same thing again. He took the bait, and she'd ultimately kicked his ass. The rider had been Ace—the quiet new agent whose demons were legendary.

From then on, they were friends.

Since that day, nothing had been awkward with Ace. Nudity? They didn't flaunt flesh, but given the active lifestyle they shared as friends, sometimes skin happened. He'd even stood watch for her when she had to pee on the side of the road on motorcycle trips. Spinach in her teeth? No embarrassment. Not with him.

He grasped her moods. Bummed and bitchy because her beloved New York Giants, the team her father had once quarterbacked, had lost a game? Not a problem. He understood post-game blues. Got them himself. Pissed because she wasn't selected for a high-stakes field job? He understood her competitiveness. He could even guess when she was on her period. Sometimes he'd bring her chocolate at that time of the month, with no words to explain the gift or the slightly teasing grin.

But, since that pedicab ride to end all pedicab rides, things were different between them. Though she'd tried hard to behave like she always had, she didn't think she was imagining that he sounded different on the phone. He'd even looked different on video chats. He seemed...distant, but not. As though he was thinking of things that he didn't want to tell her. Which wasn't the way he usually was with her. He'd tried, in a roundabout way, to talk to her about it. She considered the ease with which she'd manage to deflect his attempts were an indicator that he wasn't serious about talking about what had happened.

All because of one shot too many of tequila. Or something in the warm and humid, New Orleans air. Or...damned if she knew what had provided the impetus. The end result was she couldn't forget their kiss. Compelled by a rare moment of sentiment, she'd even written a note with his Christmas gift that told him what she thought of it. The note and the gift were wrapped and waiting for their return to headquarters, after the job. Now that a few days had passed, she was reconsidering the gift and what she'd written, and re-written.

No way am I going headfirst into the land of feelings. Ever.

She'd redo his gift when they got home. She had a backup present that wasn't nearly as special or sappy. And, for-the-love-of-God, she didn't need to say a thing about their accidental kiss in a note.

The bathroom doorknob clicked. The vanity where she stood was on the opposite side of the spacious bedroom. Glancing into the large mirror, over her shoulder, she saw steam seep into the bedroom through the crack in the door. "Are you decent?"

The formality in his question was just another indication that they'd both donned invisible costumes of politeness after stepping out of the pedicab, which they hadn't yet removed. Pre-Halloween Ace would have charged through the door, treating her...like a guy.

"Give me a second."

Ever since that night, she'd been waiting for the inevitable conversation. Especially since their job briefing in Denver, she'd known it would be coming soon. Like winter's first snow did to fall, the conversation they needed to have was going to change the friendship that, after work, was the most important thing in her life. The shift their words would make in their friendship...scared her.

Hurry. Hurry. Hurry.

If he stepped out now, he'd have a view of her butt cheeks and the black lace thong that covered absolutely nothing at all. Taking a breath, she reached behind her hips, and tried to pull up the zipper.

He opened the door, glanced her way as the front of the dress fell forward, then quickly turned towards the bed, averting his eyes. “Damn. You could’ve said no. Not dressed.”

“I did.”

“No. You said give me a second. I gave you two.” Evidently not sharing her problems with modesty, he wore a towel around his hips. He strode across the room to the bed. Without glancing her way, he slipped on a pair of briefs, then let the towel fall to the floor as he reached for his tuxedo pants. Pulling them on with ease that inspired hatred in her, he asked, “Want help?”

“No. Go back in the bathroom.” She gestured with her head to the bathroom door. “Come on. Take your clothes and go. Finish getting dressed in there.”

“Seriously?” Through the mirror, she could see he was poised. Still. His eyes met hers, puzzled.

“Come on, Ace. I’m modest—”

“Nah. There isn’t a modest bone in your body, and don’t say my name. We’re undercover.” He’d slipped into serious team leader mode. “If you slip in private, you’ll slip in public.”

She nodded, because he was correct and she should listen to him. With the rigorous training that came with preparation for field jobs, agents tended to develop a certain amount of bravado that blurred the hierarchal lines of a job when bullets weren’t flying. Facts were the facts. Technically, as second-in-command, Ace was her superior.

“Okay, Zack. My dear fiancée, I’m trying not to show you my boobs and ass while this zipper malfunctions.”

She caught the beginning of a smirk as it played at his lips. His blond hair was darkened by dampness and slicked back, making the cobalt-blue of his eyes all the more noticeable.

"Okay, so maybe it's not a malfunction. Maybe it's my recent binge on foods that start with P. Hey. Maybe that'll be one of my New Year's resolutions. No P foods."

"You wouldn't make it a week. No pizza. Pasta. French fries—"

"No fair. French fries start with F. Tater tots start with T."

He laughed and, maintaining eye contact with her through the mirror, he gave her a slow headshake. Laughing wasn't something he normally did, and if she was honest with herself, she realized that ever since she'd met him, she'd done things to provoke a chuckle. As though she was in first grade, and his laughter was a gold star by her name, his laughter made her feel the warm glow of accomplishment. "For a year? No P foods. No cheating. I'll put money that you can't do it."

She shrugged, and the dress slipped further down her body. She didn't break eye contact with him as she yanked it up and muttered, "New Year's resolutions are supposed to be a challenge."

He ran his fingers through his damp hair, styling it to effortless perfection that became even more perfect as he gave her a firm headshake. "You can't do it. You downed a two-pound bag of peanut M &M's on the last leg of the flight. Without sharing."

"Liar! You ate at least half the bag while I was sleeping." *And I still need to get this damn dress zipped.* "Go in the bathroom. I either need to make this work, without you watching, or I need to put on tomorrow night's dress."

He sat on the edge of the king size bed. Pants on. Zipped, but unbuttoned. Taut skin rippled over sleek abdominal muscles. He didn't even have an inch to pinch where his belly hit the waistline of his pants. His chest was ripped with more muscles than should be allowed on one man. Why his physique was now as much an eye-grabbing wonder as the Grand Canyon, when she'd been blind to it for two years, was officially a problem. One she didn't know how to resolve.

From across the room, the mirror's reflection conveyed his shift from light joking to serious intensity. He wasn't looking at her boobs or her butt. He simply used the mirror to gaze into her eyes.

"Maybe you could get dressed and go to the Compass Rose," she said. "It seems in keeping with our legends that you'd have a drink in the bar while I'm getting ready. Or go back to the casino."

"Nah. Stills remains in position in the casino. I checked in with him when I stepped out of the shower. He's reporting that most guests are in their rooms, getting ready for the event. Our position here is optimal, until eight. It gives us a better spread around the ship. I also checked in with the other agents and Ragno. Everything's quiet. So I thought..."

As his words trailed, she realized his tone had shifted to something less businesslike. The look in his eyes was far different than the cool, practiced look of equanimity that he, and most Black Raven agents, employed on a job. "I've muted my audio line. Thought you and I could finally talk for a few minutes."

Frozen in place, she could only stare at the person she knew to be hard-as-nails. He'd transformed into someone whose normally matter-of-fact tone actually reflected the thoughtfulness that she'd learned was his true nature. His expression now carried feelings from deep within, and it was riveting. “Women usually put on that sort of dress after their hair is dry and their makeup’s on. The fact that you’re doing it ass-backwards tells me you’re feeling just as awkward as me.”

Trying to keep her cool, she resorted to the light tone that typically went with their ‘*back-at-ya’* banter. “So you’re an expert on female dressing?”

With a shrug of broad, bare shoulders, he gave her a slow nod. “I’m thirty-nine.”

“I’m twenty-eight.” She squirmed and made about a quarter inch of zipper progress. “That doesn’t mean I know how to tie a bow tie.”

“I’ve been around in some pre-party dressing. Plus, don’t forget, I have four sisters.” He stood, crossed the room, stepped into the bathroom, and pulled a robe off a hook. Walking towards her, he held it out to her. He stopped a few inches behind her, looking into her eyes through her reflection in the vanity mirror. “Either let me zip the dress or put this on over it. It’s taken me a long while to come to my senses. Now that I have, I don’t feel like wasting time. I don’t want how I handle this to become yet another regret in my life.”

She gave up on banter and went for honesty. “You’re scaring me.”

He chuckled, but the gravity in his eyes didn’t disappear. “Nothing scares you. Some things should, but not this. We have to talk about that pedicab ride.”

She tried to force a perplexed expression. She gave up on zipping the dress, and reached for the front of it, covering her chest. “What do you mean?”

"The fact that it's taken us fifty-two days to talk about it speaks volumes."

"Oh! You mean in New Orleans, on Halloween?"

"Nice try. Your effort at surprise proves you didn't forget. Besides, it's the only time we were ever in a pedicab together."

"I made a great Trinity, didn't I?"

"Not talking about our costumes. I'm talking about what prompted us to share the best kiss I've ever had. Don't say it was the tequila. You hold liquor better than me, and I remember every second of it. I remember how badly I wanted that kiss. Remember how you kissed me back, too."

Frozen in place, looking into his eyes through the reflection in the mirror, the almost-irresistible allure of a different world called her. Yet an insistent, suddenly certain voice, told her not to go there.

It will never work, and it will destroy our friendship.

"It was a locality issue." Careful to keep her voice casual, she tried to maintain a nonchalant look. "People do crazy things in New Orleans. They blame things that happen there on the humidity. It was really steamy that night."

His eyes became even more serious. "No."

Sparkling, fresh hope sent a chill down her spine, the kind she hadn't dared to dream since she was impossibly young, before her father was killed. Before she'd become compelled to fight evil, especially the kind that struck innocent victims as they were going through their daily lives.

Shake it off. Fooling around with a co-worker is a stupid idea. A career-limiting move. Not even Ace.

Especially not Ace.

He jiggled the robe. "You putting this on?"

She turned to him. A few inches from her, his bare skin exuded the delicious scent of freshly-showered maleness. Momentarily letting go of the dress with her left hand, she pushed the heel of her palm into his chest. He stepped back an inch.

"Okay. I won't crowd you, but we need to talk."

"Even talking about it is a big mistake. Let's forget it ever happened. It's a dead end."

"Don't say that. I'm not letting you cross the finish line before the race is even started." Voice deadly serious, his gaze held hers. Intent. Focused. Determined. Not a trace of a smile on his lips.

"It won't work. Besides, it was just a kiss—"

"It was more than a kiss. You know that. That's why you're having such a hard time with it."

"It shouldn't have happened. We're great friends, but that's all."

"There's a reason we're such good friends."

"Perhaps because you, unlike most other guys, have never tried to get in my pants. So—" She drew a breath. "Don't start now."

She tried not to see the turmoil in his eyes as he ran his hand through his still-damp hair. Under his coolness, there was a tentativeness that signaled raw feelings. The look made her heart twist, because the truth was, she'd fallen hard for him the minute she met him. Pre-Halloween, there had been times when she'd wondered if he'd ever make a move towards something more intimate. But now, she realized there were far more reasons why they shouldn't go there than reasons why they should.

"I wouldn't do anything that's not mutual." He folded his arms over his chest, still clutching the robe.

"But you've never even flirted with me. What we have is like a bromance."

"Yeah. That's what makes it great, but you're not a bro. That leaves us with a romance."

"Seriously?"

"This best friend routine we've got going might be the best flirting anyone's ever done. Because we both have a few–," He paused as a shadow drifted over his eyes. "–issues, we didn't recognize it."

"I'm having a hard time here. When, exactly, did things change for you?"

"Maybe the desire has always been there. When we first met I was too messed up to go there. After Kat died, I didn't even think about sex for two years. Since then, I've mostly had one-night stands. Nothing lasting."

She'd always wondered, but their sexual habits were one of the few things they'd never talked about. "Perhaps that's too much info. Maybe we should keep our sex lives to ourselves."

"Nah. There are some things I need to tell you. See, the odd thing, now that I think about it, is that you're the person I want to talk to the most, after I've had sex, and...even before. I'm usually looking for a text from you as soon as I'm out the door. You want to know when I realized what all of this means? When I finally figured out what to tell you? About an hour ago. In the casino. As I stood next to you, and all you did was laugh."

Her mind reeled at his honesty. “It might take me a while to catch up. I might never.”

“We’ve both lost enough in our lives to know that there’s no guarantee we’ll be here for a long time. Tomorrow isn’t a certainty. I’m not banking on it. I know you’re not, either.” His gaze, deadly serious, conveyed the gravity of his words. “Let’s not waste the time we have.”

“We’re friends. Best friends. That has to be good enough, even if we only have today.”

As her firm statement registered, Leo watched pain filter into his eyes. His pain stole a few of her heartbeats, while she realized that she’d be disappointed if she lost the promise of...more. If she was truthful with herself, having more of him had been an elusive hope, ever since she met him.

He gave her a slow headshake and the beginning of a smile. “Being best friends might be good enough for some people, but I don’t do good enough. Neither do you.”

He dropped the robe to the floor, then reached out and traced a line with the tip of his index finger along her collarbone, to her neck, up to her jaw. He lifted her face so that her gaze locked on his. “I’m dying to kiss you again.”

“I’m not Kat,” she blurted, worried that the sea change she was witnessing in him was the product of a flashback. To her knowledge, he hadn’t had one in a while, but that didn’t mean he wasn’t having one now. “I won’t be a substitute for her.”

“I know. Losing her was awful. The horror of it could be why it’s taken me so long to realize how I really feel about you.” Every nerve in her body felt the force of his lips, as he touched them to her ear. "Please know that I'll never project anything that happened with Kat onto you. It all belongs in a different world now. My past."

He sounded so convincing, she believed him. Yet that didn't solve all of their problems. Drawing upon willpower, she said, "Black Raven Rule 6.9, in the section governing agent dynamics, says—"

He lifted his finger to her lower lip. "Shhhh. I know what it says."

"Two agents—as in you and me—can't be involved. No intimate relationships. No sexual relations. Friendly camaraderie only. That rule is explicit."

He held her gaze for a long second. "Forget that we're agents. Imagine a world where we can have what we want. Then let's decide if it's worth working for."

God, but every molecule in her body wanted to go along with the fantasy he was spinning. Instead, she shook her head. "Imagine? Come on. This isn't Disney. The casino atmosphere's getting to you. It must be the extra oxygen they pump into the air. Rules exist for good reason. Priorities become reordered."

"Maybe they should be. For both of us." Blue eyes held hers, before he bent to press his lips against the corner of hers, sending sizzling heat throughout her body. "Want me to stop?"

Panic welled in her gut, as did desire. There were some things about her that even Ace didn't know, and she didn't feel like having a conversation about the one thing, in particular, that was weighing heavy on her mind. Besides, her sexual status should be irrelevant. Because they shouldn't go there. "Yes."

He drew a breath and moved his lips away.

"Maybe we're imagining that our kiss was better than it was," she said.

He gave her his typical, lopsided smile. More of a smirk than a smile, the left side of his mouth went a little higher than the right. "What do you say we find out if it feels like we're kissing cardboard? You make the call. If it does, I'll stop."

With the beginning of her nod, he groaned as he pressed his mouth to hers again, pulling her in closer. Opening her lips with the force of his kiss, his tongue glided over hers. She forgot about holding up the dress. It fell to the floor as she lifted her arms over his shoulders. Just as in the pedicab, the world disappeared as she tasted him and felt his fingers thread through her hair.

She sighed and leaned into him. "Damn. Not cardboard."

Without breaking their kiss, he picked her up and carried her to the bed. He put her down, then stretched out alongside her. Their kiss, deep and glorious and way better than she remembered, lasted a lifetime.

Or maybe just minutes.

"Better than I remember," he mumbled, unhooking her bra, letting it fall away. His fingers on her nipples sparked a fire that sizzled in wild streaks, throughout her body, all the way to her toes.

"Oh," she whispered, inexplicably shivering despite the burning heat. "Feels great."

"Yeah," he said, replacing his fingers with his mouth. "You. Are. Perfect."

With his tongue, he traced lazy circles around her nipples, while his hands drifted down, blazing a trail along her abdomen, until his fingers stroked the soft skin of her inner thighs.

He slid his fingers under the narrow strip of her thong panties, into the dampness that was a sure sign of how badly she wanted him. She sighed in relief, but managed to say, "We really, really shouldn't..."

Yet she spread her legs wider, crying out as he pressed. She shuddered, flexing her hips for more.

"We're not," he mumbled, with only a slight pause in the open-mouthed kiss he was lavishing on her left breast. "Just a kiss. Or two."

"This is more than a kiss."

"Didn't say I'd just kiss your lips." He broke away from her breast, then gave her another open-mouthed kiss on her hips as his fingers probed at her opening. She felt a fingertip slide into her, and arched into him for more, as he groaned. "Mmmmm. So perfect. Didn't promise not to grope."

"But we...oh... "

He slid his finger deeper into her. He pulled out, but kept working her folds with his fingers. His touch was gentle. Less insistent. He took his mouth away from hers, lifted himself on one elbow, then met her gaze. "Anything you want to tell me?"

She felt the blush burning up her neck, into her cheeks. "No."

"Seems like I should know if this is your first time."

"Let's just get past that part without talking about it."

"It really is?"

She pushed at his shoulders, then his chest. He barely moved more than an inch off of her. "You were guessing?"

He gave a deep-throated chuckle. Usually, she was happy to hear that laugh. Now though, she wanted to crawl under the blankets and hide. "After two years of knowing you, I had an inkling."

"How?"

He shrugged. "Just a gut feeling. You're the sexiest woman I've ever met. How is it that—?"

"Come on, Ace. Drop it. You went two years without seeing me as sexy. When I was younger, I was too busy being a prodigy to pause and have sex. I started at Black Raven the minute I graduated. Until now, I never dreamed of making it with a co-worker. As I just told you, it's against the rules. Besides, I work twenty-four seven, so how would I meet any—?"

His kiss stole her words, while his hand made her forget her reluctance. He barely put the tip of his finger into her.

"More," she whispered.

His tongue glided over hers, as he did things with his fingers that made her wonder how she'd gone her entire life without anyone else ever touching her there. When her muscles started clamping on his fingers, and she was sighing into his mouth, he used his thumb on her clitoris. An orgasm ripped through her that made her sigh and scream into his mouth as he continued to kiss her.

He moved his lips away from her mouth, then slid them down her body. Planting a trail of kisses along the way, he gave her a smug smile as he positioned his shoulders between her legs. When he pulled her thong down her legs, she kicked it away. While she was still trembling from her first orgasm, he opened his mouth on her. With his lips, tongue, teeth and *yes*, his fingers, he pushed her almost to the brink of mindlessness.

Energized to act, she moved away from him, rotating as she twisted herself down his body. Lying on her side, she pushed his pants to his thighs. He shifted closer to her, then lifted her leg and resumed where he'd left off, gently thrusting his fingers inside her and using his tongue to trace lazy circles around her clitoris. She shivered as she eyed the smooth, taut skin of his full, heavy erection.

"Hey," he said, moving his mouth from her for a brief second. "Let me focus on you for a while."

"I'm better when I multitask."

His chuckle became a groan as she ran her fingers along the length of him. Like everything else in life, she didn't let the fact that she hadn't done the act before stop her. She'd figure out how to do it. Though she'd never placed her mouth on a penis, she gripped his shaft and licked at the liquid that was beading on the head. He was so large, she had to use her mouth and her hands to cover him.

"Oh," he groaned. "Yeah. Was wondering if you..." His words trailed as she squeezed her fists around him, opened her mouth wider, and took more of him in, until she could feel him at the back of her throat. "Perfect."

He shifted, rolling them so that she was on top, with her legs draped over either side of his face. She flattened her tongue along the length of him, while he gently suckled her and gripped her hips. Their hips flexed slowly, at first, then faster and faster, as they matched each other, thrust for thrust, sigh for sigh, hungry groan for hungry groan. She squeezed his shaft and took him deeper in her mouth, until she felt urgency in the movement of his hips. When his fingers inside of her lost their gentleness, when he licked her then suckled her until she felt his teeth nibbling at her clitoris, finally, an orgasm ripped through her.

As she moaned with the force of it, while squeezing him and taking as much of him as she could into her mouth, he mumbled something that sounded like, “Let go.”

Instead, she squeezed his shaft harder, holding onto the base of it with both hands as she sucked harder at the head.

“I’m...aw...yeah.” He flexed deep into her throat, pumping into her, with a long groan that matched her sighs. After his hips stopped flexing, he pulled away from her. While their bodies shook with the aftereffects, he moved her so that she was in his arms, their legs entwined. “Sorry. Meant to pull out.”

“I wasn’t going to let you. That didn’t seem like it would be the best ending...” Stunned by the force of their mutual climax, she let their noses touch, while her words trailed and her thoughts swam. Her body became heavy with lethargy. Before she could even think about what had happened, her eyes closed. Fighting sudden exhaustion, she nestled further into the warm space between his arm and his side, and whispered, “Glad that’s out of our system.”

He gave a short chuckle. He pulled her in closer, closed his arms around her, and kissed her forehead. “Not a chance.”

“It’s got to be.” With her last ounce of energy, she opened her eyes. Locked gazes with him. “Promise.”

He gave her a slow, lazy smile as he lifted her leg so that it draped over his abdomen and pulled her in snug against his hip. He bent his head to plant a lingering kiss on her forehead, "Can't make that promise. We just need to talk a bit. We'll figure something out."

She let her eyes close again, feeling a sudden, overwhelming fatigue. "That conversation would take a lifetime, and my answer will never change. It won't work."

"It will. You'll see. We're too compatible. Too good together."

"Too tired."

He closed his arms around her. In the small of her back, she felt him turning his wrist to check his watch. "I'll wake you in ten minutes, then help you zip your dress."

"Exhausted. Can't...think," she mumbled, as her mind zoomed towards an unconsciousness that was more than tiredness. Her last glimmer of thought told her something was wrong. Her drop-dead fatigue was too sudden. Yet before she could say anything, her mind crossed the thin line that separated light and awareness from darkness and unconsciousness.

Chapter Six

December 23; 12:20 a.m.

'Bomp-bomp-bomp.'

Insistent and loud, the emergency signal blasting over the ship's PA system was almost as irritating as the sharp icepick of pain that jabbed through Ace's skull. As though his lower and upper eyelids had billions of interconnected nerves, the pain intensified when he opened his eyes. Between blinding flashes of emergency lights, his and Leo's suite was pitch black.

'Bomp-bomp-bomp.'

Three blasts. Not seven, which ship's protocol indicated would have signaled an emergency requiring immediate abandonment of the ship. Three blasts signaled an emergency that required all passengers to pay attention for further instructions. They'd been told that at the muster drill.

With his mind reeling as fast as the strobe of the emergency lights, the muster drill earlier that day now seemed like a distant memory. He tried to impose order to his addled brain, but all he could think of was Leo. Kissing her. Touching her. Tasting her.

What the hell was I thinking?

Apparently, not much, other than how good it felt to have her mouth on him while his mouth had been on her. In no way was oral sex the equivalent of the conversation they needed to have. But, damn...the side trip certainly had been mind-blowingly fun. His thoughts drifted back to the moment when she'd closed her mouth on him. He shut his eyes because opening them was impossible. He was too damn sleepy.

'Bomp-bomp-bomp.'

His body jolted out of sleep, again.

Fuck!

Time.

How much had passed?

Think.

You're on a job, goddammit.

THINK!

Ace gasped, ripped open his eyelids, and realized the air was thick with a sickly-sweet tinge. Gaseous ether, having strong analgesic properties. In a murky recess of his headache-addled mind, he remembered encountering the scent before. Afghanistan. He and his recon team had infiltrated a prison where it had been used only moments earlier.

He inhaled again and wished he hadn't. Ether had been mixed with something...pungent and lingering. He couldn't identify it. But it was effective, whatever it might be, because he had no idea how long he'd been out.

Too long.

Leo was pressed against him, unmoving, in the space between his arm and his chest.

"Wake up." He managed to say the words, though his head swam and his tongue felt like it was glued to the top of his mouth. With a touch of his watch, he checked his comm settings. "All agents. Report. Ragno. Copy?"

Silence.

'Bomp-bomp-bomp.'

Leo was pliable. Limp. Too limp. Not sleeping. Unconscious. Maybe worse. While ether wasn't normally lethal, this wasn't simply ether, and she could've had a reaction...

No! Don't even think it. Get her air. Now!

He sat up, lifting her with him as he swung his legs over the side of the bed. Kicking aside the sheet that was wrapped around their legs, he fought a wave of nausea as his brain protested the sudden movement. Ace felt for a pulse. Found one at her carotid. Faint, but there. Gasping, he inhaled and almost lost a sudden, violent battle with bitter bile that rose in the back of his throat.

'Bomp-bomp-bomp.'

Fighting the ether-induced urge to lie back down, he shifted Leo into the crook of his left arm and glanced at his watch. Half past midnight.

What the fuck!

They'd been out for almost four hours. Stumbling to his feet, he lifted Leo with him. The sliding glass door that led to their balcony was a mere fifteen steps away. It was easier to get to than their equipment that was underneath the floorboard near the vanity, yet the noxious air made the distance seem like a football field.

'Bomp-bomp-bomp.'

"Emergency. Emergency. All guests. Proceed to the Clio Deck, Calliope Theater. Immediately." The voice of First Officer Raznick, the officer who'd led the muster drill when they'd first arrived on the ship that afternoon, was calm as he delivered the instructions in English.

During the muster drill, the Calliope Theater had been designated as one of two potential assembly points for emergencies requiring congregation of the guests. "If you need assistance, press the call button from any ship's phone."

Ace took unsteady steps towards the sliding glass door that led to their balcony. The suite went from dark to light to dark with the flash of the emergency strobe. Their reflection—caught like a snapshot in the glass door—stopped him in his tracks.

Her head lolled against his chest, floppy arms and legs supported by his arms. Naked. Curvy. Muscular. Beautiful, but limp. Lifeless. Through the murky recesses of his ether-addled brain, the vision of her lifeless body in his arms played the cruel trick of transporting him to another place and time.

Not again. Not Leo. I'll die this time.

With one of his classic flashback symptoms, his legs became useless, while his mind snapped into overdrive. His brain raced to four years earlier when he'd carried Kat from the battle that had killed her. He could feel her weight again. Could feel the life slipping from her. Heard himself screaming.

After Kat had died, he'd returned to the village where his unit had been ambushed. For the next twenty-four hours he'd been in stealth mode. Beyond going rogue, he'd become a hunter who lived only to kill the men who were responsible for Kat's death. He'd found them. Tested them. Determined they were complicit in the ambush. Then he killed them. In various circles, his unofficial actions were unofficially legendary. Despite all that happened, his discharge was voluntary. He kept all his medals, but had earned a reputation, behind closed doors, as a dangerous loose cannon. His rogue actions hadn't healed him.

Now, in a reel of memory-film, worthy of a sick, twisted, depressing Hollywood movie, he saw himself as he'd lived in the months after returning to the States. There had been long periods of lonely numbness. Just him, his surfboard, and the ocean. Or his motorcycle, rural roads, and no one else.

Until an old friend called, a Black Raven agent who he'd met when on a joint mission that had pulled in a few private security contractors. Gabe Hernandez. Zeus' younger brother.

Of the two Hernandez brothers, Gabe was the brother who smiled. It was something that Gabe did frequently, with warm enthusiasm that reached even into the dark corners of the worst of Ace's post-Afghanistan days. It had taken a while for Gabe to persuade Ace that Black Raven could be an option. Ace had hesitated, because only he knew the depths to which he'd sunk. After his anger finally left him, he felt profound grief. For Kat. His team members. No one had ever told him that grief could feel so much like fear.

I need to stand. Fight this paralysis.

Yet the strobe light flashed Leo's reflection again. His mind replayed the past, while forcing him to remain on his knees. The first step in the right direction had been two years earlier, when he'd arrived at Last Resort, with a grief-stricken heart and more than a little bewilderment at how his once-perfect life had imploded, so quickly.

He'd met Leo that first day. He'd pulled up alongside her at the training facility, after their motorcycle sprint. As though none of his tours of duty or the awards he'd won as a Marine meant jack shit in the hallowed world of Black Raven's elite agents, she'd laughed when he introduced himself as Ace Evans. *'We've been expecting you at Last Resort, Adam Cooper Evans. Ace is a name you'll have to earn here. Welcome. By the way, it wouldn't be a good thing if all the agents knew that I just kicked your ass. I won't tell them. You owe me one.'*

The *'bomp-bomp-bomp'* of the emergency signal jarred his mind to the present, but the memory of that day in the parking lot gave him the strength to get off his knees. Tuning out Raznick's repetitive instruction, this time in Spanish, he stood and walked to the balcony door. Opening it a few inches, he turned Leo's face to the fresh, cool air. "Come on, honey. Breathe."

Their suite was on the starboard side of the ship, the same side he'd been on when talking to Ragno earlier. There was one striking difference between then and now. When he'd been talking to Ragno, there hadn't been another ship in sight. Now, though the night was dark, he could easily see another vessel, about a mile away.

Most of the lights on the boat were off. Moonlight, though, revealed the dark, shadowy outline of a ship that seemed to be slightly behind *Imagine.*

He eyed the following ship's nighttime navigational lights. A red light was visible on the side of the vessel. Eyeing the distance between the red light and the bright white navigational light on the stern, he guesstimated that he was looking at a two-hundred-footer.

If the ship was complying with international navigational laws, the red light was a signal that the port side of the following ship was facing *Imagine.* The fact that he could see the red navigational light from the starboard side of *Imagine* meant that the two ships were travelling almost parallel to each other.

Probably not a good thing.

His night vision scope, under the floorboard with their weapons, would give him more details. But, for the moment, reviving Leo and figuring out what the hell was happening were more urgent matters.

In contrast to the darkness that cloaked the other ship, *Imagine* was lit like a Christmas tree. As strobe lights flashed in his and Leo's suite, he opened the sliding door more, dropped again to his knees, and crawled onto the balcony with Leo in his arms.

He sat her on the deck, leaned her head back, and opened her mouth, as he used his foot to ease the balcony door almost shut. Inhaling cool ocean air, he pinched her nose and exhaled into her mouth. He repeated the process a few times, until she opened her eyes and gave him a glazed, disoriented glance.

“Come on, goddammit.” He remembered how hard it had been for him to get out of the bed. It didn’t matter. He needed her better, fast. “Breathe. Deep.”

He felt her inhale, while his mouth was on hers. Finally, she grabbed his forearms, then pushed him away. She leaned to the side, clenched her stomach, and started heaving. He held her hair away from her face, giving her a few seconds of silence to shake off the initial rush of sickness.

“What...the...hell?”

“We’ve been gassed. Ether, and more. Pirates? Terrorists? I don’t think labels matter much at this point.” He let go of her and sat back.

She dropped her head into her hands. “My head’s swimming. We went through potential attacks at headquarters. Historically...piracy...isn’t successful on cruise ships.”

“I know. I think we’re at the inception of what might be a history-changing event.” With each breath that he took, his headache receded a bit more. His thoughts became clearer.

She wiped her hands and mouth on a lounge chair cushion, sat back, and breathed deeply. Wincing, she held her palm to her forehead. “Someone hammered a railroad tie into my head.”

“Based on what I just went through, and the fact that you weigh a lot less than me, you’ve got about fifteen more minutes of pure hell before you get to the other side.”

‘Bomp-bomp-bomp.’

“Is that the ship’s PA system?”

He nodded. “Your brain’s still cloudy. Breathe.”

“I thought I was dreaming it.”

"The ship's air filtration system was the perfect delivery vehicle. We were out for four hours."

Raznick's German wasn't as perfect as his Spanish, but he still sounded calm and authoritative. The man was using the languages spoken by the guests. This was Leo's first time to hear the instruction while awake. Leo didn't speak German, but Ace did. The fact that she didn't ask him for a translation told him the severity of her headache and disorientation.

She was pale, shivering, and showed no visible reaction to the jaw-dropping news that they were now four hours into a siege. She'd wrapped her arms around her legs and tucked her knees into her chest.

"Deep breathing," he said. "Work on it."

She nodded with another inhale.

Fiddling with his watch, he refreshed the comm system, then reset his comm to the open line. "Agents. Ragno. Report."

Silence.

Bleary-eyed, she shot him a questioning glance. "I'm set on the open line. I should've heard that. Have you had any contact with anyone?"

"No."

"How long were we out?"

He frowned when she couldn't remember what he'd already told her. He swallowed his frustration. He couldn't fault her for her ether-induced confusion. After all, his brain had been so addled that he'd had a flashback that had knocked him to his knees, when he was damn well past the days of flashbacks.

As a matter of fact, as a condition of his employment, he was supposed to report the occurrence of flashbacks or PTSD episodes to the Black Raven psychiatrists. He thought about the episode he'd just had, with her naked in his arms, when he couldn't get off his knees. Full circumstances were typically relevant in flashback analysis.

Yeah. Details of that one aren't making it to an evaluation.

"A little over four hours," he repeated. "Take deep breaths."

"It's freezing out here." She eyed him from head to toe, then glanced down, at her own nude body.

He was sitting about two feet from her. Keeping his ass planted next to the deck chair, he fought the urge to move closer to her, hold her, and warm her up. She wouldn't appreciate the gesture. Plus, the cool air would help her shake off the noxious after-effects of the gas quicker.

"To think I was worried about..." As her words trailed, she shook her head. Drawing her knees tight to her chest, she clutched her stomach with one hand, while holding her forehead with the other. "...that damn zipper. Look at us now."

It was hard not to look at her. She was turned a little sideways from him. He had a partial view of the curve of her right breast, the delicate slope where her waist met her hip, and the graceful lines of muscular thigh and calf. Realizing she was staring at his body with the same level of distraction, he felt a moment of relief. His immediate next thought was that they both needed to take in more fresh air, because there was no room for distraction right now aboard *Imagine.*

'Bomp-bomp-bomp.'

This time, the announcement was being repeated in English. She set her jaw as she listened intently, as though she was noticing the instructions for the first time.

"Let me guess." Her gaze returned to his. Her tone remained shaky, but her words were less tentative. "We're not walking into the Calliope Theater as Chloe and Zack."

His worry over her condition eased a bit with her statement, which he took as a clear sign her brain was starting to reassemble. "Correct. We're Ace and Leo from here on out."

She shut her eyes and held her head in the palms of her hands. "Jesus. This pain needs to go away."

"You have at least eight more minutes of it."

As the strobe of the emergency lights continued, each illumination of her face revealed that she was shifting into agent mode. Some of the glaze of pain and fatigue left her eyes. Her jaw became set. Her eyes drifted over his shoulder. "Wouldn't the door be better open, since we need to get in there and suit up? Noxious fumes take a while to dissipate."

"I left it open a crack, but we should give the room a few more minutes to air out. Right now, keep breathing, as deeply as you can." He paused. "If I gave it any more than an inch, the open door would be seen."

"Ship's cameras?"

As their pre-job preparation, they'd both studied camera positions. Outside starboard cameras were angled to encompass a view of the balconies. Onboard cameras wouldn't reveal their current position on the floor of the balcony, nor would the cameras reveal a slight crack in the balcony door. If it wasn't for her ether-induced confusion, Leo would know that as well.

He gestured with his chin toward the direction of the open sea and the other ship, but the solid balcony wall blocked her view. He lifted himself a bit and peeked over the railing. The red nav light seemed to be in the same position as before.

"We've got company cruising with us. Slightly behind, as though it's following. I want to stay out of their line of sight."

She nodded as though she was well on her way to shaking off the effects of the ether and absorbing the facts. "With our comms down, we should signal them. It might be our easiest way of making a Mayday."

"Can't tell whether they're friend or foe. They're a little less than a mile away. My gut's telling me foe, because their position hasn't changed. They're cruising at the same speed as us."

She absorbed the news with a nod. "That's close enough to interfere with *Imagine*'s radar and electronics. It's probably equipped with a jammer and is sending false signals." She took a long-measured breath, then exhaled. "That could be why we can't use our comm system. Ours is dependent upon the ship's system."

"Any chance you can restore comms without going to the radio room?"

"Doubtful. Under the floorboard, I have a laptop, tablets, radios. I need to access radio signals to figure out what's jamming us. The radio room is probably the only place I'll be able to do that. Plus, once I'm there, I could also disable the ship's surveillance cameras."

He nodded. “Cameras definitely need to be shut down so we can move around the ship without alerting the powers that be. Since I doubt the ship’s coffee shop has a Wi-Fi hotspot—”

She chuckled, interrupting him, but her humor was short-lived. She pressed her fingertips to her temples and winced. “It’s a little more complicated than that, but you’ve got the right idea.”

‘Bomp-bomp-bomp.’

“Getting to the radio room seems like the most productive option. We don’t have a lot of time here,” Ace raised his voice to be heard over Raznick’s repetition of the instructions. “They’ll eventually do a cabin check.”

“Understood.”

“For now, we have to assume that the only fact that Ragno and headquarters know is that our comms are down. I’m betting the pirates have radar duping capabilities. Ragno probably sees a false radar reading.”

She nodded in agreement. “Which means even if we are off course, headquarters has no way of knowing where we’re going.”

“Okay then. Let’s get moving. The most direct route to the radio room will take us past the Calliope Theater.”

“No,” she said, with a firm headshake. “The theater’s on the Clio Deck. That’s two decks below us. The radio room is on the Erato deck. Two decks above.”

“Keep breathing. Your brain’s still cloudy. Due to the damn effective gassing, and because Raznick and whomever he’s working with are trying to corral all the guests in the theater, we have to assume we’re in a hostage situation. Which means we’ve got to avoid the ship's cameras until we sabotage the surveillance system. Once they know about us, and perceive us as a threat—

"We look real threatening."

He chuckled. "That'll change soon."

"Anyway, once they see us as a threat, odds are they'll start killing hostages to make us surrender."

She closed her eyes for a second, then gave him a bleary-eyed nod. "Geez. Sorry. I know we can't go straight there."

"Correct. To avoid the surveillance cameras we'll have to go down to go up. That plan works in our favor, because the only path that we can take will lead us right over the theater. We'll get an eyeful of what's happening there and plant a camera that will give us a view of the action. That way, when we do establish communication with Ragno, we know what to tell her."

She gave a slow nod, then winced. "Still chasing my thoughts."

"You need a few more minutes out here, because the room will have residual gas. Our O2 saturation levels need to be high."

'Bomp-bomp-bomp.'

"I was...unnaturally tired before it happened," she said. "I mean, I didn't smell ether while we...were, you know...Did you?"

"No. Though it may have been taking effect while we were...otherwise occupied. God—" He couldn't help but smile as he thought about being in bed with her. "That was incredible."

She shifted closer to him, then kicked her heel into his shin. It didn't hurt, but she used enough power to jolt the smile from his face. "Incredible? Really? We didn't even speak in full sentences just now. How the hell will we write an after-action report?"

He chuckled. “Seems like your head’s getting clearer.”

“This job will be scrutinized from every angle. Imagine the look on Zeus’ face if he’d read an AAR with this sentence: *‘As Agent Evans and I were engaging in mutual oral sex, I started to smell ether. Instead of being alarmed, I continued sucking, because he had his mouth between my legs and it felt too good to stop.’*”

Somehow, Ace couldn’t see Zeus laughing at that.

Leo pounded her fists on the floor of the deck. “Say something.”

“I didn’t have a warning, either.”

She kicked him again. “You’re missing the point.”

“Not at all. We’re on a three-day job. We were exactly where we were supposed to be. In our suite. Agents do things on a three-day job, like sleep, shower, sh—”

“Understood, though sex is an s-word that isn’t supposed to happen. We’re getting paid to work. Not have sex with each other.”

“Not all details make it into after-action reports. I know the bulk of your work has been in the cyber division, but—”

“Don’t give me that bullshit. I know how to write an AAR. I’m not simply a desk agent—”

“My point is you’ve been in the field enough to know that some details aren’t relevant in an AAR, and our detour, as noteworthy as it might be in our lives, doesn’t need to see the light of day, no matter what happens on this job. How’s your head?”

“Bad, but thoughts are getting clearer.”

“Obviously.”

“I can work around the pain in my head. What we did, though...”

'Bomp-bomp-bomp.'

"Keep breathing. Your head will get better. We're both intelligent. After this job, we'll figure out what we need to do about our situation."

"Don't worry about our situation," she snapped. "I know the fix for it. No matter how great it felt—"

"Pretty damn incredible—"

"You're missing the point," she said. "What we did in that bed isn't happening ag—"

"It won't stop our feelings for one another. It would be just like ignoring our kiss. If you're honest with yourself, how effective was that?"

From the direction of the ship's bow, maybe two decks down, a man's harsh, guttural yell interrupted them. The man's words, unintelligible, were followed by a pop-pop-pop of gunfire from an assault weapon. Leo's eyes hardened and her jaw set. Just as quickly, he watched her eyes cloud with another wave of post-anesthetic grogginess. She needed more time outside, but they damn well had to get dressed and armed.

"Give me a few minutes inside to access the crawl space and our equipment. Take that time to clear your head. On my signal, follow me in. Shut the door behind you."

"Roger."

"When you're gearing up, carry as much firepower as possible. Put on your gas mask first."

"No need to state the obvious."

"No need to be sensitive. Sorry if I sounded patronizing. It wasn't intended that way. Stating the obvious helps me think."

"I didn't take it as patronizing. I took it as overprotectiveness. I thought maybe what happened earlier between us was getting in the way of proper agent to agent interaction."

"It won't."

"Good. Don't let it. Act like I'm a guy. Like you always did before."

He'd been turning to the door when she dropped that verbal bomb. He glanced back at her. She'd dropped her head to her knees and folded her arms over her shins, a sure sign that she was in more pain than she was letting on. "Never thought I was treating you like a guy. I was just treating you like...you."

Chapter Seven

12:44 a.m.

A minute earlier than they'd planned, his second-in-command stepped into the stateroom with two additional men. They wore camo-gear and carried assault rifles. Their gas masks, firmly in place, answered whether he should remove the mask he'd put on more than four hours earlier.

On the ship's manifest, his second-in-command had been identified as Chad Ting. In their real-life world, the tall, pale-skinned, dark-haired man, of mixed Asian heritage, went by Skylar. The executioner. He planned to retire with his share of the proceeds from the job.

It was good to have a highly motivated co-conspirator.

Skylar stepped forward. His two men stayed behind him, at the door. They stood with their backs erect, their beefy arms dangling at their sides.

"Roundup of guests and security?" he asked, tuning out the repetitive bomp-bomp-bomp of the emergency signal and the directions that followed.

"Proceeding as planned." Skylar said, nodding coolly, seemingly dismissive of the violence that was part of their 'roundup' plan.

Casino guests were integral to the operation, for a while. Everyone else was immediately expendable.

Despite the violence that the plan required, he felt no remorse. No excitement. If anything, he felt relief that the operation was finally underway, with underlying anticipation of how wealthy he'd be after the next four hours.

Skylar apparently felt the same. The glint in his dark eyes was just as hard and humorless as ever. There was no sweat on his brow, or anywhere else that he could see. Showing no outward signs of nerves, the man appeared just as cool as he had in any of their lengthy planning meetings. For that, the man was worth every dollar of his steep fee.

"From here on out you and I will communicate through our mics," Skylar said. "Testing. Line four."

"Copy," he answered, hearing Skylar though his ear mic, loud and clear. He dropped his voice to a low whisper. "Testing."

"Copy," Skylar said. "Our encryption's in place. Be careful when around others. Take off your mask."

He glanced at his watch. "It's early for free breathing."

"The gas has almost dissipated," Skylar said. "You won't inhale enough to pass out. A bit of sickness will help you stay in role."

He unstrapped his gas mask, removed it from his face, and breathed air that smelled sickly sweet. When he moved towards the door, Skylar's firm grip on his forearm halted his forward progress. "Mess up your tuxedo. Trust me, none of the other guests look so cool and crisp. Scared shitless is in order. When you're around the guests, you need to act like one."

Chapter Eight

12:45 a.m.

When Ace indicated, Leo began the trek back into their room. Trying to ignore the *bomp-bomp-bomp* of the emergency signal, and Raznick's repetitive instructions, Leo stayed on her hands and knees. Using her foot, she shut the balcony door behind her. Her head still throbbed, but the sharpest spikes of pain had diminished. While her brain fog hadn't fully dissipated, she was managing to put together more and more thoughts.

Ace had removed a floorboard near the vanity. He stood, visible from the hips up in a crawl space, one of several possible ways for them to exit their suite undetected. He'd dressed in a tight base layer of black body armor, made of material that provided anti-ballistic protective coverage. Fibers in the clothing made it almost impervious to small arms fire.

"Catch." Ace tossed her a full-face mask, with an attached safety helmet, identical to the one he wore. Strapping it on, she breathed in filtered air through the respirator, then started crawling his way.

Moving on autopilot, inch by inch, she stayed on all fours until she was away from the sight line provided by the balcony's glass doors, just in case anyone on the nearby ship could see.

Ace paused as he fitted a bulletproof chest plate into the pocket that covered his chest. Nodding in her direction, with a slight smile, he said, “See? You’re not shy at all.”

Through the comm system built into the helmet, his voice resonated. For a second, her murky thoughts didn’t give her a clue as to what he was talking about. Then she remembered she was naked, but for the helmet and respirator, and he was gloating, because he’d been correct earlier. She wasn’t modest. Not in the least. There’d been good cause for him to call her out when she’d been shy about getting into an evening gown in front of him. “Be professional, Agent Evans.”

He chuckled, then refocused on assembling gear. All agents on board had access to the cache of weapons and gear that had been stowed in the crawl space under ‘Chloe and Zack’s suite, prior to boarding, by a Black Raven ‘crew member.’ It was one of two such stashes Black Raven had onboard. The other was in Agent Kamin’s room, on another deck, on the opposite end of the ship.

“Others should be showing up here for weapon power.”

“Yeah. It’s odd that no one has come yet.” In the illuminating strobe of the emergency lights, the shift in their relationship was reflected in Ace’s eyes, easily visible through the polycarbonate lens of his respirator mask. His gaze as he glanced her way to check her progress was...

Assessing?

Yes, but that wasn’t a problem. Given the gassing that they’d just experienced, he’d assess any agent on his team.

Worried?

Yes, but a bit of worry was typical territory on any problematic job. Each agent played an integral role in the work of the team. If there was a weak link, the leader needed to be aware and work around it.

With one more bright flash of emergency light, Ace's dark blue eyes were illuminated again, and *Bingo!* the problematic emotion zinged her way.

Lingering tenderness.

Tenderness was an issue because it was a close cousin to caring. Worse, tenderness was in the family of...that dangerous four-letter l-word, which hadn't escaped her lips since September 11, 2001, when she'd hung on to her phone with all her might as her father told her goodbye for the last time. Her head renewed its incessant pounding, keeping pace with the strobe of the emergency light.

Look on the bright side. He hasn't said 'I love you.' Unfortunately...or maybe fortunately...he's got as many problems with that issue as me.

But tenderness and its attendant other emotions, even without the l-word, were trouble. None signaled logic or rational thought. Such heartfelt emotions had no place on any Black Raven job.

"You okay?" His voice was loud, clear, and signified too much concern for her well-being.

'Bomp-bomp-bomp.'

Over the emergency instruction, this time in Spanish, she said, "Stop worrying about me."

"I would ask any agent who was coming out of ether-induced analgesia, and who wasn't moving, that question. I'm assuming they're coming for Chloe and Zack, since we haven't made an appearance at the theater. If you're okay, move your ass. If you're not okay, tell me. I've got first aid to help with the aftereffects."

She hadn't realized that she'd stopped moving. Unlike her, he was in action, making two stacks of gear and clothes on the suite's carpeted floor from trunks that were nestled in the crawl space. Black slacks, times two. Armor plates for her, since his were already on his chest and back. Boots, times two.

"You sound different."

"The mic system with these helmet respirators is pretty unsophisticated." He glanced again in her direction, before bending down, then coming up with two knives, sheathed in black leather holsters, connected to thigh straps. "You know that, though. What do you mean, different?"

"It sounds like you're thinking of me differently."

He paused, a grenade in each hand, and glanced her way. "Paranoid?"

"No."

"Look, I intended to talk things through a helluva lot better. Could be you're just hearing me differently, now that we—"

"That's not it. We're bickering. Like a long-married couple."

He shrugged, adding transparent nylon bags of climbing rope and carabiners to their piles. "Seems a lot like one of our typical discussions to me."

"No. We're acting like a couple—"

"That was my point earlier. We've acted like a couple from the beginning, except for one big omission."

A visual flashed through her mind, of what they'd done in bed earlier. Where their mouths had been. Where hers had been, in particular. "How was I so oblivious?"

Her words were low, barely a mumble, but his chuckle indicated that he heard her. "We were both oblivious. Issues, Leo. Issues. We both have them. We just need to work through them."

'Bomp-bomp-bomp.'

Shaking off her frustration with the annoying sound of the PA system, she resumed crawling again, as the emergency instructions were repeated in Chinese. "I'll gladly shoot Raznick to get him to shut up. Don't you think anyone planning on following that damn instruction would have done so by now?"

"Probably not. I opened my eyes about forty minutes ago. It was a long time before I was well enough to get you out of the room." He paused, gave her a look she couldn't read, then cocked his head, watching her forward progress. "You've had the benefit of being carried to the balcony, and breathing fresh air, and you're still moving slow. I bet half the guests are just waking from their ether nap. They don't have our training and aren't in the shape we're in. It's going to take them a long time to get all one hundred fifty guests to the theater."

"Stop looking at my boobs."

He dragged his gaze back to her eyes. "I'm guessing irritability means you're starting to feel better?"

"Yes." She grimaced as she reached the stack he'd laid out for her. "The wooziness is gone. I still need this splitting headache to go away, though. And, I damn well need to figure out how to cure the problem we've created for ourselves."

"You said we wouldn't fall into bed again, as though you're thinking that's a cure."

"Yes. That's a given. But you need to stop looking at me like, like...with..."

He bent down. When he reappeared, each hand held a Springfield Armory M1A close quarter combat rifle. "Use your words."

"Screw you. Tenderness. That kind of feeling has no place on a job."

"I can't help how I feel about you, and I'm not going to fight it. It's like you're..." He placed a rifle next to her pile, then added extra clips to both piles. "...my endless summer. Hey. I'm liking this. I can't believe I was so speechless after our kiss. It's as though you're the ocean, on a warm August morning. Together, we'll experience the most perfect waves imaginable."

"I might've liked it better when you were speechless," she mumbled. The truth was, she was touched by his words, but logic quickly prevailed. His sentimental analogy, equating her with his surfer's version of nirvana, not only showed her how deep his feelings ran, it added another layer of concern. If only her head wasn't hurting so badly, maybe she could think through a way to make him focus on the task at hand.

Dammit. Think!

As he added M84s—flashbang grenades—and a handheld thermal imaging scope to his backpack, he glanced at her. "Sig Sauer or Glock?"

Hell. He is focusing. I'm the one with the problem.

There'd be time to worry about the emotions that had inspired his surfing sentiment later. The more pressing question was which handgun she felt like carrying. She liked that the 9mm Sig Sauer P226 required a more deliberate trigger press to launch the first shot. Other times, she wanted her hand on a Glock 19.

"Earth to Agent Leon. With your comms and your tablet, you're up to over twenty pounds of gear so far. You'll be belly crawling through narrow spaces with your backpack and your rifle, so—"

"Both."

He put both handguns in her pile. "I don't think you should take a night vision scope too. It'll add too much bulkiness."

"Agreed. I'd prefer the extra firepower. Including cameras. They don't weigh much and might be useful after I reestablish connectivity." She picked up the Sig Sauer and continued crawling past him.

"Where are you going?"

"Fifteen-second bathroom break." Glancing behind her, she realized she was well past the visual range of the balcony door. No one from the neighboring ship would see her walking across the room to the bathroom. She stood, lifting the hand that carried the gun. Once her head caught up to her movement, she started walking, unsteadily, to the bathroom. "If they come for us, I'm ready."

She was almost to the door when she heard the muffled *pop-pop-pop* of gunfire. She glanced over her shoulder at Ace, whose gaze was locked on her butt. "Hey. Surfer boy. Focus on the task. That was from the floor below us. Agree?"

His gaze lifted to meet hers. Grimness in his eyes told her that while her butt might have provided a focal point, his brain was on the job. He nodded, confirming her guess as to where the gunfire, which was now followed by screams, originated. "Midship. Based on earlier gunfire, it sounds like they're moving towards the stern."

"So we know a few things. Raznick's trying to get everyone to the theater," she said.

He nodded. "And we know he's calm about it. Doesn't sound coerced."

"But he's damn persistent." She stepped into the bathroom. "So, my guess is not everyone has shown up there."

"Agree. Guests may have been detouring elsewhere, with the assistance of security. I seriously doubt any of the security personnel on this ship would follow his instruction."

"Unless they're in on it," she said. "And we know they're using weapons to assist in the search."

"They–whomever they are–are likely only searching the rooms of people who haven't arrived at the theater. Like us. Let's assume the search team we're hearing has almost finished with the floor below us. They'll likely climb the stairwell that's in the stern and start on our floor."

As she used the toilet and the sink, through the audio system in her helmet, she listened to Ace's calm breathing. It helped her collect her thoughts, as her brain started firing normally. "Our ether nap started around 1930 hours. correct?"

"Closer to eight o'clock. I'd put it at 1945. Right before I passed out, I had promised to wake you in ten minutes. I checked my watch."

"When you were in the shower, you had just confirmed with Stills that most guests were in their rooms. Our agents were disbursed around the ship."

"Yes. Hopefully, that works in our favor. It would be good if our team had all hands on deck. No pun intended. We also know that the disbursement of guests must have worked in their favor, too. We'll have to figure out why."

"Disbursement of guests would have helped to separate guests from security." She took an extra few seconds to wash her hands, then risked lifting the helmet to splash cold water in her mouth.

By the time she emerged, Ace was dressed and strapping a knife above his ankle, underneath his cargo pants. She shimmied into tight body armor, then pulled on looser pants and a shirt, all black. With each added ounce of gear, Leo felt more like herself. When she strapped on a tool belt containing a stun gun, a clip with a grenade, hand ties, and a holster for her Sig Sauer, her head was finally free from the fuzziness caused by the sedative.

"Catch." He tossed a compact battery-operated, pivoting power tool in her direction. With controls and an eyepiece on the handle, the working end was a fully retractable, pivoting camera and screwdriver, capable of angling in any direction. In the handle were alternate heads–flat ones of varying dimensions and Phillips heads. Engineered by Black Raven, the device was necessary for maneuvering quickly through areas where they'd have to unscrew panels and vents from inside crawl spaces. Four screws were a standard configuration on *Imagine*'s crawl space and access panels. "And another for backup."

As she caught the second screwdriver and slipped it into one of the pockets at her thigh, she asked, "Superstitious?"

"No. Prepared."

Armed and equipped, she started to feel less like a woman who'd fallen prey to emotional weakness. Which she had, the second she'd let kissing Ace seem like an idea worth entertaining.

Okay. So, I'm human. Snap out of it. Be better next time.

She'd sort through her feelings after the job, when she was on her couch, eating pizza, peanut M&M's, and popcorn, and catching up on the football she'd missed while working. She watched him put a Glock into a shoulder harness. He handed it to her. As she strapped it on, she promised herself that no matter the end result, she wouldn't let her feelings for him become a weakness. "Thanks for the help with the gear."

"Under the circumstances, I'd have provided an assist to any agent suffering aftereffects of sedation." He studied her for a split second, then bent to replace the wood panel over the crawl space. "You're better now, right?"

"Yep. Ready to kick some ass. Once we figure out whose ass to kick." Lacing her combat boots, then reaching into her backpack for her hand-held navigation system, laptop, tablet, and phone, she said, "I thought we'd use the crawl space beneath the floor."

He gave a quick headshake as he replaced the screws that held the floor panel in place. "No. That won't lead where we want to go. You need to get to the radio room without them spotting you on surveillance. Plus, re-rolling the rug's slightly problematic if we both go out through the floor. I don't want to give them a reason to look in there and spot weapons. We don't want to let them know we're here."

"Care to share the plan?" She had ideas, but he was her superior.

"The crawl space above us leads to the aft service stairwell, which isn't on surveillance. From there, we can access the crawl space that's above the Clio Deck. You'll go all the way to the bow, where you'll go through the forward service stairwell to get to the radio room and do your thing."

"What will you do, while I'm doing all the work?"

"Assess the enemy." He shrugged, with a smile. "Regain control of the ship."

"Sounds easy. A few details are missing though. Like how."

He gave her a serious, distant look, as he thought through scenarios. He knew the only acceptable ending. So did she. Disable the bad guys, whatever it took, while losing no innocents. Black Ravens return home safely. Multiple avenues could lead to the ending, each with drawbacks.

"Going into the helm station isn't an option," she said. "Agreed?"

He nodded. "Yep. By now, accessibility is an issue. Even if we could get past their firepower there, electronic and manual locks would slow us down for too long."

She nodded. "And by now, they've changed the exterior override codes. With just two of us there, we'd be easy targets while we tried to figure it out."

From outside their suite, further down the hall, someone pounded on a door. The crack of a doorjamb giving way reverberated, as a man yelled words that were almost unintelligible. She heard enough. While Ace didn't speak Mandarin, she was fluent. "Mandarin. Directing hands in the air."

"It's the primary language of one-fifth of the guests, and the primary language of most of the employees of Quan Security," he said, referring to the private company that was *Imagine*'s Tier One security, hired by Imagine Casinos Worldwide. There was a *pop-pop-pop* of gunfire, followed by more yelling. From the opposite direction in the hallway, there was more pounding on doors. "Two search teams are working now."

"Sounds like it," she said. "If we took out whoever is getting ready to come into our room, we could use their comm system. At least to hear them communicate with one another."

Ace glanced at her as he rerolled the rug and smoothed the edges out with his feet. "No. I thought we might stick around for that, but now that I know there's more than one team working our hallway, it doesn't make sense. I don't want to be in a firefight with an unknown number of combatants. We're blind in here, and our priority has to be to establish a Mayday. Not kill one or two of these fuckers. Plus, once we start shooting, I want to do it in a way that doesn't alert the enemy to our presence. We need to put that off as long as possible."

She nodded her agreement as she powered up her laptop and her handheld navigation system, while he jumped on top of the vanity and started unscrewing the entry panel. "Because once we start killing them, they'll start killing hostages to get us to stop."

"Correct. But only if they figure out we're killing them," he said. "Right now, they're still in assembly mode, which gives us time. We don't know if they've made any demands yet. I don't want them to find out about us until you're well on the way to alerting Ragno and the outside world to the hijacking. Or whatever this siege might be classified as."

"Sounds logical." Glancing at the laptop screen, she clicked through commands that would provide access to *Imagine*'s satellite-driven internet and telecommunications capabilities. "As we expected, access is disabled. There's no connection."

"What about opening a line with our agents aboard *Imagine*?"

"Without connectivity and transmission capability, I can't open a comm channel with our agents on the ship through our implants—that's the way we need to be communicating with the other agents. Our safety helmet comm system is fine for us, but it works the same way a child's walkie-talkie would. If you and I were more than fifty yards away from each other, the helmet comms would be useless. If the following ship has satellite access..." She clicked through dead ends on her laptop. "I can't find it."

"GPS reading?"

Glancing at her handheld nav system, she studied the GPS data, then shoved all the devices into her backpack, zipping it as she crossed the room. "They're sending a false signal. Radar signal shows that *Imagine* is on course, a hundred fifty miles Southeast of Macau."

"How do you know that's false?"

"Easy. The radar image is showing no sign of the following ship. God knows where we're really headed. We were knocked out for four hours. We could be anywhere by now." She lifted her backpack and tossed it his way. "Here. Catch."

She watched Ace catch her backpack, then heft it up and into the overhead crawl space. "The South China Sea provides access to any number of places that could be a safe haven for kidnappers and a ship full of billionaire hostages. Indonesia. Malaysia. Singapore Straits."

"Agreed. Even North Korea? You can never tell what they're up to. Plus, there are any number of pirate friendly ports in North Africa. None of which would take very long to get to for the ship behind us, assuming it has serious horsepower in its engines."

As he talked, Leo stepped on the vanity stool, then onto the marble counter, facing him as she lifted her arms to the ceiling. "Boost me up." When they were at eye level, she added, "I'm betting they're going to transfer the guests to the other ship."

Chapter Nine

1:00 a.m.

While Ace considered her statement, Leo managed to pull herself upwards, with only slight help from him. "Using the following ship as a transport vessel is a clever idea. Mobility enhances the likelihood of success in hostage negotiations."

His mind raced with scenarios, as she moved in the metal space above him for a few moments, until her face appeared, directly overhead.

"Think Entebbe," she said.

He nodded, remembering the mass kidnapping that had sparked a rescue operation led by Israeli commandoes that, more than forty years later, remained a textbook problem for security strategists. "Got it. Assuming we have another mass kidnapping—which at this time seems damn well likely—then Entebbe could be a similar situation. The plane was hijacked over Greece, but the terrorists rerouted the flight all the way to Uganda, where Idi Amin welcomed them."

She nodded. "*Imagine*'s top speed is nineteen knots. Relatively slow. Right?"

"Correct. The following ship—let's name it *Follower*—is smaller and probably faster. If I were taking the guests aboard *Imagine* hostage, I'd transfer them to *Follower*. The smaller ship would be easier to conceal. I'd take them to my safe harbor, wherever that might be, leaving *Imagine* behind as a decoy. So, this situation has the potential to become an Entebbe-type situation, with the twist of a second transport vehicle."

She nodded, a grim expression in her eyes. "Brilliant. If you were a pirate, you might get away with it. Hand me your backpack."

He bent, lifted his backpack, then hoisted it overhead. As she grabbed it, his fingers grazed hers. Their gazes locked. "No wild heroics, Leo."

"Understood."

"Seriously. Keep your ass safe. I will be..." He had to clear his throat to spit out the words. "...fucking pissed if you get...hurt."

Behind her face mask, something flashed in her eyes as she looked down at him. Concern. Uncertainty. After all, she knew his goddamn history. While her eyes reflected worry for him, though, her tone was one of pure irritation. "And you'd say this to Kamin, Stills, or Ryan? Any of our other agents onboard?"

Crap. She has me. I mixed personal feelings with business, and I didn't even realize I was doing it.

"You're lucky I didn't punch you in the nose for that lapse. Be glad you're wearing a mask that would've broken my hand. I'm ready to go kick some pirate ass. Don't distract me. Let's do this."

She was fierce, his Leo. Fierce and well trained. He had to take his emotions, high at the moment, out of the equation. She was right. Of course, she was. A bam-bam sounded as the door of the suite next to them banged open. Pounding of heavy footsteps echoed.

"Hurry." The helmet mic picked up urgency in her low hiss.

"No shit. Get moving," he said. "Towards the stern."

He was damn glad he hadn't let up on pull-ups, arm exercises, or Parkour drills in recent months. Using hand and arm strength, core strength, and every muscle fiber he could call upon, he jumped and pulled himself up and into the tunnel-like space. When his feet were in, he belly-crawled backwards, then slid the cover into place and reinserted the entry panel's screws. As he worked on the third screw, pounding on the door of their suite echoed.

With their backpacks on, Ace and Leo barely had space to move. Walls, floor, and ceiling of the crawl space were stainless steel, covered with a hard, marine quality composite. The floor held tubes that contained the complex wiring required for various systems—electrical, inter-ship comms, routers and boosters for Wi-Fi. The HVAC system ran overhead, composed of rectangular, sheet-metal ducts through which heating, cooling, air filtration, and ozone injection systems worked. The proliferation of access panels to the crawl space, in every suite, hallway, and stairwell, were an indication of how many things could go wrong with the ship's systems.

Below them, as he finished with the fourth screw, the door to their suite gave way with a sharp crack. He lingered long enough over the vent to see five men spill inside, speaking a mix of Mandarin and English. Doors bounced as they were flung open. Shit was thrown around as they searched. The balcony door slid until it thudded. Chairs thumped on carpet as they were overturned.

As he and Leo silently retreated directly over their heads, Ace whispered, "Five males. What was that reference to Skylar?"

"They're reporting to him. They were telling him there was no sign of Chloe and Zack in the room. It seems that other guests are missing from the roundup too. I couldn't catch names."

Ace caught up to her where the crawl space widened enough for them to move side by side. "Mandarin again," he said. "Not only are they speaking the primary language of Quan Security, that company had access to the ship for weeks."

"Correct. It's walking like a duck, Ace. It makes sense that Quan would be involved, in some capacity. Maybe it isn't the entirety of the security company that's corrupt, but the team that is aboard *Imagine* is the likely culprit. Quan had the same intel we had. Passenger data. Ship schematics and systems." She shot Ace a sideways glance. "Including the air handlers."

He nodded. Wiring system tubes rolled under his hands and knees as he crawled. They had thirty yards to go. Not comfortable, but doable. "And Quan had access to information regarding the guests—who's who, and how much wealth they represent."

"The security company was hired by Imagine Casinos Worldwide," she said. "Could Baru be behind this?"

Ace considered whether Baru could be the perp, as a faint *pop-pop-pop* of gunfire erupted from over their heads, on the Melpomene Deck. They halted. Given the distance they'd travelled through the crawl space, he pegged the firefight as being in the vicinity of the spa. When the gunfire quieted, they continued on.

In a low whisper, he said, "I'm not sure what Baru would gain from it. This cruise is giving him even more of the prestige he craves in the gambling world, putting him on par with all of the big houses. I don't think he'd sabotage it. Have you noticed how proud he is?"

"Beaming. As though he's spit-polished every inch of this ship himself." She paused as they reached a vertical return vent. With the connected ductwork, the apparatus took up half the space.

"You first."

She slipped off her backpack, then turned to her side to slide around it.

"I'd vote for the pirates wanting Ling and May Wen." Ace moved around the ductwork, then caught up to her. "They're the biggest ticket items on board. The rest of the guests might simply be bonus extras."

She nodded. "But the rest of the guests are high ticket leverage to use in the negotiation process."

"About ten more yards in here, then we open the panel at the end and go down one flight of stairs. From there, we'll access the crawl space above the Clio deck. We'll see what's happening in the theater, then split up at the forward stairwell."

About five feet before the end of the crawl space, there was enough room for him to crawl past Leo. He directed her to hang back as he got to work removing the entry panel on the vertical wall. "It's pretty tight."

Klunk.

"Our tool's silent, but given that we're working with heavy metal, gravity will cause that klunk. Which means you're risking exposure if someone's within earshot on the other side."

He glanced over his shoulder in time to catch her eye roll.

"Stating the obvious again." A bit of a smile played at her lips. "I get it. It's a quirk. You do it even when you're not a team leader, you know. Sometimes it's irritating." She shrugged. "Mostly it's not."

He scowled. As he slid the panel aside, from overhead in the stairwell, he heard footsteps.

"Ace—"

"Got it. Stand down."

Glock drawn, he slipped through the opening. Disobeying his instruction, Leo immediately came through, on his right. Just as he rose to his feet, two men, wearing camouflage gear, walked down the stairs, side by side. Chatting, with no situational awareness. *Mistake.* One was a blond Caucasian. The other was Asian. No respirators. *Good to know.* No safety helmets. *Big mistake.* The two men were gripping assault rifles. They started to lift them. *Fatal mistake.*

Leo shot the one on the right between his eyebrows. Ace took out the guy on the left. Both tumbled down the stairs, coming to rest on the landing at their feet.

Ace checked for pulses. Both dead. "You didn't follow orders. I told you to stand down. That means to maintain your position, which—"

"I know what it means." She unstrapped the dead men's watches. "You were being protective."

"Damn straight, and that has nothing to do with what's happening between us. It's all about your role being critical to our mission. Of the two of us, you're more likely to establish a connection to the outside world. Your mission won't be accomplished if you unnecessarily throw yourself in harm's way without regard to safety. Understand?"

"Understood. Should I remain at attention for your reprimand, or may I figure out their comm system?"

As anger flashed in her eyes, he told himself not to let personal feelings interfere. Yet no matter how much firepower or gear she carried, no matter how serious their situation, he couldn't help but notice the wisps of chestnut hair escaping her helmet to curl towards her jawline and cheekbones.

While her eyes conveyed the gritty determination he'd expect from any agent, she couldn't control the flush of pink in her cheeks. He knew her well enough to know that it came from excitement, stress, and the incredible energy produced by her incomparable brain. Fuck-it-all-to-hell, to him, her flush made her human.

Not superhuman.

Which made her vulnerable. Which made him think of how precarious their position was and how easy it would be for a well-aimed bullet to mortally strike her in any one of a number of places, despite her protective gear.

"Well?" She held up the hand that held the watch and earbud, wiggling the equipment in his direction.

Cocky. Gorgeous. Confident, and damn well focused on her mission. Goddammit, but he was totally into her. Every single facet of her, even the part of her that would make her a handful on any job, for any team leader. Given her brilliance, her unparalleled technical capabilities, and off-the-charts field skills, having her on a job was well worth a bit of attitude. He wasn't the only agent who thought so. To his knowledge, they all did. "Carry on."

After stripping the dark-haired man of his earbud, she sat on the bottom stair. He removed the blonde man's comm gear and handed the guy's watch to her. He kept the blond guy's earbud, though. He studied the small plastic device. "Looks similar to what we had before we moved to implants."

"Yep, and their watches are similar to what we use now. Capacitive touchscreen. Won't work with gloves. Hopefully, it's not fingerprint enabled. That would be a real pain in the ass." She touched the watch face with her index finger and pressed. "Nope. We'll be able to manipulate. It's got cellular and Wi-Fi capabilities. Defaulting to their comm system and operating on a closed channel. When we insert the buds into our ears, we'll be live. So, don't put it in until I figure out how to mute it."

Ace slipped the bud into his pocket for safekeeping until she directed otherwise. He went through the two men's pockets as she studied their comm system. He pulled out phones and tossed them to her. He found metal clips with identification cards. He glanced at the cards briefly. "Steffan Wendt, from Frankfurt. Lee Yang. Beijing."

"Lucky."

"That occurred to me as well." They were in luck from a communication perspective, because Ace spoke German fluently. He could speak English with a slight German accent almost as easily as he spoke English without any accent at all. "Mute button? Figured it out yet?"

"Testing it."

"Override buttons are on the side." She turned the thick watches sideways, holding them up and squinting. "Red's probably mute."

"Probably? Doesn't sound very analytical." Ace lifted Wendt, then slid him into the crawl space he and Leo had just come from to enter the stairwell.

"Sometimes even Ragno makes a guess. You know that, don't you?" She pressed the watch, then inserted Yang's earbud into her ear. "Yep. Red button mutes the system. Green means go. Channels are manipulated on the watch face. There are plenty of options programmed, but these watches both default to their comm system. Earbud's good to go."

Ace lifted Yang and shoved him into the crawl space next to Wendt. "What channels are active?" he asked, as he slipped Wendt's earbud into his ear.

"There are varying degrees of static on a few lines, channel four in particular. Your earbud is on line four now."

He listened to hums, clicks, and static. "Encryption?"

"Possibly. It would take me some time to crack it. I'd have to route the calls to Ragno's encryption team to do it. Bingo. Line sixteen. Clear chatter. I'm setting Wendt's comm to that line now."

On line sixteen, Ace heard a male voice, English. Midwestern twang. "Childs. Calling Skylar."

He glanced at Leo.

She nodded. "I hear it."

"Copy," a male answered, in terse English. "Skylar to Childs. Proceed."

"Medics and assistance needed on the Euterpe Deck," Childs said. "Suite 510. Blackwell. Todd and Nina. The Blackwells are gone."

Leo handed Ace the watch and smartphone that had belonged to Wendt. "I disabled GPS capabilities."

"The Blackwells apparently left their suite through an access panel in the floor," Childs was saying. "Phuong is dead. Shot in the chest. Bei was shot in the neck. He needs a medic. ASAP."

"Goddammit. We knew the Blackwells both carried weapons," Skylar said. "Bei and Phuong should have been more careful."

"James is going after the Blackwells," Childs said. "I'll apply pressure on Bei's wound till the medics arrive."

"No," Skylar said. "Go with James."

Leo and Ace locked glances. Skylar's order might've just been a death knell for his man, Bei. He'd given the order without hesitating. Even with a bit of irritation underlying his words.

Skylar continued, "Keep me updated. Attention. All operatives. The guests who are unaccounted for are now Ling Wen, May Wen, Todd Blackwell, Nina Blackwell, Chloe St. Laurent, and Zack Abrams. Here are your orders. Childs and James, continue searching for the Blackwells." Skylar rattled through an extensive list of names and directed them to find the Wens. A shorter list was to find St. Laurent and Abrams. "We cannot commence Phase Two without these people. Find. Them. Now."

Line sixteen went silent.

"Good to know they're still in Phase One," Leo said.

"Whatever that means." Ace replaced the panel that led to the crawl space, while Leo rechecked the other lines on the comm system.

"Other than their line four, the only other line currently in use is channel sixteen. Line four remains a series of clicks and static. Sixteen is the only line that is clear."

"Bei, Phuong, Childs, James, Wendt, Yang, Skylar." Ace repeated the names that they'd heard. "Those names mean anything to you?"

"No. Adam Evans and Sylvia Leon wouldn't mean anything to them either. Seems like we aren't the only ones aboard using fake names."

After replacing the bolts, Ace used the ball of his fist on each corner of the panel, until the seams blended with the adjoining wall. He glanced around. "No surveillance cams, here or down these stairs, which will take us to the crawl space above the Clio Deck. It's a long crawl space, spanning the entire enclosed area on the deck, almost from stern to bow. Gives us a straight shot over the casino, the foyer between the casino and the theater, and then over the theater. We'll check out what's happening there. Then we'll go our separate ways."

As she nodded, he followed her gaze upwards, to the white walls of the stairwell. His glance took in the telltale signs of the two close-range shots that had taken down Wendt and Yang. Red splatter. Definitely visible. Larger drops, red blood and gray matter, were on the stairs. Although the bodies were hidden, in the crawl space, Ace and Leo didn't have time to deal with the rest of the cleanup.

"No time to worry about that." He gestured with his chin to the descending stairs. "Let's go."

As they ran down the stairs, they detached their respirators from their helmets and strapped them onto their tool belts. At the next landing, he paused at an entry panel that provided access to the crawl space above the Clio deck, while she faced the opposite way, standing guard at his side with her Sig drawn.

She asked, "What do you think Skylar's Phase Two is?"

"Kidnappings typically require communicating with a third party to let them know that you have hostages, correct?"

"Correct. Kidnappers have to make demand to a third party—'I've hijacked *Imagine*. Pay up. Free prisoners. Give my country a nuclear weapon. A billion dollars.' Or whatever."

He removed the first screw that held the access panel to the wall. As he answered her, he slipped it in his pocket for refastening from the inside. "And given the diverse nationalities of *Imagine*'s guests, and their wealth and importance, the demand will provoke an international incident."

She nodded. "Macau is a Special Administrative Region of China, a huge revenue generator. Both Macau and China would be involved. Given the number of Americans aboard, the U.S. would cooperate."

"Sure hope so," Ace said, removing the second screw, then getting to work on the third. "China should deploy everything it has to keep Macau appearing safe. There is also the Ling Wen factor. He's got folk hero status, given the philanthropic reforms he pushed through the Chinese government. The scholarship system that he personally funds makes him a celebrity."

"China will lead. People's Liberation Army Air Force is pretty damn awesome."

He nodded as he worked on the panel. "Agreed. The PLA is mighty, and China would deploy jets, ships, and submarines to protect Wen. Intel has been telling us for years that China is building up military installations in the South China Sea. Now could be the time for them to flex their muscle. U.S. military installations in the area are scant, but there are enough in the Philippines to provide aid. Even with a false radar image and false coordinates, the cavalry will find *Imagine* in a matter of hours once the ransom demand is made. The likelihood of getting away once the cavalry focuses on *Imagine* is pretty slim—that is, if the operation is still aboard this ship."

"You're assuming we're not dealing with people who are willing to commit suicide for their cause?"

"Yep. Assume Quan Security is implicated," he said. "Quan started this cruise with sixty operatives. Their ranks may have increased if they had undercover people among the staff or in Tier Two security. That's way too large a number to believe suicide is acceptable to all."

"Agreed. Plus," she said, "given the value of the hostages, money is the likely incentive. You can't spend money from the grave. That means once the demand is made, the window of time for their escape commences. So, I agree with your assessment. They haven't made the demand yet. Plus, as Skylar's chatter on line sixteen just told us, they don't have control of their hostages yet."

"It all adds fuel to our theory that we have an Entebbe-type situation of transporting hostages, with the twist of moving the operation to *Follower*. Plus, who's to say the kidnappers need all of *Imagine*'s guests? Looking at the comparative net worth of the hostages who are on the loose, the Blackwells might be expendable. Chloe St. Laurent might also be expendable. Zack Abrams certainly is." He glanced at her as he removed the fourth and final screw. "But the kidnappers definitely want Ling and May Wen. They're not going to start Phase Two, the evacuation, until they have the Wens under their control. Which gives me a window for stopping them while you're sending a Mayday to headquarters."

"Ideally, your action won't immediately start an execution of hostages, which the hijackers would do to make you stop. Right?" she asked.

"Correct. I can't move easily while surveillance cams are up. So, while you're disabling the surveillance system, I'll take their hostage evacuation option off the table. I know that might trigger an alert." He glanced at her. She wasn't looking at him. Her gaze was focused up, then down, covering the stairwell, exactly as she was supposed to be doing. "I'll just have to disable anyone who comes my way."

"Okay. Risky, but worth it," she said. "How do you plan to remove their evacuation option?"

"Sabotage the hydraulic system. That'll disable the lifeboats—"

"But what if we need to evacuate the hostages later?"

"I won't permanently disable the hydraulics. I'll do it in a way that enables me to fix it, if I need to. It'll disable the system just enough to slow them down. Lifeboats can't be launched without hydraulics. The water garage can't open, either, because the door won't open without hydraulics."

"Smart, but I'm not sure you'll be able to succeed," she said. "There are plenty of surveillance cameras around the engine room."

"Get ready to enter. I'll go first." He slid the panel aside and glanced down the long, narrow crawl space. *Empty*. No enemy. *Good.* No Black Raven Agents. *Bad.*

The tunnel-like space was similar in design and function to the crawl space above their suite, except this one was longer. Wedged between the Clio Deck and the Euterpe Deck, the long crawl space dead-ended at the forward service stairwell, where they'd part ways. Leo would access the stairwell and get to the radio room, four decks above them. He'd go two decks below, to access the engine room, where the hydraulic system was located.

"Hey. Stop ignoring my concern." A slight scowl line bisected her eyebrows. "There are plenty of surveillance cams in the engine room."

"You know what you have to do—disable the surveillance system once you get to the radio room."

"I understand that," she said. "But what's the priority? Mayday, reestablishing comms with our agents, or disabling surveillance? Three discrete tasks, Evans. I'm only one person."

"You're capable of multitasking."

Her cheeks flushed, and she shook her head. Then he remembered her comment in bed when he'd told her that he wanted to focus on her for a while.

Oh. Fuck!

"Hey. I wasn't referring—

She rolled her shoulders, holding his gaze for the briefest of seconds, then glancing away and scanning the stairway. *No footsteps.* "Drop it. It's just that I can't disable surveillance while I'm trying to figure out a way around a damn impressive communications logjam."

"We'll work around it. Mayday is your priority. Inter-agent coms are next. Surveillance system is third. It will all come together. We're a good team, Leo." *In more ways than one.* "Not that I wouldn't mind having a few more of our agents show up."

"Where the hell are they?"

Flicking his head to the crawl space, he answered, "Not in here."

While he was still in the stairwell, he handed her the screws to the entry panel. "Practice sealing it from the inside. You'll run into a few more of these panels when you're alone. Turning around to face forward will be a bitch, but you're smaller than me—you'll be able to do it." As he hoisted himself into the tunnel-like space, head first, he added, "It's likely the others are headed to the radio room for a Mayday, just like us. Get in."

As she followed him in and started working on the entry panel, he started belly crawling. Inside the dim space, he smelled the coppery, bitter tinge of bloodshed and death.

"Do you smell that?" she asked, as she worked at the entry panel.

Even though he was a few yards from her, the helmet audio systems picked up her low whisper. "Yep."

With each shimmy forward, the air seemed to thicken with the stink. He knew what came with that odor, and he knew she did, as well. They'd both been trained not to have physical reactions to bloodshed, he as a Marine and she as a Black Raven agent.

An instrumental version of "The Little Drummer Boy" seeped through the vents that were above the casino, providing an out-of-place reminder of the season. Ahead of Leo, Ace paused at the first vent that provided a view of the casino below them.

Forget training. Forget field experience. His gut did a hard twist at the carnage that greeted him. When he felt her hand on his shin, he shifted to the side. He pressed himself against the wall, giving her room to slide in alongside him. “Brace yourself.”

Chapter Ten

1:20 a.m.

As she crawled into position at Ace's side, the grim tone in his voice chilled her. The Christmas carol's repetitive *rum-pum-pum-pum* sounded, with a drumroll, as she inhaled a fresh blast of coppery death. Their overhead vantage point was within twenty feet of where she'd spent the better part of the late afternoon playing craps. The grating revealed gambling tables, chandeliers, Christmas trees...

And bodies.

"Oh. God." Swallowing hard, she fought to maintain the cool control needed for job performance as she gazed into the once-frenetic space, where now all was still.

Leo had been with Black Raven long enough to have firsthand knowledge of evil, and her personal history had introduced her to evil in one of the worse ways possible. Despite her experience and training, the killing field that unfolded below her sent her mind reeling, as her gaze crawled from one lifeless body to another.

Like discarded dolls, people were strewn on the floor of the casino. Cocktail waitresses, dressed as Santa's elves. Waiters, dressed as nutcrackers. Some with bullet wounds in their foreheads. Some with throats slashed. Dealers, in tuxedos. Security personnel, wearing tuxedos and red bow ties.

"Eyes closed. No signs of resistance." Ace's whisper was bitter, but his words were calm and matter-of-fact. "Executed while in an ether-induced sleep."

She cleared her throat, trying to do her job. Observe. Analyze. Learn about the enemy from the trail they'd left. She focused on getting an estimate of the bodies, as "The Little Drummer Boy" faded out and the music shifted to the soft plucking of string instruments that marked the beginning of Tchaikovsky's "Dance of the Sugar Plum Fairy."

Hell.

The xylophone came in with the main melody of the tune, and she involuntarily gave in to roiling emotions triggered by the carnage below her. The depth of those emotions was exacerbated by the painful memories inspired by the song.

Going to the Nutcracker on Broadway had been an annual outing for she and her dad, from when she was old enough to sit still through the performance until he died. Her mom had always been too busy with work. Tickets for the December 15, 2001, performance, which they'd already purchased for the annual father-daughter date, were framed on her vanity.

"Leo. You with me?"

Ace knew that sorry slice of her history, because no matter how much she was resisting the idea of them being more than friends, the truth was he was the rare guy—the one and only, so far—who'd gotten close enough to her and taken the time to learn almost everything about her. That's why he'd figured out that while she could calmly shoot to kill someone, the poignant sweetness of the "Dance of the

Sugar Plum Fairy" inspired a haunting sadness that could bring her to her knees on even the best of days.

Which clearly, this isn't.

Once he'd known the reason behind it, he hadn't teased her. Now, she cleared her throat. Didn't dare look in his eyes. She forced her gaze to stay on the casino floor. Clearing the emotion from the back of her throat, she tried like heck to shove some tough coolness into her voice. "Yes. Don't worry about me. I'm with you, but I still hate that damn song. A hundred and twenty souls?"

"More. Looks like most of the casino staff. Over to the starboard side, there are officer's whites. I can't make out faces from here." He was in agent mode as he voiced his observations, while she was trying hard to reassemble her professionalism. "Son of a bitch. Look three bodies down from furthest craps table. Kamin?"

She dragged her gaze to where Ace stated, looking for the dark-haired agent who was head of Omega team and undercover as one of the ship's engineers. "Hard to tell from here. But...no. That's not him."

"See any gamblers and their guests?"

She forced her eyes to go from face to face, looking for the people whose faces she'd memorized. "No."

"Left of the trophy. Paul Stills."

The crystal vase depicting the nine muses was undisturbed on its pedestal, as sparkling as it had been when she'd been throwing dice at the craps table. On the carpet in the walkway near it, Agent Stills—the overall team leader—lay flat on his back, as though he'd fallen asleep.

"Confirm." She swallowed hard. "Looks like you're team leader now."

"Copy that. Not the way I ever wanted to get here."

As her eyes bounced from person to person, she listened as Skylar talked intermittently to his operatives on channel sixteen. The man switched easily between Mandarin and English. She listened to the cool, controlled chatter of his men as they responded to him and talked amongst each other, while she craned to see through the grating, and around the gambling tables. Her gaze rested on two familiar faces.

"Shit. That's Jacks and McMillan." Her pulse raced as she said names of Black Raven agents who'd been in Tier Two security, personal bodyguards to Ali and Samantha Bandel, of Zurich, Switzerland.

"Where?"

"Near the baccarat tables."

Ace shifted his body slightly for a better view. "Confirm. Andros and Payne." As he pointed out the two agents who'd been personal bodyguards to Mark and Liz Bates, from Seattle, Washington, his tone remained steady, yet she could hear the anger building.

"Where?"

"Fifteen yards from Jacks and McMillan. Other side of the blackjack table."

"Confirm." She forced herself to start over, using the furthest point in the room as the beginning. "Look towards the main entrance. Double doors." Choking back emotion, she almost lost it. Again. "That's a pile of...at least twenty. Tuxedos, with green bow ties."

"Got it. That's Tier Two security. Looks like they were killed elsewhere. The casino must have been chosen as a dumping ground. Possibly for keeping inventory?"

She lifted her eyes, meeting his gaze for a second. His eyes reflected her assessment of the carnage. *Created by evil that needs to be stopped. No matter the cost.* "Based on what's below us, we're still working with the assumption that Quan Security is behind this? And Skylar's with them?"

He looked down again. "See anyone down there with a red tie?"

She scanned the floor, looking for the red bowtie that had marked the Quan Security operatives earlier in the day. "No."

"About twenty-five percent of the communications on channel sixteen are in Mandarin. Skylar, whose German accent is heavy enough for me to think that German is his native language, is also fluent in Mandarin. Wendt and Yang were carrying QBZ-95s. That's the favored assault rifle of the People's Liberation Army, Chinese triads, and Chinese private military contracting groups. With the notable absence of red bow ties down there, I'd say the assumption's a pretty safe bet. Skylar and his operatives have to be from Quan's ranks. Agree?"

"Yes."

"Goddammit to hell," he said. "Talbot. On our side of the baccarat tables."

Agent Dirk Talbot. Former Marine. An elite agent who loved his Harley and his dog. Recently engaged. She'd met Talbot's fiancée and liked her. "Confirm."

She forced her eyes to keep scrolling across the bodies until her gaze screeched to a decisive halt. A lump in her throat kept her from voicing aloud Agent Amy Ryan's name, the brilliant, energetic agent who'd been Leo's backup. When roles had been assigned, Ryan had grumbled, good-naturedly, about her cocktail waitress legend. She'd grumbled even more about the green-velvet micro shorts that went with her risqué Santa's elf costume.

Swallowing, hard, Leo managed to say, "Furthest craps table. Ten feet to the left. Amy."

"Confirm."

Unaware of when she'd reached out for Ace, she realized she was gripping his hand, hard. She had to look away from Amy. She found solace in the cool, controlled rage that simmered in Ace's eyes. There was also concern. Empathy, and yes, that dreaded emotion she'd called him out for earlier. Despite the cool exterior he showed to the world and the firm set of his jaw, in his steady gaze there was tenderness. Towards her.

She was overcome with profound relief that Ace hadn't left their suite when she'd been in her snit over the stuck zipper. He'd have been exposed when the ether was released, and he'd be on the floor of the casino.

Dead.

He closed his hand over hers and squeezed hard. She shut her eyes.

Stop. Stop imagining the worst. Stop!

"You okay?"

No. I'm losing it.

He squeezed her hand harder. She wanted to ask, '*why do we do this*?' But she knew the answer. It was because hell had unleashed an evil on earth. As long as her soul burned with the fire that had started on September 11, 2001, she was going to fight it.

"Leo?"

"I'm fine." She opened her eyes and locked gazes with her best friend. He gave her a slow nod of encouragement.

Focusing on the strength to overcome that he was imparting to her with his grip on her hand and his solid gaze, she was able to channel the potentially debilitating force of her emotions into something workable.

"It's okay to be ups—"

"I'm not upset," she said, drawing upon defense mechanisms she'd learned as a child, when waves of dread and uncertainty had forced her to face the obvious—that her father hadn't survived the terror attack. At the age of thirteen, she hadn't been able to join the war against Osama Bin Laden, but she'd set herself on a mission to fight terrorism with her brainpower. Later, at Black Raven, she'd found a way to combine her brainpower with fighting skills.

Get mad. Channel anger into cool, rational thought. Strive. Thrive. With every ounce of your being, find a target. Make it a goal. Hit it. Get even. Win. "I'm furious. I'm not stopping until I kill the person who is behind this."

He nodded. "We. We will kill the fucker."

As he let go of her hand, she glanced through the vent as the casino doors opened. Four men entered the casino, each wearing camo gear, similar to the outfits worn by the two guards that they'd just killed in the stairwell. QBZ-95s were slung over their shoulders. Pistols were holstered at their hips. Between the four of them, on stretchers, they carried two bodies, dressed in tuxedos and green ties. Tier two bodyguards. Glancing at the faces of the men on the stretchers, she recognized one of Wen's bodyguards. In Mandarin, the men kept a running stream of chatter going over "*White Christmas*."

Through the earbud in her ear, line sixteen, which had been silent for a while, crackled to life. "Childs. Calling Skylar."

She glanced at Ace. Keeping her voice low, she asked, "You hear this?"

He nodded while keeping his eyes on the men on the casino floor, two of whom were laughing at something one of the others said.

"Go ahead," Skylar responded.

"Trail's gone cold for the Blackwells," Childs said.

"Where are you?" Skylar asked.

"Erato Deck. Library," Childs said. "We know the Blackwells entered it from the crawl space. The vent was open. Don't know where else they could have gone from here. Unless they've accessed the aft service stairwell."

"Copy. Skylar, calling Wendt."

Ace gave her a *here goes* nod.

He touched the green button on his watch, unmuting the comm system. "Wendt to Skylar."

Pronouncing his W like a V, Ace gave his response in English, with a slight German accent. She gave Ace a thumb's up, hoping like hell that Ace had guessed correctly that Wendt, from Frankfurt, would not have answered Skylar in Mandarin.

"Wendt. Need you and Yang to provide an assist to Childs. Aft service stairwell, then library. Over."

"Copy. On our way. Over." Ace said, then re-muted the system.

Line sixteen went silent. She checked the other lines. All were silent, except for line four, which hummed with a short burst of static and a few clicks. She glanced through the vent. Quan operatives on the casino floor were walking towards the bow of the ship.

"Let's go," he said.

They moved forward, side by side, shoulder to shoulder. The ship's gentle roll reminded her that even though seas remained calm, they were still in a moving vessel. When they were further down the crawl space, almost to the next ceiling vent, a vertical entry panel rattled. Her mind raced through the ship's schematics, approximating where the sound was coming from, as she and Ace froze. "Mid-ship service stairwell." She glanced sideways, into Ace's eyes. "Another area without surveillance cameras?"

"Correct. Get ready." As he shifted sideways and unholstered his Glock, she reached over her shoulder and pulled hers out of its holster. "Company's coming."

Chapter Eleven

1:30 a.m.

Klunk.

Ace held up a finger, then four, indicating that the first of four screws had been removed from the access panel.

"Assumes we heard the first," she whispered. "Staying where we are, or backing up? I vote staying."

Her face was only a few inches from his. Distracted by a gleam in her eyes, he didn't focus on her words. Instead, he thought about how she had looked in his arms as he'd tried to carry her out of their suite. Lifeless. In his core, he felt a strong premonition that her time was running out, as surely as gravity would pull the last grains of sand through the top of an hourglass to the bottom.

"Evans?" Her whisper was worried. Her eyes, doubly so. Her use of his last name underscored her concern that he was no longer thinking as an agent.

His mental detour had lasted only a second or two, but it was long enough to make him wonder what-in-the-name-of-hell he was doing getting so distracted while on a job that had gone sideways. He didn't have to wonder for long, because he'd had four years of learning about the problem.

PTSD, rearing its ugly head in a way that it shouldn't. Here I am, four years later, distracted by being in love when I'm supposed to be focusing.

He mentally shook his thoughts clear. "Yeah. Weighing options."

He glanced over his shoulder. They'd entered through a similar panel, which was now a solid fifteen yards behind them. Getting out that way wasn't an option. It would take too much time to backtrack. Dropping into the casino through the vent they'd been looking through, now five yards behind them, also wasn't an option. With four Quan operatives beneath them, getting to it and unscrewing it would take too long.

"Staying. We'll neutralize the immediate threat coming to join us. Move forward. Next vent. Double time." The next vent that looked down into the casino, ten yards ahead of them, would give him a better firing position at the operatives on the casino floor. "Need to see action below us while we focus forward."

Side by side, they crawled forward. Her movements were smooth, lithe, and super fast. More important than fast, she moved quietly. Quite a feat, considering they were in full battle gear, plus some, and the tubing and ductwork in the crawl space made movement a challenge.

Klunk.

She made it to the vent at the same time he did. Looking through the narrow slats of the panel, he spotted the four Quan Security operatives taking their sweet-ass time as they walked through the sea of bodies littering the casino floor. Presumably, they were looking to see whether the guests that Skylar had said were missing–the

Blackwells, the Wens, or Chloe and Zack— were hiding among the dead. One stopped, using the barrel of his rifle to nudge a face for a better view.

If he and Leo had to fire at whomever was coming through the entry panel, their gunfire would resonate in the close quarters, even with silencers. Despite their nonstop chatter, intermittent laughter, and "*O Holy Night*" playing on the casino speakers, the operatives on the floor below them would hear the shots coming from overhead. Repetitive rounds from the QBZ-95s that the operatives carried would weaken, crack, then penetrate the stainless-steel crawl space. Which meant the four men needed to die before Ace and Leo fired their first shot.

"You take the panel," he whispered, eye to eye with her.

She nodded.

"I'll take the casino. Zero margin for error. These guys are wearing chest and back plates. If you don't have a head shot, go for femoral, carotid, or brachial arteries."

"You're stating the obvious."

Unperturbed, he continued, "Might take more than one shot, if their anti-ballistic material's as good as ours. Even ours isn't impenetrable. Theirs won't be, either."

Sliding forward, she lifted her body over the ceiling panel, then crawled forward into a better position for firing. "Hey. Want to show me how to pull a trigger?"

Her sarcasm wasn't lost on him. He deserved the pushback, because he was telling her things she damn well knew. And why? Hell if he knew. It might be because he was having a hard time simply thinking of her as an agent, and not someone he loved. As she glared at him, he realized that she evidently wasn't having the same sort of difficulty. "Nah. Think you have that covered."

Klunk.

"One more," she said.

Imagine had departed Macau with sixteen Black Raven agents aboard. Those agents had consisted of Ace's twelve-agent team, which included him and Leo, plus four agents in Tier Two security, as personal bodyguards to two of the guests. They'd just counted seven agents on the floor of the casino, and their vantage point didn't give him confidence that their body count was complete. Despite that, he remained hopeful that some of their agents had survived. "It could be Black Raven agents coming through that panel."

"Understood. Friendly fire concerns are present." Leo's whisper was low enough that he only heard it on his helmet comm.

"It could also be the Blackwells. Or, more likely, Ling Wen. His shipyard built *Imagine*. We have to assume he knows about this crawl space and how it avoids ship's surveillance.

"Roger," she said. "You handle your end. I'll handle mine."

He kept his gaze focused on the casino floor. "It would be damn helpful to talk to any of our remaining agents and ask if it's them on the other side of that panel."

"If they're Black Raven, and if they've suited up," she whispered, "helmet comms should work as soon as their heads break the plane of the crawl space. Steel walls are interfering with transmission."

Beneath them, one of the Quan operatives eyed a stack of bodies. Another pulled a cigarette out of a pocket of his cargo pants. Yet another talked rapidly in Mandarin, waving his hands. The others listened.

"Are they saying anything helpful?" Ace asked.

After a second, she whispered, "No. Dumb guy stuff, which, under the circumstances, makes me really want to kill them."

"Such as?"

"Jokes. Boobs, vaginas, and fucking someone's mother. Can't believe they can joke while walking through a killing field."

His stomach twisted with anger over their callousness. He shifted position to keep the men, who were now backtracking, within his sights. It was hard to make a U-turn in the tunnel-like space, but he slipped off his backpack, compressed his body, and managed. Leo moved forward to make room for him as he swung around the vent. He and Leo were now facing in opposite directions. His left leg was pressed along her left side. To him, she felt small. Fragile. He knew better.

Relatively small, yes.

Fragile? Like a charging rhino.

Ace stilled his breath, forcing himself to ignore the repetitive clang of warning signals over their personal situation. More immediate issue: his kill order for the guys below him. First–skinny Cigarette Smoker, who was eyeing bodies as he walked slowly ahead of the others. Second–the asshole standing over Agent Ryan's body. Third and Fourth–the two nearby, eyeing stacks of chips on the craps tables. The distance between them didn't shut them up. It only made the one whose turn it was to tell a joke talk louder. Which was working in his and Leo's favor.

"Counting on your eyes on the entry panel. Good guys won't be wearing camo."

"Understood."

"Assume casino's surveillance cameras remain live. My gunfire will draw more enemy there."

"Copy."

"If I give you the order to abandon this scene and get to the radio room, move as fast as possible. Do not hesitate. Mayday is your priority. Leave while I draw their fire to me."

For as long as I can.

Silence.

Yeah. I wouldn't like that order from her, or anyone, either.

"Agent?"

"Copy," she said, with tangible reluctance.

Klunk.

Through the sights of his Glock, he focused on the round head and jet-black hair of Cigarette Smoker, who was now walking further away.

"Panel's removed," she said. "Can't identify. Yet."

He drew a deep breath. Kept his trigger finger still, but ready.

"Not wearing camo," she said.

"Need more."

"Black Raven." Leo's tone was steady and certain. "Stand down. Agents. Acknowledge. Black Raven. Agent. Acknow—"

"Black Raven. Kamin. Copy."

As Kamin's voice registered through the speaker in his helmet, a loud clunk reverberated through the crawl space. Cigarette Smoker stopped walking, glanced up, eyed the ceiling in the vicinity of the entry panel, and cocked his head to listen.

Ace gave his trigger finger a little more pressure. Cigarette Smoker took a drag, then exhaled a long plume of gray smoke as he continued walking towards the door. Ace eased his trigger finger, slightly, but kept his aim focused until the four exited the casino.

"Gone." As soon as the casino door shut behind them, Ace turned around to face Kamin and three additional Black Raven agents—Marks, Branch, and Scott—all in full battle gear, but without respirators covering their face. They were lined up on the left side of the crawl space.

Ace pressed himself against the right wall to address them, keeping his voice low so he wouldn't be overheard in the casino below, but loud enough to carry through the helmet mic.

Kamin, undercover as the ship's engineer, had been the leader of Omega team. He'd started out the job as third in command, which now made him second. Within a minute, they'd traded information. Ace provided a few details of the massacre in the casino, the names of the Black Raven agents who were dead, and the names of the guests who remained out of Skylar's grasp. Kamin and Marks had killed two Quan Security agents and hidden their bodies in Kamin's stateroom. Like Ace and Leo, Kamin also had seen *Follower*. He reported that as of ten minutes ago, the smaller ship remained on the starboard side of *Imagine*.

"Sixty Quan Security agents were aboard at the inception of the cruise. Quan radio transmissions indicate that the Blackwells killed one and disabled another. Between us, we've killed four. Which means there are a minimum of fifty-four still standing. We also have to assume that there were other Quan agents among the staff and Tier Two security."

Kamin had been thinking along the same lines as Ace and Leo. "Yes, sir. Agreed. Numbers aren't in our favor, yet. We were using this crawl space to head to the forward service stairwell. We were hoping we'd come across Leo or Ryan."

The dark-haired agent set his jaw after speaking Ryan's name. Then he rolled his shoulders and shook his head, having to visibly force away his emotion. Ace knew how Kamin felt. He was damn sure they all felt the same way about the death of the young, smart agent with the nice, bright smile. And they were all friends with the other agents who had been killed. While Black Raven was an enormous company with plenty of agents, those agents who were considered elite—and all aboard *Imagine* fit that category—were part of a smaller subset. But no matter how they felt about their fallen colleagues, there wouldn't be time for mourning until the job's end. Ace, whose eyes were locked with Kamin's, watched the man recover, with a hard glint in his gaze that echoed Ace's thoughts.

This isn't the time for grief. It's the time to make the bastards pay.

"We were headed to the radio room," Kamin continued. "I have rudimentary knowledge of how to establish a connection for a Mayday and how to disable the surveillance system, but Leo's expertise far surpasses mine. Then we were going to start killing these fuckers."

Ace thought through the ship's schematics and the relative strengths and weakness of his team members. "This is how we'll do it. All actions run concurrently. We have three immediate goals. One—send Mayday, restore our agent-to-agent comms, and take out ship's surveillance. Two—reduce enemy numbers. Our presence needs to be undetected until the numbers are better. Once Quan Security knows about us, they'll start killing hostages to make us stop. Three—disable hydraulics to halt any sort of evacuation to *Follower*."

As he spoke, his agents returned his gaze with glances full of grimness and resolve. When he looked into Leo's eyes, the foreboding returned. In a split second, he saw himself carrying Kat away from a battlefield. Instead of Kat, the person in his arms was Leo.

Fuck.

He cleared his throat, rolled his shoulders, and managed to shake off his misplaced personal concerns over Leo, her safety, and their future. For a second or two, he let his gaze run along the tubing and ductwork in the cramped space. As his resolve built, he focused his gaze on the other agents. "Keep in mind our ultimate goal is to free the hostages. Then we'll work on gaining control of the helm. For as long as possible, we will try not to alert the powers that be to our presence. Innocent souls depend upon us. Trust your instincts, knowledge, and weapons. Improvise as needed. Let's outsmart them."

Ace looked at the two agents who had entered the crawl space last. "Branch. Scott. You're now Omega team. You'll work the stern area, in the aft service stairwell. Take out as many Quan Security personnel as possible. Without detection."

Ace explained the potential for immediate live action in the stern area, as Skylar had directed Wendt and Yang to assist another team there in their search for the Blackwells. "Obviously, Wendt and Yang haven't shown up, so other Quan operatives will soon be doing recon. Plus, Leo and I left blood splatter in the aft service stairwell when we were there, which could draw more Quan operatives to the area if it's noticed. We have to assume it will be. Move elsewhere as needed. Remember, until we disable the system, once you exit that stairwell, unless you're in a crawl space, you're likely under camera surveillance. Once our comms are reestablished, we'll reassess positioning. Go."

Branch and Scott eased past the other agents, nodding as they belly-crawled past him. He glanced over his shoulder at their progress, watching them pause briefly at the first vent they came to that provided a view of the casino floor. They didn't linger.

He refocused on the remaining agents. Marks. Kamin. Leo. Of the three, he saw only one. She was looking over her shoulder at him as she waited for his order.

"Kamin and Leo. You're Delta team. Your goal is to get to the radio room, where you will make a Mayday call, then reestablish agent-to-agent comms. Disable the ship's surveillance."

"Yes, sir," Kamin said.

"Yes, sir," she echoed.

Ace couldn't help but let his gaze linger on her, as a flash of '*I've got this*' lightened her caramel-colored eyes. Before she turned away from him and started moving forward, she gave him a confident, cocky nod that made his breath catch and his heart sink.

It's as though she thinks she's goddamn invincible.

Her confidence didn't bother him one bit. Her cockiness made him want to pull her back to him and tell her that odds were against them. That she was human. That she wasn't infallible. But those were things that she already knew, and the fact that he felt an urge to say them now told him something about the possibility of a future for the two of them that he wasn't ready to admit.

And he sure as hell didn't have time to dwell on it now.

Chapter Twelve

1:45 a.m.

Leo and Kamin paused at a vent, looking through the slats into the theater. They were positioned above the tenth row of seats, towards the left of the stage. Ceiling height varied as the floor sloped towards the stage. They were a little more than twenty feet above the floor, with a view of two-thirds of the theater, from the middle rows to the stage. A syrupy version of "*White Christmas,*" playing on theater speakers, provided low background music that juxtaposed a layer of surrealism over the drama unfolding below them.

Her hand slipped, as one of the wiring tubes that ran along the floor of the crawl space rolled from her weight and the ship's movement. She readjusted her body, using her forearms for balance and her core strength to stay still.

The theater had seating capacity for two hundred. Plush, forest-green drapes, with gold trim, were drawn across the stage. A cluster of three blue spruce trees, flocked lightly with a dusting of white snow, stood in a grouping at center stage, on platforms that could be moved as needed for performances. Golden bows, sprays of holly, and twinkling, star-like lights made the trees picture perfect. Ornaments in varying sizes, all red, green, gold, and white, reflected the lights.

Guests sat in burgundy-velvet, theater-style seats, looking smaller than they had when they'd been in the casino. Most wore the cocktail clothes they'd planned to wear to the opening night's festivities—glittering, low cut gowns, and tuxedos. Some wore casual clothes they'd worn in their rooms as they dressed for the night's festivities. Others wore plush, cream-colored robes that had been in their staterooms. Some were pale. A few were crying. All had their attention focused forward, towards the stage.

Eight men in camouflage stood in the orchestra pit, with QBZ-95s hoisted and aimed at their captive audience. Five more armed men roamed the aisles, their weapons pointed at the guests.

A tall man, also in camo-gear, stood center stage on the semi-circle portion in front of the drapes. Pale skin. Dark hair and eyes. Mixed Asian heritage. On the ship's manifest, he'd been identified as Chad Ting, head of Quan Security. Leo hadn't had the opportunity to talk to Ting before the siege. Now, Ting was speaking in English, with a trace of a German accent.

He spoke loudly enough for her to clearly hear that his voice was the same as Skylar's, which she and Ace had been hearing on line sixteen. "They damn well didn't jump in the ocean and swim away. I'll double the pay for the man who brings Ling Wen to me."

Leo tuned out the responses, as she focused on the closed, leather-bound folder that Skylar/Ting held in his left hand. Her gaze was drawn to, and then riveted upon, the table on stage next to him, in front of the Christmas trees. There were several dozen or more black-leather bound folders stacked neatly in piles on the table. Four men in business suits flanked the table.

Those definitely aren't Christmas presents.

The objects looked like leather-bound portfolios. Or slender books. Or, what would have looked like a book twenty years ago. She knew better, though, and Skylar confirmed her suspicion, as he opened the folder in his hand, then glanced at the screen.

Tablets. Electronic devices.

Her veins came alive with the pump of adrenaline. “Holy crap.”

“Well, well,” Kamin said, under his breath.

“Evans,” she whispered, glancing over her shoulder. Ace was easing around an HVAC duct. He was moving ahead of Marks, ten feet from where she and Kamin were poised over the theater. “They’re using tablets. Like iPads.”

“Implies Wi-Fi connectivity.”

“Correct.” She and Kamin made double time crawling to the next vent so that Ace and Marks would have a view. She fell into position in time to see Skylar focus his attention on the front row, where two people were seated in front of the stage.

Keeping her gaze on the drama unfolding below, she eased her backpack straps off her shoulders. As her gaze bounced from Quan security agent to agent, she recognized several of them as people who had been part of what they had once considered to be a legitimate, Tier One security force.

Knowing the due diligence that the Howard Underwriting Group and Black Raven had performed prior to the job’s commencement, she acknowledged, with a sinking feeling, that the Quan operatives had been superior with their deception. Black Raven normally detected oddities that led to criminal behavior. When she thought of how good Quan security had been with implementation of the siege, from effectively gassing the entire ship, rounding up and killing Tier Two security and any ship employees who weren't relevant to their objective, and corralling most of the guests into the theater, she felt queasy. Her gut told her that what they were now seeing of the Quan Security operation was just the beginning. It was going to get worse if Black Raven didn't stop it.

Which begged the question of what was in store for the guests, and, more specifically: where was the first officer who'd given the post-gassing, repetitive, and annoying-as-hell, multi-lingual emergency instruction for the guests to proceed to the theater. "Evans? From your vantage point, do you see Raznick?"

"That's a negative."

With a head-nod from Skylar, a business-suited man picked up a tablet. He used the stairs at stage left to step onto the floor, as the music changed to Elvis Presley's "Blue Christmas."

"Someone turn off that damn music!" Skylar yelled as his man reached the front row of seats. The man in the suit sat next to Randy Howell and his fiancée, Miranda Lake. He handed Howell the tablet, opened it, and said something in a voice that was too low for Leo to hear.

Presley was cut off in mid-verse as Leo's mind raced with details about Howell, who'd been playing craps across the table from her earlier that evening. The forty-nine-year-old entrepreneur had gained notoriety in his early teens as a video game designer. He'd brought new complexity to video gaming, patented his innovations, and had become a multi-millionaire by twenty. In recent years, he'd made significant investments in Chinese tech manufacturing facilities and software research and development. Black Raven's due diligence for the cruise had confirmed rumors of hard times and crafty financing. His first wife had died in a boating accident, five years earlier. He was legendary in gambling circles. Originally from Seattle, Washington, he now lived an international lifestyle, with residences in Vegas, Monte Carlo, and Macau. He was a HUG client, with K & R coverage of five hundred million dollars.

Dressed in a tuxedo, Howell had dark hair that was graying slightly at the temples. If he'd had time to put on a tie before the ether hit him, it was long gone. His collar was unbuttoned and his shirt was rumpled. He lifted his black-rimmed glasses from his mottled face to rub his eyes, ending the gesture with a two-handed pull at his thick hair that mussed it even more.

Below them, despite the weapons aimed at him, Randy Howell gave Skylar a defiant headshake and pushed the tablet from his lap. As it fell to the carpeted floor with a resounding thud, Leo glanced over her shoulder. Ace and Marks had reached the vent. They were watching what was happening below.

Glancing again into the theater, she watched the guy in the suit reach forward and pick up the tablet. He checked the screen, then calmly handed it back to Howell, while the nearest Quan Security operative stepped forward, aiming the muzzle of his assault rifle at Miranda's forehead.

Skylar walked close to where Howell was seated. "Mr. Howell, you will proceed as directed at the prompts."

"How dare you! You'll never get away with this."

Skylar stood directly in front of Howell, looking down at him. "When I want your opinion, I'll ask for it."

Black Raven provided cyber security to businesses in the financial sector, and Leo knew that banks were constantly updating security measures to prevent hacking thefts. Personalized passcodes. Retinal scans. Live-time fingerprint scanning. Some banks used all three, and more. With access to Howell, and a weapon aimed at him, or someone he cared about, Skylar would have access to all the man's assets. As long as Howell complied with his demands.

"At the prompts, Mr. Howell," Skylar glanced at the audience, his gaze panning the crowd, as though he was an actor who was enjoying his performance, "and rest assured, we will get away with this."

From further back in the audience, someone yelled, "You can't do this!"

Focusing on pulling her laptop and tablet out of her backpack, Leo didn't see who yelled. She glanced down in time to see a Quan operative punish Le Yarles, of Singapore, seated ten rows back from the stage, for his outburst with a closed-fist punch to his cheek. Yarles' wife, a petite, dark-haired woman wearing a bathrobe, started sobbing. Others grumbled. A few gasped.

Leo powered up her laptop and tablet, then backed away from the vent as her screens flashed. "Evans. Kamin. I might have access for a Mayday here, piggybacking on whatever Wi-Fi connection they're using. I'll have to break through whatever security or firewalls they've established, though. Could be tricky, but once I'm on, I might also be able to re-establish our agent-to-agent comms from here. Can't hurt if we're trying to accomplish those tasks from two separate avenues of connectivity."

Kamin, at her side, said, "Copy that, Leo. Evans? Looks like Leo and I should split up here."

"Roger that," Ace said, his voice a low whisper through her helmet mic. "Kamin, move forward to the radio room to disable surveillance. Once the cameras are down, hold position in the radio room and start working on a Mayday and our comms from there. Leo may be joining you there if she can't accomplish anything here. If you do hear from Leo on our comms, reposition accordingly."

"Copy," Kamin said.

"Roger that," Leo said, clicking on her keyboard.

As Kamin slipped away from her side, Ace shimmied forward. He fell into position with his face over the vent, his body on his side, along hers. His gaze was focused downwards, on the events in the theater. Leo peered down in time to see Howell jump to his feet, his cheeks flushed beet red.

Howell yelled, "I will not."

One operative held the muzzle of a pistol steady at Miranda's forehead, while another jabbed a rifle muzzle into Howell's chest. All of the flush left Howell's face, as three operatives grabbed Miranda and hauled her, shrieking as she tried to pull away from them, on to the stage. With tears falling, she yelled, "Give them what they want!"

Acutely aware of what was going to happen next if Howell didn't act fast and comply, Leo had to fight the urge to grab her Glock. Beads of sweat broke out on her forehead, as she struggled with the urge to stop the killing from unfolding.

As though reading her mind, Ace reached out, gripped her right hand, and squeezed hard. Miranda's hysterical screams filled the crawl space, joined by the screams of the other guests and Howell's yells of indignant rage. She glanced back, through the crawl space.

Marks was looking through the vent. Ahead of them, Kamin was at the entry panel that would lead to the forward service stairwell, loosening the screws. Neither seemed to be fighting the urge to lift a weapon and fire.

"Leo." Grim resolve and steely determination glinted in Ace's eyes as he whispered to her. "Stand down. Collateral damage would be too great. Four of us. Eighteen of them in the theater now. We know there could be at least fifty-four Quan Security operatives aboard. We're outnumbered, which means we're also outweaponed."

"But our position is great—"

"No. It will delay our Mayday." *And if we don't survive, the delay might damn well be indefinite.* "Our position isn't optimal. We don't have a view of more than a third of the theater—"

"But—"

"The minute we start firing, surveillance cameras will pick it up. All the Quan Security operatives who are now scattered around this ship, looking for the Wens, the Blackwells, and Chloe and Zack, will return. If we try to stop this, there's no telling how many hostages will die."

She swallowed. Nodded. Knowing that Ace was correct didn't make his *stand-down* directive easy. Below them, the *pop-pop-pop* of gunfire sounded. It silenced Miranda's cries, but the yells of the other guests reached a deafening crescendo, before dissipating to harsh cries. After a few seconds, the room fell into eerie silence. It was as though they were holding their collective breaths, waiting for the next scream-worthy scene in a horror show.

"Mr. Howell." Skylar's tone was calm. Cool. So low, Leo almost didn't hear him. "You have exactly five seconds to reconsider."

Quan Security operatives dragged Howell up the stairs and onto the stage. The operatives threw Howell to the ground, next to the body of his fiancée, and aimed their weapons at him.

"Three seconds."

Howell reached for his fiancée, cradling her face in his hands.

"One second."

"I'll do it," Howell yelled, choking back a sob.

Leo shook her head, clearing her rage away as she reached for her laptop. "I'm on task."

"I know you are." Ace reached out and lifted her chin with his index finger. He gave her a nod of encouragement and a look that conveyed more tenderness than she'd ever thought she'd see on a job.

"If they're getting their money from the hostages now..." Her voice trailed as she tried to predict Skylar's next step. Glancing sideways at Ace, she met his gaze. "Maybe they're not going to evacuate the hostages to *Follower*."

He nodded. "Thought of that. However, it could be their escape route, and they'll take a few hostages there for cover. To use as bargaining chips to guarantee an escape. Until I know what the reason is for *Follower*, I'm taking out their access to it, as I whittle down Quan Security's numbers."

He paused as he glanced in her eyes one last time before moving away.

She gave him a nod. "Be talking to you soon, sir."

Something flickered in his gaze. What, she couldn't tell. Then it was gone, and he was all business. Hard jaw. Flat eyes. Grim resolve in the set of his lips. He returned her nod, then turned and moved towards the entry panel. Marks nodded as he moved past her. When Kamin had the panel open, light from the forward service stairwell made the crawl space a little less dim. As they disappeared into the stairwell, Leo got to work on her laptop and tablet.

A sudden, high-pitched scream from the theater distracted her. A feminine voice said, "Let. Me. Go. You son of a bitch!"

Guests gasped, and there was a rustling of people shifting position. Mumbling. A man's voice said, "No."

Leo shifted so that she had a better view through the grating. Her chest tightened, as she looked at the couple who were being dragged through the theater's center aisle. One Quan Operative had his hand wound through Nina Blackwell's long blonde hair, pulling it as he pushed her forward. Todd Blackwell was behind her. Two burly men, both of whom Leo recognized as being in the casino earlier, walking and joking among the dead, pushed him forward. He fell and turned onto his back.

For a brief second, before one of the men hefted him up onto his feet, Leo had a view of his face. His eyes, a blackened mess of swollen flesh, were barely open. His nose was a bloody mess. His lips were split and oozing. Glancing towards the stage, where Skylar stood over Miranda's body, Leo didn't have to guess the fate of the Blackwells. She saw it in the grimness of Skylar's thin-lipped smile.

"Fuck," Leo whispered.

She glanced up. On her left, at the end of the crawl space, the entry panel leading to the ship's stairwell in the bow had been reattached. Ace, Marks, and Kamin were on the other side, on their way to complete the tasks. To her right, Branch and Scott were long gone. They'd made it past the casino and, on the far end of the crawl space, through the entry panel that led to the stern of the ship.

"Welcome to the Calliope Theater, Mr. and Mrs. Blackwell," Skylar said. His tone, full of self-satisfaction, sounded more chilling than welcoming. "Bring them to the stage. Let's show them, and our audience, what happens to people who kill members of Quan Security."

A fresh scream from Nina Blackwell, loud and unrelenting, drifted through the vent and resonated in the crawl space, the horror that it carried echoing along the stainless-steel walls. Leo gritted her teeth against the urge to do something to stop Skylar and his men. She grabbed her laptop, reminding herself that she had orders, that she was powerless to stop the drama or the execution unfolding below her.

Not now.

But later...

She focused on her tasks. Mayday. Restore agent-to-agent comms. But Mayday first.

If ever a ship needed such a call, it was *Imagine*, now.

Chapter Thirteen

2:06 a.m.

Ace slid head first into the narrow stairwell that was between the Clio and Euterpe Decks. After the dimness of the crawl space, he had to narrow his eyes against the bright lights and the stark white composite painted on the steel walls. He sprang to his feet, then adjusted his stance for the slight roll of the ship in the two-foot seas. Bouncing action as the vessel moved in the ocean's slight swells was more apparent in the bow than at any other point in the ship. From behind him, in the crawl space he'd just exited, a fresh round of chilling screams echoed. In the stairwell, above and below, there were no footsteps. No weapon fire. Only silence.

Marks slid out to stand beside him. He was twenty-eight years old, with an army background and two years in Black Raven. His helmet concealed most of his auburn hair. Freckles on his nose seemed dark compared to the paleness of his skin. He glanced at Ace with a grim look in his green eyes.

Stretching out kinks in his arms, shoulders, and neck, Ace said, "Damn well thrilled not to be belly crawling any longer."

"Agreed."

Glock in hand, Ace stayed alert while Marks bent to lift the entry panel so he could replace it. Ace allowed himself one last look down the crawl space before Marks set the entry panel in place. Fifteen yards away, lying on her belly and poised on her elbows, Leo was hunched behind the open screen of her laptop and focused on her task. As expected.

He tried to tell himself she wasn't the woman he loved. She was simply a well-trained agent. Smart. Intuitive. With great field skills. Rationally, he knew she could handle herself as well as, or better than, any agent aboard *Imagine*. He tried to tell himself that his worry over her wasn't rational. His worry, though, had nothing to do with her capabilities, and he knew there wasn't a goddamn thing he could do about it. The gnawing worry that was eating at his insides...he was going to damn well feel it, until the second they were reunited. And probably for a lot longer.

For now, though, she's simply an agent doing her job. Just do yours.

Ace slipped his Glock back into its holster and unstrapped his M1A. He checked that the rifle's 20-round magazine was secure. He had two more mags in his backpack. For his Glock, he had four mags, with 15-rounds apiece, minus the two rounds he'd fired earlier. Adjusting his backpack, he wrapped his palm around the rifle's grip.

"We're going two flights down, along a short hallway. We've got to go through the control room to get to the engine room. Perfect place to reduce their numbers."

Stating the obvious. Just like she said I do.

Marks didn't seem bothered. "Yes, sir."

Even as Ace turned at the first stair landing, with Marks behind him, his thoughts were on the difficulties of Leo's tasks. He knew enough about satellite systems, communications networking, and Wi-Fi frequency jamming technology to know that she needed to focus. Which meant she might not hear danger approaching...

Fucking hell. If she's on her A-game, I'll hear her voice within twenty-nine minutes, tops. Because my girl will want to boast that she managed the impossible in under thirty.

He glanced at his watch. He'd crawled away from her side a mere five minutes earlier. Twenty-nine minutes from the time that he'd left her would be at 0233 hours. Which meant he had twenty-four more minutes to go before he'd worry if he wasn't hearing her—loud, clear, and damn well alive—on his embedded ear mic. He told himself to focus on his own shit. Because if he let it, his worry over her would awaken every one of his demons. With those demons in play, he'd freeze. He'd be no good to anyone.

The sound of footsteps ascending the metal stairs snapped his mind back to reality. Hard-soled shoes. One person. Relatively light. In good shape. Surefooted. Fast.

Raising his rifle, and holding his breath, he pressed his index finger within a hair of firing. The man reached the landing, with an immediate turn to face Ace. His eyes widened with surprise as he saw Ace and Marks. In the millisecond before Ace fired at the man on the stairwell, his brain absorbed who the guy was, and more importantly, who he wasn't.

Black hair, graying at the temples. Asian. No camo. Tuxedo. Shirt unbuttoned. No tie.

Kill?

No!

Not a Quan Security operative.

Ling Wen.

As Ace realized he was within a hair of killing a guest who happened to be one of HUG's most prized clients, Ling Wen assumed a squared firing stance and lifted a QBZ-95 to point it at Ace.

"Don't fire!" Ace raised his arms, and his rifle, overhead, while Marks, eased forward to stand on the same step as Ace, rifle lifted and aimed at Wen.

"We're friendly," Ace said. "Put down your weapon."

"Prove it."

Fair enough.

With a sideways glance at Marks, Ace said, "Stand down."

As Marks raised his arms and his weapon, matching Ace's conciliatory stance, Ace locked eyes with Wen. "It took one hell of a lot of skill for me not to blow your brains out. You're handling that weapon well enough to know that. Don't make me regret my decision. Put the rifle down."

Wen kept the butt of his rifle at his shoulder. If the man was nervous, he did a damn good job of hiding it. Arms lifted, with no tremble. Steady focus through the sights. His right cheek was firmly planted against the smooth cheek surface on the stock, as he slowly shifted his aim from Ace's face, to Marks, and back again. He had a solid stance, as though he knew what he was doing and wouldn't flinch when he did it. Digging a fact on Wen from his memory bank, Ace remembered that the man owned weapons manufacturing facilities. *Shit.* Wen built the QBZ-95, for God's sake.

“I’m worth more alive than dead to you. Or your boss.” Wen spoke perfect English, without a trace of an accent. His tone was calm and cool. “For a while, at least.”

“I’m not a hijacker, goddammit. I’m a guest. Zack Abrams,” Ace kept his voice low, mindful that even small sounds carried in the stairwell and, at any moment, the enemy could approach from above or below. “At six fifteen this evening my fiancée was playing craps two tables down from you. Golden skin. Metal halter top. Your wife kissed you before you rolled. You spotted me looking at the two of you. Right after we made eye contact, you rolled a ten.”

Wen, studying Ace, kept the assault rifle aimed. “I recognize you. Explain why you packed combat gear for a gambling cruise.”

Great question.

“I’m a security contractor. I was undercover as a guest. Actually, I’m Adam Evans. You’re one of HUG’s clients. Your K & R coverage, and your wife’s, tops out at two billion Hong Kong dollars. Apiece. HUG hired my company to cover their ass in the event a kidnapping involves a ransom demand. So please, put down the goddamn rifle. I’ve got work to do.”

“Name of your company?”

“Black Raven.”

As Wen eased the weapon down, Ace asked, “Where’s your wife?”

“Where she won’t be found.”

Ace sure hoped the man was right, but on his next breath, he had a sinking feeling in the pit of his stomach. “Please don’t say in a crawl space.”

Wen visibly flinched. “She is.”

Aw. Hell. "They know other guests have hidden in crawl spaces, so they're already searching them.

He watched the man grow pale. His shoulders dropped, before his moment of weakness passed. "She's not anywhere near our cabin."

"That might buy her some time, but I wouldn't count on much."

"How many of you are there?"

"Not enough," Ace said, "yet. We're working on making the odds better."

"We need to end this. We should go to the radio room." Wen slung the rifle behind his shoulder.

We? Great. A billionaire boy scout.

Wen continued, "I was headed there to make a Mayday call."

"Got that covered." Ace reached into his pocket for his extra screwdriver. "Catch."

Wen caught it with his left hand, looked at it, and glanced at Ace with what Ace thought was a puzzled look.

"Screwdriver," Ace explained. "Pivoting, telescoping head. You can use it from outside and inside the crawl spaces."

"I know what this is."

"Use it at the next entry panel. Slip into the crawl space. One of my agents is in there. I wouldn't surprise her if I were you. Hide there until the ship's secure, or use that crawl space to get back to your wife. If you do that, be ready to use that rifle."

"I'm not hiding."

“You should, and be prepared, because if they find your wife, they’ll use her as leverage against you. I just watched them kill one of the guest’s fiancée to get him to comply with their demands.”

Anger sparked in Wen’s eyes. “If you think I’m going to hide, you have severely underestimated my capabilities.”

Wen’s insistence that he would not cower proved that the man hadn’t accumulated his vast wealth without more than the usual dose of tenacity, coupled with a pair of balls that would have made a goddamn bull elephant envious.

“Hide. Or don’t. My advice is hide. Whatever you do, stay out of our way. And let me be clear. Aiming a weapon at any Black Raven agent is a mistake, one that may prove lethal if you do it again.” He paused, eyeing Wen. “One more thing. Where did you get that rifle?”

“My security. My men weren’t in their room when I awakened. But I knew where they kept their weapons.”

Somewhat satisfied, and disappointed that Wen hadn’t acquired the rifle after killing a member of Quan security, Ace nodded in the direction of the descending stairwell. “Marks. Move out.”

Chapter Fourteen

2:07 a.m.

As Ace and Marks replaced the entry panel, Leo realized that the steel walls of the crawl space provided too much interference with the signal Skylar was using. The signal wasn't totally blocked, like the walls did with the Black Raven comm system in their helmets. The signal strength indicator on her laptop showed that her position gave her one of four possible bars of strength. She shimmied forward, moving her laptop closer to the vent. There, the indicator light showed two bars of strength.

Shit!

As tempted as she was to try, she knew that half strength wouldn't be enough. To piggyback effectively on Skylar's signal, and do it undetected, she'd need maximum signal strength. The signal's two bars flashed, then became one, confirming her decision.

No choice but to proceed to the radio room.

She reached into her backpack, feeling for one of the small remote cameras. Finding it, she attached the orb-like camera to the vent. Once she established connectivity, she'd be able to pick up the camera's signal and see what was happening in the theater, almost as though she'd stayed in position above the vent. Assuming she was able to reestablish a connection.

After repacking her laptop and tablet, she belly-crawled forward, then turned sideways to get around an HVAC duct. As she turned, a smaller passageway leading off the main crawl space caught her attention. Her pre-job study of *Imagine*'s schematics indicated that the passageway led directly above the backstage area and dead-ended there. If she could get to the end, she'd be able to drop through a vent into a booth that housed stage props.

The props booth was behind the drapes that were now drawn across the stage, as well as behind the on-stage acting area. It was essentially part of the stage, but designed so that theatergoers wouldn't notice it, even when the curtains weren't drawn. Through design tricks of sliding walls, black paint, and dark mirrors, the booth functioned as a closet of sorts for stage props. It was virtually invisible to theatergoers. Most important for Leo's purpose, the walls of the booth were not reinforced with steel. The thin walls, designed for maneuverability, would provide virtually no interference with jumping on Skylar's Wi-Fi signal. It would be as though she and Skylar were both on stage, in the same room. Because they would be. Most importantly, there would be minimal interference with the signal he was using.

Eyes straining, she studied the narrow passageway, jam-packed with tubes, wiring, and shiny silver HVAC apparatus. It was too small for Evans or any of the others. She'd only fit through it if she stripped off most of her gear. Even then, it would be tight. Yet she could do it, with bare-bones equipment. The next hurdle she'd face would be a significant drop from the ceiling to the floor of the props booth. If she remembered the schematics correctly, the ceiling over the stage sloped. At the props booth, it could be anywhere from twenty feet to thirty feet. Fortunately, Ace had added climbing rope to her stash of gear, when her mind hadn't been functioning properly in their suite.

On the plus side, she could get there faster than she could get to the radio room, and Skylar's signal, if she could access it, was potentially a surer shot for a Mayday call. With Kamin already attempting a Mayday from the radio room, there was no down side.

Except that Ace wouldn't like the idea of one agent advancing into the theater alone.

Unfortunately, until she restored comms, there was no way to run the idea by him. Besides, when Ace deemed that the number of Quan operatives was sufficiently reduced, he and the other Black Raven agents would be entering the theater. It would help if she was already inside, at a point where she'd have full firing range of the room.

Decision made, Leo quickly stripped down to the essentials. She kept her Glock and Sig Sauer, but left her rifle behind. She stripped off her backpack. Her laptop was encased with a material that was similar to the flexible body armor that she wore. She could use it in place of either her chest plate or back plate. She removed her back plate and shoved her laptop into the pocket where it had been. She tucked her other comm gear into the front of her shirt, along with her handgun clips. She slid climbing rope into the waistband of her pants and shoved carabiners into her pockets.

As she contorted her body forward, moving as fast as she could, she breathed easier with each inch of forward progress. She focused on the tasks that she'd accomplish once in the props booth, which had to be performed quickly. Mayday. Restoration of agent-to-agent comms.

Upon which many lives damn well depended.

Chapter Fifteen

2:14 a.m.

Ace and Marks ran down the stairs, leaving Wen behind. On line sixteen, Skylar was silent, presumably preoccupied with the demands he was putting upon the hostages. Ace wondered how far Skylar had gotten in his wealth accumulation. How many hostages had been killed for incentive. Whether the brutal murder of Howell's fiancée had been enough incentive for all of the hostages to comply with Skylar's demands. And, what the hell Skylar was going to do with the hostages when he met his financial quota.

Would he kill them anyway?

Two Quan operatives talked as they climbed the stairs and rounded the landing. Focused more on each other than their surroundings, Ace realized that their lack of attention meant that the other agents hadn't yet done anything to sound alarms.

Could be a good or a bad sign.

It did mean that Ace and Marks had surprise working in their favor. Ace fired at the one on the left, between the eyebrows. Marks killed the one on the right.

Eight Quan operatives down. Maybe more, depending on Omega team's success. As many as fifty-two remaining. Still too many.

Sprinting over them, Ace and Marks continued down the stairs until they reached the bottom floor. They didn't encounter any more Quan operatives on their way to the control area, which was a self-contained room. To get into the engine room, he and Marks had to go through the control room. Normal operation of the ship required two engineers monitoring systems that ran everything from toilet flushing to engine oil pressure.

The control room door was open. Ace and Marks approached, slowly. Two camo-wearing Quan operatives were seated on either side of the closed engine room door, their backs to Ace and Marks. They weren't paying attention to what was happening behind them.

The one on the left said, in English, "Fuck. Cameras are on the blink."

"Again?" The one on the right said, without glancing at his co-worker.

Over the Quan operative's shoulder, Ace saw monitors that should've shown video feeds from internal engine room cams and elsewhere around the ship. Rather than showing live video, the monitors were dark. Good—Kamin had succeeded.

As if sensing that they had company, the Quan operatives lurched to their feet, fumbling for their assault rifles. Ace and Marks fired while the Quan operatives were dicking around. One fell on the still-blank surveillance monitors. The other hit the workstation before sliding to the floor, leaving streaks of blood over blinking green numbers that revealed engine output data.

Ten Quan operatives down. Maybe more, depending on Omega's success. Fifty remaining. Still too many.

Signaling Marks to shut the control room door, Ace crossed the narrow room to the engine room door, which was centered in the wall, between the two workstations. A round window in the door provided a view of the vast area containing *Imagine*'s four diesel engines, generators, HVAC units, fuel and bilge tanks, hydraulic systems, spare parts, and more. Composed of three platforms that stretched across the beam of the ship and spanned its length, the cavernous room was as large as the casino and twice the height.

While his Black Raven comm remained dead silent, the Quan Security earbud crackled to life with the voice of an operative, speaking hurriedly in Mandarin.

Skylar replied, in English, with a terse, "Repeat that."

As he listened, Ace peered through the window, into the engine room. At first glance, he didn't see any Quan operatives. Only a wide expanse of a room, gleaming with white industrial paint and pristine equipment, silver-gridded pathways that provided access around the equipment, and yellow, red, and green safety lights. He refocused, then spotted a flash of camo. Port side. Second platform. Side walkway. Three Quan operatives were moving cautiously towards the engine room door, weapons lifted, as though they were expecting someone to come charging through, guns blazing.

On line sixteen, the Quan operative whose excitement was getting in the way of effective communication, repeated his statements, this time in a mix of Mandarin and heavily accented English.

Ace understood only a bit. Something about "controls," "forward stairwell," "dead," and "two." He heard enough to know why the Quan operatives in the engine room had raised their weapons and were more on guard than any he'd seen thus far. Evidently, the bodies of the two men that he and Marks had killed only moments earlier, in the forward stairwell, had been discovered.

Skylar replied, "Ling. Tam. Go investigate. Bottom deck."

There was no reply to Skylar's directive. The silence lasted long enough to make Ace pretty certain that the now-dead operatives who'd been working in the control room were Ling and Tam. Skylar confirmed Ace's hunch by yelling for all available operatives to proceed to the control room and the forward service stairwell.

Ace tuned out the replies, except to be aware that the number of different voices meant that he and his agents damn well had work to do before they had a prayer of overtaking Skylar in the theater and freeing the hostages. As Ace flipped the latches on the engine room door, Marks fired off a volley of shots that killed an Asian man who burst through the door of the control room.

Marks once again shut the door. "Eleven Quans down. Maybe more, depending on Omega."

"Getting better," Ace said. "We have three Quans in the engine room, ready to fire at us as soon as we go through the door, which opens on the middle platform. The two hydraulic pumps are on the bottom platform."

Marks nodded. "Positioned twenty feet from the KVMB12s."

The younger agent's technical reference to the Bergen-type main engines gave Ace a measure of comfort that Marks, who'd been undercover in the ship's jewelry store, knew exactly where to go, what to do, and that he'd accomplish his task no matter the stress. "Once we get through the door, you'll take port side. I'll go to starboard. We'll disable at the power take-off clutch." Ace explained how he wanted connections severed. "We have to be able to put it back together, just in case we need to get the hostages off *Imagine* via life boats later."

"Yes, sir."

Ace glanced again in the engine room through the circular window and found what he was looking for. "Three Quan operatives. Partially concealed. Port side, at a water expansion tank and hot well. Poised for firing."

"There's access to the engine room on the stern," Marks observed.

"Correct. So the fact that there are only three is good news." Ace thought about the agents that he'd sent to the stern of the ship, with the open-ended directive to whittle down Quan's numbers. "Let's take it as a sign that Omega team's doing good work."

Three Quan operatives were enough of a problem to be a speed bump for getting through the engine room door. Ace intended to comply with what he considered to be a primary rule of close quarter combat; when entering a room, damn well live through the perilous act of crossing the threshold.

Cons were that he and Marks faced three men with powerful weapons, superior tactical position, who were already in kill position, expecting someone to enter. *I've faced worse.* One pro for him and Marks was that both the expansion tank and hot well where the Quan operatives were hiding were designed to collect and release steam. *Stupid hiding place.* Also, the wall between the engine room and the control room was reinforced steel, designed to protect the ship in the event of catastrophic, explosive engine failure. Which meant he and Marks had some protection.

"Tank and hot well hold one hell of a lot of boiling water and steam," Marks' lips were a thin, tense slash as he voiced Ace's own thoughts. "Can we hit the apparatus from here without risking exposure?"

Ace considered the angles, distance, and the position from which they'd need to fire. Awkward. He'd be off balance. Plus, he needed to shoot with his left hand, when he was right-handed.

I've done it before.

He returned Marks' tense smile with a nod, then placed his rifle on the floor next to him and pulled the Glock out of his shoulder holster. "Fuck, yeah."

They heard footsteps in the hallway.

"I've got this," Ace said. "Hallway is yours."

Meanwhile, his Black Raven ear mic was silent. If the agents were in their intended positions, Kamin was almost directly above them, five decks up. Branch and Scott were on the stern side of the ship. And Leo. She was either two decks up, in the crawl space above the theater. Or, she'd given up there and was on her way to the radio room.

Hell. Come on, Leo. I'd love to communicate with the team, and you. It would be nice to know whether you managed a Mayday call. Even nicer to damn well know you're okay. That everyone is okay.

While Marks took care of the Quan operative in the hallway, Ace slid to the floor, positioning himself on the port side of the door. Face against the wall, he pushed open the engine room door, then let the thick wall shield him against the barrage of gunfire that the Quan operatives sent his way. Amidst the loud whir of the engines, he listened for a rhythm in their gunfire.

Pop-pop-pop-pop-pop. Pause. *Pop-pop-pop-pop.* Pause. *Pop-pop-pop-pop.* Pause.

From his position he couldn't see the men or the apparatus providing their cover. Didn't matter. The expansion tank and hot well were large enough targets, and he knew the direction to fire. At the next pause in their gunfire, he held his Glock in the doorway, just inches from the floor, aimed it towards the hot well, and fired. Yells sounded as boiling hot water and scalding steam escaped the tanks.

With Marks behind him, Ace advanced into the engine room. They both fired at the tank as they ran through, then took the stairs leading to the bottom platform at a run. The Quans had fallen from the elevated platform, and were screaming as they writhed in pain on the engine room floor, near the wastewater system. One of the Quans sat up and lifted his rifle. The other two crawled for their weapons. Ace and Marks fired three shots as they took the stairs leading to the bottom platform at a run. When they reached the floor, Ace went right, to the starboard side. Marks went left, to the port side.

Three more Quans, down.

Ace got to his knees when he reached the hydraulic system, as Skylar, on the ship's PA system and on line sixteen, said, "Ling Wen. Surrender. We have your wife. She has only fifteen minutes to live. Get your ass to the theater. Now."

Given the engine noise, Ace wouldn't have been able to make out Skylar's words if he'd only been listening to the ship's PA system. With Wendt's earbud firmly in place, Ace not only heard Skylar's demand to Ling Wen, he also heard May Wen's screams of horror that followed Skylar's demands. Sure as hell, her screams were confirmation that Skylar wasn't bluffing about having her. When May Wen quieted, Skylar called five names, whom he directed to proceed to the life rafts and ready them for evacuation. Ace ground his teeth, wondering if Wen had heard the announcement and what he'd do.

Ace unscrewed the components of the power take-off clutch assembly, and disconnected the wires. When the starboard hydraulic system was disabled, he rose. Marks was hunched over the port side hydraulic system, pulling the components apart. Overhead, two men entered the engine room through the stern access door, hoisting their weapons as they ran along the grated walkway. Ace fired as the men aimed their weapons. They were on the third level and had reached the spare parts area. Some of Ace's bullets pinged off spare propellers. At least two hit their target. The men fell over the railing.

Before the two men thudded to the engine room floor, gunfire whizzed past Ace. A bullet grazed his backpack, providing a solid clue that his plan to draw Quan personnel to him was working.

Maybe a little too well.

Ace crouched, spun, and ducked behind a steel beam, then peered around it to see two Quan operatives running through the control room door. Two more were on their heels. He and Marks killed all four. Ace counted that twenty-one Quan operatives were down. It was a sizable dent in their forces.

Time to move on.

Engine whir suddenly quieted, marking a change in forward speed. Ace's position in the engine room was almost at midship. The boat started rolling, from side to side. The gentle rocking motion told Ace that forward speed hadn't simply slowed the ship—it had stopped it. Presumably, Skylar wanted to facilitate an evacuation.

Good luck with that.

Ace noted the time.

0222.

Eleven minutes before he'd allow himself to worry about not hearing from Leo. Twelve minutes before May Wen would lose her life, unless Skylar was stopped.

In Ace's mind, his immediate objective became the man he now knew to be Skylar. A tall man, in camo-gear. Pale skin. Dark hair and eyes. Standing on a stage terrorizing innocents.

Stop Skylar. Figure out who's pulling his strings.

He had a lot to do in very little time. He inhaled the engine room's scents of oil, diesel, and moist air. At least he'd made some progress. Unless Skylar and his company had rope ladders, they were going to have a damn hard time getting the hostages, or themselves, off the ship without hydraulic assistance.

Gesturing for Marks to follow him, Ace ran to the engine room's midship doorway, which opened on the Thalia Deck, directly beneath the Clio deck. Now that he no longer needed to worry about surveillance cams, the midship doorway would provide the fastest access to return to the theater. The route might coincide with the one route that Wen would take to get into the theater, assuming he was headed there.

At the door, Ace unzipped the side pocket of his backpack and pulled out his thermal imaging scope. As he opened the door, Skylar, on the PA system, said, "Ling Wen. Surrender. Your wife has ten minutes to live. Tick. Tock."

A fresh batch of screams came from May Wen. Ace blocked out her terror as he stepped into the cool night air and ran towards a deck-to-deck support beam for cover. While Ace didn't need to worry about surveillance cams along the exterior starboard side of the ship, he had the same concern there as he and Leo had when they'd been on their balcony; he didn't want anyone on *Follower* to see them.

With Marks beside him, standing guard, Ace lifted his scope and edged forward so that could peer around the support beam. Not more than a mile away, *Follower*, with its lights out, was parallel to *Imagine*. Both ships rocked side to side in the ocean's gentle swells, with almost no forward motion.

Thermal imaging made details visible. It had three decks above the waterline, holding at least twenty men, at various points along the vessel. All of them carried rifles. Two men were on the top deck, in front of the radar arch. Ace squinted, studying objects on the ground next to them. Not rifles. Too big. "Surface-to-air missiles."

Marks gave a low whistle. "Interesting."

"Not in a good way."

A small helicopter sat on the top deck, behind the radar arch. With its large cabin shape and tail rotor, the chopper looked like an Airbus H-135. Easily maneuverable. The rotors weren't spinning now, but he knew it could be aboard *Imagine* within minutes. Six passengers could fit in it easily. Eight if they pushed.

"Chopper's going to be their fallback when they figure out lifeboats won't work," Ace said, reminding himself to keep most of his body behind a support beam. He scanned the deck, left and right. No sign of Wen, or anyone else.

"Copy that."

Thermal imaging revealed that on the bow, bulky housing looked out of place on the otherwise sleek ship. The apparatus was square, approximately five feet tall and five feet wide. A matching apparatus was on the stern. Two missiles were in place in each housing, poised for firing towards *Imagine*, each approximately six feet long with a diameter of approximately twenty inches, give or take an inch. Two men were at the missile housing on the bow. More were on the stern. "Looks like anti-ship missiles. Four. At the ready."

"Holy fucking crap."

"Not exactly helpful, Marks. Do some thinking here."

"Yes, sir. They're going to scuttle *Imagine*."

"No, Marks." Ace took cover again behind the beam and turned to the younger agent. "They're planning to scuttle her. We're here to stop that from happening."

Marks nodded, fighting past the uncertainty Ace read in his eyes. "Yes, sir. Okay. I'm with you. But...how?"

Wendt's earpiece crackled to life, with Skylar yelling for someone to fix the hydraulic system so that the lifeboats could launch. Ace smiled and told Marks what he'd just heard, then continued with the scuttling scenario. "Before they'd scuttle this ship, someone like Skylar, at least, will try to evacuate. We're not going to let that happen. Which also means I can't kill Skylar right away."

Fucking hell, but I'm walking a tightrope.

Ace edged forward again and refocused his scope. They were probably of the surface skimming variety, radar-guided. He couldn't pick out more details. Then again, he didn't need many more. The missiles were sizable enough to pack serious destructive force. "Can't tell exactly the type. Or how they'll be guided. Given the short distance the missiles have to travel to reach *Imagine*, I'd say details don't matter."

"Given the amount of time that we've been out to sea, the depth here could be anywhere from a thousand to five thousand feet. Or more." Marks' tone had grown calmer, more matter-of-fact. "It would be hard to recover evidence at that depth."

Ace nodded. "Save for elusive transfers of money through complex financial transactions that could be impossible to trace, the bombing might very well destroy all evidence of the mass-hijacking and murder. Unless we succeed." Ace lowered the scope, returned it to his backpack, and searched for one of the small, orb-like cameras he'd packed. The device auto-focused and had thermal-imaging capabilities. He attached the camera on the exterior of the support beam, with full view of *Follower*. For now, the camera was useless. But once Leo reestablished comms, they'd be able to send the video feed to Ragno and the cyber department in Denver.

"Let's end Skylar's show. With just the two of us advancing into the theater, we don't have many options. We'll detonate flashbangs, then move in. Once in, we'll get an assist from Leo, who's in the crawl space above the theater."

As Marks nodded, Skylar's voice, on the PA system, interrupted any response. "Ling Wen," Skylar said. "Your wife has seven minutes to live."

A fresh round of May Wen's screams and pleas for her husband's help filled the ship in reverberating surround-sound, compliments of *Imagine*'s state-of-the-art PA system. Before her screams faded, Ace and Marks were on their way to the theater, climbing the exterior stairwell that would open onto the Clio Deck. Double doors there would lead to the foyer that separated the casino and the theater.

As Ace reached the deck, he saw Wen and Kamin running towards the same doors. They saw Ace and slowed their forward momentum.

"I disabled the surveillance cams, but couldn't signal Mayday. Or restore our comms," Kamin reported. "No sign of Leo."

"We need to stop them," Wen said.

"We will." Ace incorporated them into his plan and told them the logistics. He noted the time—0231. Well past high time to alert the world as to what was happening aboard *Imagine*. Goddamn time to have agent-to-agent comms restored. If he didn't hear from Leo soon, he'd implode. Yet the only sound he heard on his embedded ear mic was silence.

"Goddammit, Leo." Ace muttered. "Where the fuck are you?"

Chapter Sixteen

2:20 a.m.

With her laptop perched on the oversized, shiny black boots of a larger-than-life Christmas nutcracker, Leo sat lotus-style in the props booth. She glanced up, into the lifeless eyes of the figurine that was to play a part in the Christmas show.

Fairytales. Useless. As usual.

She was wedged between wheeled platforms that held a top-hatted snowman and a red-nosed reindeer. The wheels had brakes that kept them stationary. Various stage flats, painted with idyllic scenes of a Norman Rockwell-ish, small-town Main Street at Christmas, were behind the statues.

Without Christmas music in the theater, every sound was amplified. Each click that she made on her keyboard seemed loud. As did Skylar's footsteps, as he moved along the front of the stage and threatened the audience, and May Wen's sniffles between yells. Every now and then, she heard heavy footsteps of Quan operatives in the backstage crossover area, behind the props booth, as they followed Skylar's orders and moved out to other areas of the ship.

The front wall of the booth was a portion of the lightweight, plywood wall that bordered the rear of the stage. Painted black, it blended seamlessly with the rear stage wall. Aside from that thin piece of plywood, only a few feet of stage, the green velvet house drapes, and the three Christmas trees that were in front of the drapes, separated Leo from Skylar.

She whispered her second attempt at agent-to-agent contact. “Leo to Alpha, Omega, Kamin. Copy?”

Silence.

Hell.

“Could the problem be our encryption?”

Leo’s whispered question was directed at Ragno. She was pretty certain the answer was no, but when in doubt and in a hurry, she was plenty happy to ask others their opinion. She’d reestablished communications with headquarters a few minutes earlier, with the completion of the most important task she’d ever performed as a Black Raven agent. Mayday.

Now, all agents who worked cyber support for field ops were hanging on the silence that had been the reply to her radio check, while also urgently working on the tasks required by *Imagine’s* predicament. Ragno led the cyber-support team, with Zeus’ troubleshooting team working alongside them.

“Shouldn’t be.” Ragno’s voice was clear through Leo’s ear mic, as though she was sitting next to Leo. “And let’s hope not, because our lines need encryption, at least until I manage to isolate Skylar’s comms and shut him down. Starting at ground zero would be at least a fifteen-minute task. Let’s try a couple more times within existing parameters. This should work.”

Leo clicked quietly at her laptop, as she and Ragno both tackled the problem of reconnecting Ace and the other agents. Her laptop screen had three windows open. One window showed the commands she and Ragno were entering to open the agent-to-agent comm line. Another showed the video feed of the theater from the camera she'd left in the overhead vent. The third showed ongoing dialogue in the form of instant messaging thought bubbles between cyber-support agents in Denver, as they tackled the myriad tasks that would lead to who-what-and-how-the-hell-we're-fixing-this.

As she worked, Leo felt a shift in the ship's movement. Stage flats and props creaked as the ship rolled right to left. The stabilizers adjusted to the different movement, and the ship became steadier. She glanced at the time on the computer screen—*0222*.

"We're slowing," she told Ragno. "Virtually stopping. That has to mean Skylar's making some kind of move. Probably an evacuation. But why now? He's only gotten money from about a third of the hostages."

"Yes, but he's got May Wen, so he knows her husband's coming," Ragno said. "Odd, though, that Ling Wen hasn't appeared already. On another note, with the number of operatives Skylar is calling who aren't responding, he's got to be worried about sabotage. I suspect he'll abandon his efforts with the other hostages entirely once Wen shows up."

"Bank transactions with endless security combos take a while, even when hostages are sweating bullets in their eagerness to comply."

Leo clicked through several more commands, then waited for the cursor signal to reappear, which would signify that the comm line was open. When the cursor didn't appear, she rolled her shoulders, rubbed her hands together, and started over. While she worked, she watched Skylar through the video feed. He paced a slow path in front of the Christmas trees and in front of May Wen.

In the IM dialogue that ran along the left margin of her screen, Denver-based agents were discussing the ongoing attempt to determine with whom Skylar was communicating on line four.

"Haven't determined the encryption program Quan is using."

"You try Inviso-Crypto? Latest greatest."

"Trying I-C now."

"Skylar's listening on line four at least as much as he's talking. Maybe listening more."

Leo's pulse quickened at that observation. Why hadn't she thought of it herself? She typed. "*Good point. Listening as much as talking suggests that Skylar isn't the guy in charge, right?*"

"Would seem that way."

"Skylar's line 4—most comms are definitely coming from locations on Imagine."

Thinking of First Officer Raznick, who'd become even more of a person of interest once Leo gave Denver the man's name and preliminary searches started showing odd banking transactions, Leo typed, "*Could comms be coming from helm station?*"

The agent replied, "*Don't know. Yet. Stay tuned.*"

"Investigate First Officer Raznick."

A fresh batch of chilling screams from May Wen stole her attention. Each new octave of horror strengthened Leo's resolve to figure out a way to stop Skylar from executing the woman.

Even if I have to go it alone. Even if it proves to be the last thing I do.

Her cursor appeared, which should be a signal that the line was open–if her commands had worked. Before she could open her mouth for a radio check, an additional video line opened on her laptop screen, providing a view of *Follower*. As she absorbed the grim details of the weapons on *Follower* revealed by the video camera, Ace's voice came through, loud and clear, in a growl that conveyed full-throttle urgency.

"Goddammit, Leo. Where the fuck are you?"

From Denver, there was a collective sigh of relief, but Leo frowned as she took in the impatience and frustration in his tone. Those traits were uncharacteristic for Ace, especially in high-stress situations. Yet she didn't fault him. The situation needed to be resolved. The sooner, the better.

She replied, in her lowest whisper, "Copy that, Evans. Radio check. Leon to Evans, Marks, Kamin, Branch, Scott. Roll call. Over."

"Copy. Evans."

"Copy. Marks."

"Copy. Kamin."

"Copy. Branch."

"Copy. Scott."

"That's an affirmative from all agents," Leo said. "I accomplished the Mayday at 0215 hours. Copy?"

"Copy." Ace's voice had regained cool calmness. "Marks and Kamin are with me. Ling Wen is with us."

"Evans, we have Ragno on line with us. Zeus is also monitoring this line, while making calls."

"Copy that. Branch and Scott. Give me a status report," Ace said.

"Scott was hit," Branch said. "Upper thigh. Two bullets. Finishing field dressing now."

Hell.

"How is he?" Ace asked.

"Mobility's reduced to hobbling, but otherwise he's—"

"Irritated that I can't walk, but fine," Scott chimed in, finishing Branch's statement. His voice was strong. Leo's palms tingled with relief.

"Nice to hear from you, Scott," Ace said. "But I'd like to hear that from our medic."

"He'll be fine," Branch answered. "He's tough. Doesn't even want morphine."

"Blood loss?" Ace asked, concern apparent in his voice.

Leo's breath caught as she waited for the answer. Blood loss was always a worry in the field. Though they'd all signed up for action that included mortal risk, no one liked to have a reminder of it while the job was ongoing.

"I bleed steel, sir," Scott said, "and not much."

"There's muscle damage," Branch said. "He's in pain, there's been some blood loss, but no arteries are in play."

Leo felt the collective easier breathing from all the agents in Denver who were hanging on every word from the team on *Imagine*.

"Position?" Ace asked.

"Melpomene Deck. Compass Rose," Branch said.

Leo knew exactly where they were. Positioning themselves in the Compass Rose Bar was a smart move on their part. The Melpomene deck was the second highest deck. The only deck above it was the Erato deck, where the radio room and the helm station were located. Both the Melpomene and Erato decks were shorter than the full length of the ship.

The Compass Rose was perched on the stern side of the Melpomene Deck. The bar had floor to ceiling windows, designed to provide a great view of the wide-open ocean and the stern of the ship. From there, someone in the bar could look out to the ocean or, even better for Black Raven's purpose, watch any action on the wide-open space on the Terpischore Deck that served as *Imagine*'s helipad. Leo kept working as she listened to Ace and the others.

"Branch. When Scott's set," Ace said, "advance to the theater. Meet us at the rear doors, in the main hallway. We're gaining access now. By the time you're here, we'll have eliminated sentries. You might encounter a Quan or two on the way."

"Roger. On my way."

"Scott. You're our eyes on the stern," Ace said. "You have firing ability?"

"Yes, sir. Ready. Able. More than willing, in honor of our guys in the casino. I'm in position at the windows. I have my rifle plus the rifles of a few Quan operatives. Plenty of ammo. If action ends up on the helipad, I'll cover it."

"Copy that, Scott. I've set a cam with a view, but I no longer have eyes on *Follower*. I managed to get a visual on their weapons." Ace's tone was matter-of-fact as he relayed observations about the firepower he'd observed aboard *Follower*.

"We've got your camera view." Leo glanced at IM dialogue, confirming that Denver-based agents were on task with it. "Denver is analyzing the missiles."

"Ragno. Leo. Any chance you'll be able to disable their comms but keep ours intact? Would be good if Skylar had no opportunity to call for help once we advance into the theater."

"We're working on that," Ragno said. "It's involving some crafty manipulation on our part, finding the link Skylar's using for the financials, satellite access, and...you don't need details at this point."

"Keep me posted," Ace said. "Give me a nutshell on external rescue efforts."

With his shift in focus, Leo realized Ace was assuming she was in the crawl space where he'd left her. She'd need to tell him her present position. But there were more important issues on his list, and he wouldn't be pleased when he figured out that she was on the stage, in the props booth. She'd get to it. For now, she'd let him focus on the other issues.

"We've alerted China, Macau, United States. Zeus is on task. The People's Liberation Army is pulling together resources and forming an advance team. Aircraft first, boats shortly after. Our contact is PLA Navy Deputy Commissar Linn Ming, the leader of the joint operation," Ragno said. "Chinese authorities are not communicating clearly with us yet. Zeus is working hard for some positive traction in that regard. We have confirmed that Commissar Ming is not contacting *Imagine*'s helm at this time, believing that no contact will work in favor of rescue efforts. Advance notice will put hostages at risk. Ming will wait until you have secured the theater and hostages. Copy?"

"Copy," Ace said.

"We've reestablished a live GPS link for *Imagine*," Leo said.

"Do we have *Follower's* identity?" Ace asked.

"Remains unknown, though Denver is analyzing it," Leo said, glancing at thermal images from the video feed of *Follower*. Men were performing an external check on the chopper. Two others were approaching the helipad. Walking, not running.

"Evans," Leo said. "*Follower* is now readying its helicopter for departure. There doesn't appear to be an immediate rush. Copy?"

"Roger."

"So far, Skylar isn't alarmed," Leo said.

As Ace and the other agents moved into position, Leo kept an eye on the video feed of the front of the stage from the cam that she'd set in the crawl space. She clicked on her keyboard, remotely adjusting her camera. For the moment, Skylar was still, watching as his men in business suits directed hostages to transfer funds. He stood at center stage, his right shoulder almost touching one of the Christmas trees.

At most, Skylar was fourteen feet from where she sat. Hostages who'd completed their financial transactions were now being seated at stage right. About fifteen of them were huddled close together in the third, fourth, and fifth rows. Randy Howell sat in the first row, in the aisle seat, with his face buried in his hands. Every now and then, he'd look up. The camera angle didn't give her a view of the front of his face, but it seemed as if he was looking towards Miranda's body.

An agent from Denver sent Leo an IM. *"Scroll slower. Facial rec running. Include hostages."*

Leo reset the camera as Skylar turned. He touched his earpiece, and then his watch, and started walking across the stage. The camera caught his lips moving. He wasn't using the PA system and wasn't talking on line sixteen. Leo changed the comm channel on the watch that she'd taken from the Quan operative. She listened to the bursts of static, pops, and clicks on line four.

She IM'd Denver, *"S.'s using line 4 now. Any progress in decrypting that channel or figuring out who he's talking to?"*

"Not yet."

Leo watched as Skylar's path across the front of the stage took him in front of Miranda, who was lying, face up. The Blackwells lay next to her. Proving the theory that Skylar considered some of the hostages expendable to his money-making scheme, he had executed the Blackwells without first obtaining money. Their brutal killings had been an effective persuasion tool, and the remaining hostages had complied with Skylar's demands, without resistance and with the implicit hope that if they complied, he would let them live.

Yet the weapons aboard *Follower* confirmed that Skylar's plan was that there would be no survivors, no matter how much money he stole.

May Wen, wearing a long, emerald green dress, was in a chair next to Skylar. Mascara, mixed with tears, streamed down her face. Her glossy hair was tangled and disheveled. Her hands were tied in front of her, while her legs were secured at the ankles. Only one high-heeled shoe remained on. Her screams, for the moment, had subsided.

"Marks to Evans. Ling Wen and I are now in firing position. Crawl space. Above the theater. Leo isn't here."

"Leo—where are you?" Ace asked.

Before Leo could answer, Ragno broke into the conversation. "Marks. Did you say you and *Ling Wen* are in firing position?"

"That's an affirmative," Marks replied.

"Evans," Ragno said. "Clarify."

"He's on our side and can handle the QBZ-95. He was personally involved in its design," Ace said. "It's a team leader's prerogative to make a call like this, and I'm making it. Having Wen on our side will outweigh the cons of his lack of training as a Black Raven agent. I don't have time to give you more."

"Hold it a second. Someone is working with Skylar, and we don't know who. We're analyzing Wen's data now and haven't determined that he's on our side, at least not yet." Ragno hesitated. "His financials are impenetrable. How have you ruled him out as a co-conspirator?"

"Personal observation in a situation that left no doubt," Ace said, his curt tone giving the solid impression that he considered the conversation about Wen over. "Plus, Skylar's been looking for him."

"Innocence could be a ruse," Ragno said.

"To what end?"

"There are potential witnesses in the theater," Ragno retorted. "Whoever is behind this is damn well planning on getting away with it."

"Skylar isn't planning for these witnesses to live to tell the story of what they're seeing," Ace said.

"And I doubt he's thinking all his men will die. They could be the witnesses that the boss man is trying to avoid. Would have been simpler to stay off the ship, but we all know gamblers like thrills..."

Ace's groan was barely audible, but Leo heard it.

"No. Ling Wen is on our side," he said, sounding like he had no doubt. "Leo. Care to share your present position?"

"Props booth. Backstage area." Leo braced for attitude from Ace. He was too professional to tell her his real thoughts on the open mic, even if he had time, which he didn't. "Slightly stage right of center—"

"Clarify. Did you say props booth?"

In his clipped words she detected thinly-veiled incredulity, as May Wen let loose a fresh scream.

"Yes, sir. I left a camera on the vent, so I'd have video feed. It's a small booth that's built into the rear of the stage, and..." Leo glanced up, at the nutcracker's coal-black lifeless eyes, as she let her voice trail. Ace damn well knew the where and what of the props booth, and they didn't have time for her to waste. "It was the best option for signal strength."

"You didn't get there with your rifle."

"Correct." *Hell.* He'd comprehended what her position meant, in terms of what she'd had to do to get there. Later, when he wasn't worried about her safety, he'd appreciate that being in the props booth had meant that, upon her arrival, she was almost immediately able to signal mayday.

"I have both handguns."

"Armor?"

The rule that agents who were in active fire situations were supposed to wear both a chest plate and a back plate, meant that she shouldn't have considered the props booth an option. "Had to leave a plate behind. I adjusted. Laptop provides a measure of protection. Have my helmet."

"Damn glad to hear that." Like crimson red warning flags marked beach-going danger, the sarcasm flag flew high in his tone, while anger simmered in his terseness. She'd get an earful from him later, when she wasn't on an open line with any number of agents in Denver and field agents. "In addition to Skylar, how many Quan operatives are on stage?"

"Three." Which meant gunfire was coming her way. To gain control of the theater, all Quan operatives—especially Skylar—had to be taken down. "May Wen is in a chair, on stage, stage left of center. Upon your entry, she will be on your right. Copy?"

"Copy. Tied to a chair?"

"Negative, but her ankles are bound." Once bullets started flying, May Wen's movements would be anyone's guess. "Copy?"

"Copy," Ace answered. "How many Quans are in the theater?"

"Twenty, though that number is fluid. It includes Skylar and the three on stage with him. There were more, but a few minutes ago Skylar directed men to fix the hydraulic system."

"If you return to the crawl space, how long would it take for you to be in a safer position from which you could fire? Both prerequisites are necessary. Safety and firing position."

Leo eyed the rope she'd used to climb down into the booth, which she'd left attached. Ascending would be a bitch, but she'd practiced enough climbs to know she could do it. Problem was, it would eat up time. Another problem was that once she made it back into the ceiling, with the drapes shut, she wouldn't have a view of anything but the area behind the drapes. To have her eyes on Skylar and the other operatives, she'd need to be at a vent on the other side of the drapes. The nearest vent that had a firing position was back at the original crawl space, where she'd parted ways with Ace and the others, and where she'd left the camera.

"Three minutes remain on Skylar's countdown for May Wen. You plan to enter the theater in under three?" She hoped Ace said yes. He'd directed her to stand down when Miranda had been killed, and she'd self-directed herself throughout Skylar's execution of the Blackwells. She didn't have it in her to stand by and allow him to kill another person.

"Yes."

"Then I wouldn't make it to an overhead firing position." In contrast, if she stayed on the stage, all she had to do was push open the rear sliding door of the booth, run through the crossover area, and get to the wings on either side of the stage where she'd have a great firing position. Even better, she could slip out of the front sliding wall of the props booth, get into position behind the drapes, and cover Skylar from there.

"Maintain present position," Ace said. "When M84s go off, get in firing position off the stage, whether you've killed Skylar or not. Go right—"

"Left's better. That's Skylar's shortest route out of here, presumably to the helipad." She glanced at her laptop screen. "*Follower* is prepping the chopper. Still not in a rush."

"Because Skylar doesn't realize his control is about to end," Ace said. "Go stage left. Give us one minute to get in position, then I'll need your eyes before I give the three-count."

"Roger."

Notably absent from Ace's instruction was where her precise position should be when they threw the M84s. Leo took his silence on the issue as implicit trust that, like any other agent, she'd damn well use her best judgment.

Thinking, she glanced at her watch.

0236 hours.

Firing from behind the drapes was the best option for killing Skylar and then pulling May Wen to safety. But an on-stage position would expose her to enemy gunfire. Except, it was Christmas. Trees were on the stage. The decorative trees, with their gold bows and glass ornaments, wouldn't make her bulletproof, but they'd provide a measure of concealment for the few milliseconds that she'd need.

She looked up again, into the nutcracker's coal black eyes. So far, her life had proved her father correct on most things, including that courage in her own reasoning beat self-doubt every time. He'd taught her to be like a lion. Fearless.

Decision made.

She noted Skylar's position. He'd stopped pacing and stood next to May Wen, slightly to the left of dead center stage.

Glancing at her laptop before shutting it, IM thought bubbles from Denver caught her eye— *"No such thing as coincidences;" "Facial rec says prostitute;" "Double check."*

There was no time to scroll up and see more of what the agents were talking about. She had to have confidence that Ragno and the agents in Denver, aided by Black Raven's data assimilation programs, would find answers as they scoured the bits and pieces of information, followed the trails, and sniffed out clues. After shutting the laptop, she reached behind her and slipped it into the pocket of her shirt that spanned her back, where her armor plate should go.

Inch by inch, she pushed open the sliding door of the props booth. The stage between the booth and the drapes was dark, lit only by the thin sliver of light that ran along the seam where the drapery panels met. Gripping her pistol, she crossed the stage, then stood to the side of the seam in the drapes.

"Leo. Marks," Ace said. "Tell us where we're throwing M84s."

Like other field agents, as part of her training and in fieldwork, Leo had been repeatedly exposed to M84 detonation. She was desensitized to the blinding flash of light and deafening bang that came with it. When seconds counted, and with bad guys and innocents so close together, the flash bang produced by the grenade could be an excellent distraction. They risked injuring an innocent if detonation occurred too close.

Using a finger to part the drapes, Leo scanned the positions of the players. "Your left. Port side. Seats are clear for twenty feet from the center doorway, all the way to the port side wall."

"Roger that." Marks, in the crawl space above the theater, confirmed based on his different viewpoint. "Skylar's on the move with May Wen, heading towards stage stairs. I don't have a clear shot at him. Copy."

"Copy. Leo. If you don't have a shot at Skylar, get off the stage now. You're too exposed."

"Copy." She parted the drapes a little more with her index finger. Her sliver of a view was made even slimmer by fat boughs of blue spruce trees, bows, and ornaments. She had enough clearance to observe Skylar on the stairs at stage left. May Wen screamed and clawed at his hands as he dragged her with him. Her emerald-green dress clung to her delicate curves, making her seem small, too weak to fight off the larger man.

No shot at Skylar, thanks to a wriggling May Wen and Christmas trees. However, if he turned slightly...

Leo held position, hoping for a better shot. It all depended on where Skylar was going, and how fast she could track his movements.

"Three M84s will detonate on my count of one. Hostage safety is top priority. Right up there with us not killing each other. Sure shots only. Employing sector room clearance." Leo felt the gravity underlying Ace's words. It was one thing to disable enemy operatives when outnumbered. It was another thing entirely to do it with more than one hundred innocents in the room. People under duress and untrained in combat tended to move unpredictably when bullets started flying.

"Marks and Wen—your sector's all encompassing. Fire at anything you have a shot at from above. Work from stage to rear.

Kamin—your sector's port side, from rear to stage. Branch—you're starboard, rear to stage. Leo—stage area. I'm going straight up the middle aisle. Communicate, people."

Through the slit in the drapes, Leo watched Howell shrink into the chair as Skylar, between the front of the stage and the first row, moved in his direction. A Quan operative bent towards him. In the rows behind Howell, hostages with wide eyes and mottled cheeks huddled into their seats. Wrenching her eyes back to the stage, Leo eyed the man who'd be her first camo-wearing target. He stood five feet to her left, three feet in front of her. Tall. Heavyset. Broad shoulders. Cantaloupe-sized head. No helmet.

Easy.

"Three," Ace said, as fresh screams erupted from May Wen.

She'd fire through the fabric rather than risk exposure by aiming her pistol through the opening. Pressing her muzzle against the firm backing of the drapes, she aimed at the Quan operative's bare head.

"Two."

Checking her muzzle position, she confirmed that the trajectory of her bullet would be over the heads of the hostages in the seats at stage left if she missed. Which she damn well didn't plan on doing. Adjusting her weapon to the right and slightly lower, she willed her target not to move. She took a deep, calming breath.

"One."

In the milliseconds before flash-bang detonation, instantaneous happenings registered separately as the theater doors burst open.

Leo fired at Melon-head.

The *pop-pop-pop, pop-pop-pop* of gunfire exploded from above.

People screamed.

Ace yelled, “Get down! Down!”

“Rear doors. All men. Theater,” Skylar yelled. “NOW!”

She briefly shut her eyes against blinding bursts of light, then felt the repercussive *boom! boom! boooooom!* of the grenades. She shook with the force of the sounds and light, but confirmed that Melon-head was face down on the stage. Unmoving. The other two men who’d been on the stage with Skylar were also face down.

She moved forward, through the drapes, as rapid-fire *pop-pop-pops* sounded from all sectors. Fat branches of the densely-needled trees provided a measure of concealment. As she shifted position and peered around branches, the crisp, fresh scent of pine seemed odd, given the hell that was erupting in front of her. Smoky haze drifted forward from the M84s, blocking her view and making her eyes burn. She blinked back the tears as she looked for more Quan operatives. The haze hit a smoke detector, causing fire alarms to screech.

The sprinkler system went off, exacerbating the chaos and noise. The water would ultimately drain through the bilge system, where pumps would dispose of it. For now, though, the water had the effect of clearing the cloud that had wrapped around her. She would’ve been happy for it, but it was also giving the bad guys a better view.

“Leo to Evans. Stage is clear. For now. Skylar’s in front of the stage. He’s crouched, midway to the floor. He’s now directly in front of Howell’s seat. May Wen is struggling against Skylar’s chokehold.”

“Copy.”

“No clear shot at Skylar.” Damn it. Not at Skylar, but she did have a clear shot at a short, squat Quan operative who was huddled in the seats, in Branch's sector, about thirty feet behind where Howell was sitting. A quick glance down the aisle told her Branch's attention was on two operatives who'd come through the rear door of the theater. Unlike Branch, the operative hiding in the seats was facing the stage. Aiming. She glanced towards the center aisle and spotted Ace, with his rifle lifted. Between gunfire, she thought he might have glanced in her direction, but there was too much haze to be sure.

"Leo. Get the fuck off the stage!"

She ducked down low as she aimed her Glock at the operative who'd taken cover in the seats. With a fast *pop-pop-pop,* a cluster of Christmas ornaments that were close to her right arm exploded into shards of thin glass. Tree branches splintered. Needles stung her eyes. Before she could fire, all the air left her body with a whoosh of an exhale, as bullets thudded into her chest.

Shit!

She reeled back, as though an unseen hand had given her a hard shove. She fought to stay upright. For a fleeting second, she was glad she'd kept her one armor plate on her chest.

Her confident relief that she'd protected herself faded as she tried to inhale and couldn't. She looked down. There was a long gash in the loose black shirt that covered the thinner, anti-ballistic layer that fit close to her body. Both layers of clothes were ripped, exposing torn skin and flesh through which red blood started flowing. More pain than she'd ever imagined overtook her in waves, spreading from her right arm to her right shoulder. Gritting her teeth, she opened her mouth and tried hard again to inhale. And couldn't.

It's just a scratch. Shake it off. Keep moving.

Chapter Seventeen

2:36 a.m.

Before starting the downward count of three, Ace braced his foot flat against the gold-painted theater door, ready to push it forward. Due to the curvature of the rear wall, Kamin, on his left, and Branch, on his right, were out of his line of sight. Two Quan operatives who'd been guarding the hallway that led into the theater were dead, three feet behind him. May Wen's screams sounded loud through Leo's open line.

Ace believed in God, but details were beyond him. That was fine with him. He figured that if someone as smart as Albert Einstein believed that God and religiousness were mind-bending puzzles that defied simplistic explanations, his own mind wouldn't figure out the definitive answer.

Now, in the split seconds before entering the theater, the one thing he was certain of as he collected his breath and leaned his weight into his heel, was that some men were evil. To combat that, God had given Ace the capability of killing them.

Please, God. Guide me. My agents. Let us save every hostage.

"Three." Since his early days of Marine Corps Special Forces training, the downward three-count was usually calming. When calling it, no matter the operation, with the count of three he was able to quiet his mind. Demons disappeared. Doubts became nonexistent.

This job, though, wasn't usual. He tried to ignore the nagging, foreboding-like worry that wouldn't let go of his mind. He tried not to remember the weight of Kat in his arms, tried not to remember watching her take her last breath. Tried not to superimpose Leo's face over his last love's death mask. *Fuck it.* He clenched his jaw, and hesitated for a second before the two count, failing to find calm.

Leo's not Kat. The woman you now love is one of Black Raven's best. She's damn well got this. STOP WORRYING ABOUT HER!

"Two."

Ace focused on pulse-lowering breaths until his thoughts cleared. He forced his mind to click through his next actions: kick the door open, pitch the M84, clear the middle sector, get on the stage, and liberate the hostages. Kill Quan operatives until only a room full of innocent hostages and Black Raven agents was left.

"One."

While kicking the door open, he yelled, "Get down! Down!"

He crossed the threshold at a run, pulled the pin, and tossed the grenade towards the bank of empty theater seats on his left. In the milliseconds before detonation, he started running along the wide middle aisle. Lifting his rifle, his gaze crawled right, left, and forward, to the stage, where decorated Christmas trees were lit with twinkling lights.

"Rear doors," Skylar yelled. "All men. Theater. NOW!"

Gunfire erupted, echoing as the grenades exploded with heaven's light and hell's thunder. More than a million candela of light and 170 decibels of noise scared most of the hostages enough that they huddled in the foot space in front of their seats. Others were slumped in their seats, heads down, not moving. Most Quan operatives, also taken by surprise, hunched down in place.

Through smoky gray haze, Ace saw a Quan operative rise to his feet, ten feet ahead of him. Ace fired as he ran. While his gaze was focused on his sector, Ace heard everything in the theater. As the M84 booms faded, *pop-pop-pop* sounded. From above. *Pop-pop-pop*. From the stage. More gunfire sounded on his right and his left.

When smoke alarms went off, water from the ship's sprinkler system helped to clear the haze. Without breaking his stride, and with his eyes burning, Ace aimed at a camo-wearing Quan operative who was getting to his feet, about fifteen feet ahead of him. As the operative stood, he lifted his rifle and aimed towards the stage.

Leo.

Ace fired three times. One for certain. Two for insurance. The Quan operative went down. Ace ran forward, leapt over the man, while glancing to the left of his sector. Another Quan operative was jogging, somewhat unsteady, towards the center aisle between empty seats. Apparently suffering from the repercussive effects of the flash-bang explosion, the jogger had lost his rifle. He reached out to grab Ace, while fumbling at his hip for his pistol. Dodging the man's reach, Ace slowed his stride, twisted to his left, and fired.

As the man dropped, Ace continued running towards the stage, noting the sounds of gunfire from all sectors. The Black Raven-issued M1-A, with its shorter barrel length, fired slightly faster and louder than the QBZ-95s carried by the Quan operatives. The good guys were firing more, as yells, cries, and screams sounded from all around the theater.

"Leo to Evans. Stage is clear. For now." He shifted his gaze. Through sprinkling water and clearing haze, he saw Skylar standing exactly where Leo indicated—to the right of the stage, crouched low and holding May Wen in a chokehold, surrounded by three Quan operatives who were providing protective cover.

"Copy."

"No clear shot at Skylar," she said.

He glanced up at the stage, where he could see Leo. Christmas trees provided partial coverage, but not enough now that smoke was clearing. If he could see her, so could Quan operatives, and she made a damn easy target.

"Leo. Get the fuck off the stage!"

Tearing his eyes off her, he saw another Quan grabbing Randy Howell and pulling the man to his feet. He lifted his rifle at Skylar's group as he ran forward, but realized, like Leo, he didn't have a sure shot at any of the Quan operatives. Not with them moving towards the exit, as a unit, holding May Wen and Howell so that they shielded the rear of the group.

"Scott." As he called the agent who was nestled in the Compass Rose bar, he hoped to God the agent hadn't passed out from the pain of his gunshot wound.

"Yes, sir."

Scott's voice sounded alert. Steady. Ready. Ace's blood pulsed a little easier, as he tried again for a shot at any of the Quan operatives in Skylar's group, who were now just a few feet from the exit. "Standby. Action's coming to the helipad."

No shot. Not without risk to May Wen or Randy Howell.

Ace ran forward, watching as Leo finally gave up on getting a shot at Skylar and started moving to safety. She moved to the periphery of one of the Christmas trees, lifting her pistol and aiming into the theater seats as she started to run.

With a QBZ-95 *pop-pop-pop* sounding to his right, Christmas tree ornaments around Leo exploded. He looked to his right. Through the sprinkling water, at first he didn't see who was shooting at her.

He shook his head, blinking water out of his eyes. Foreboding exploded in his gut, snaked upwards, and threatened to choke him. He glanced over the heads of hostages who had now recovered from their disorientation and were moving. Some stood. Others sat upright.

Branch, who'd advanced to midway through his aisle, had his back to the stage and was aiming towards the rear of the room. Two Quan operatives had entered the theater from the door that Branch had entered. Further up, hunched about thirty feet from the first row, a Quan operative had hunched down low and was aiming at Leo. Ace aimed.

Fuck.

In his sights, a woman in a red dress stood and screamed, blocking his shot. As a tuxedo-clad man pulled the red-dress woman roughly back into her seat, the two of them solidly blocked his shot. Ace adjusted, stepping forward. Another hostage stood, this one a male in a bathrobe, wiping his eyes and blocking his shot.

"Marks! Branch's sector. About thirty feet from the stage. In the seats. Now!"

"Yes, sir."

"Get. Down. NOW!" Ace yelled to the hostages, as another *pop-pop-pop* sounded from the operative's rifle. Ace ran forward. He reached the first row and, without breaking stride, he turned and bolted towards the right. As he ran in front of the stage, he adjusted his aim over huddled hostages and dead Quan operatives.

Thankfully, all the hostages between Ace and his target stayed still. Marks' rifle fire mingled with his. The operative who'd been shooting at Leo went down.

Ace glanced behind him, onto the stage, where tree limbs were snapped and mangled. Bows were tattered, dripping wet. Broken ornaments were scattered on the stage floor. A couple of feet from the mess of holiday decorations, Leo had stopped, seemingly in mid-stride. He didn't think he heard her weapon fire. If she'd managed to get off her shot, she'd missed. She was glancing down, at her right arm.

Fuck!

Feeling like his windpipe had collapsed, he only managed to breathe when she shook her head and continued moving towards the side of the stage. Slowly. Too slowly. His breath caught again in his throat. "Leo?"

Silence.

"Answer, goddammit."

"I'm...f-fine."

Not having the luxury of immediately running to her side to check on her, Ace shifted his rifle aim to the side door in time to see Skylar and his group slip through it. Given the positions of the hostages, he didn't have a clear shot at Skylar. "Scott. Skylar's moving out of the theater with at least five Quans. Two hostages. Randy Howell and May Wen."

"Copy," Scott answered.

Ace breathed easier when he glanced over his shoulder and saw that the stage was empty. Leo had managed to move. He took it as a good sign, having no choice but to face the audience again and stay focused on the task at hand. "Given the firepower that *Follower* has aimed at *Imagine,* we have to assume that as soon as Skylar's in the chopper, and it lifts off, *Imagine* will be blown to hell. Have you ever disabled a chopper with rifle fire?"

"No, sir. No Quans are on the helipad yet. It's lit, like the rest of the ship, but the landing lights aren't on."

"Copy," Ace replied, managing to keep his voice calm, while fighting the ever-growing urge to run to Leo. "If you see anyone, hold your fire. We don't want to reveal your position yet. Talk to Denver. Figure out how to shoot down a chopper. Every second will count when the chopper's landing, but the Compass Rose will give you a bird's eye. You'll be my backup."

"Yes, sir."

"I'm heading to the helipad. ASAP." *And I'll check on Leo along the way.* "Ragno. Has the chopper lifted?"

He lowered his rifle so as not to scare the shit out of the hostages, and let his gaze crawl over the audience as he looked for the enemy.

For the moment, one agent, no matter how important that agent was to him, was not as important as securing the hostages.

"No," Ragno answered. "Chopper remains in prep mode. Rotors are still."

"Tell me when the rotors start." Ace fired at a Quan operative who was reaching for a hostage, managing to kill him before he succeeded in using a hostage as a shield.

"Will do."

"Were you able to disable Skylar's comms?"

"Yes, immediately before your entry to the theater."

"Evans. What the..." Scott's words trailed. "Ling Wen's on the helipad, running toward the port side of ship. He's moved out of eyesight, presumably taking cover."

"Wen left the crawl space when it was clear Skylar was going to make it out the theater door with May," Marks reported.

"For the record," Ace said, "I stand by my belief that he's on our side."

Though, fuck! Could I be wrong?

He shook his head against the self-doubt. No time to worry about that now. He'd figure it all out soon enough. Drawing a breath, Ace leapt onto the stage. Amidst hostages who were stirring, moving slowly while looking dazed and scared, there were plenty of dead Quans. In aisles. Hunched over theater seats. No live ones. He did a quick mental tally. By his best guesstimate, aside from Skylar and the Quans who were with him, only a few remained alive. "Agents. Report."

"Clear," Kamin said. "No live Quans."

"Clear," Branch said.

Marks said, "From overhead, all clear."

Personally, the fact that Leo didn't report tore at his chest. Professionally, he pushed his emotions where they belonged–firmly to the side. "Kamin. Head to the stage. You'll hold the theater. Manage the hostages. Keep your eyes on the doors. Marks. Get down here now. You'll assist Kamin. Branch. Leo needs medical attention ASAP. Ragno?"

"Copy."

"Theater is under Black Raven control."

His eyes lingered on Baru. The owner of Imagine Casinos Worldwide was sitting in his seat, his wife at his side, with a vacant, stunned expression on his face. In shock, like many of the others. He talked loud enough for everyone to hear him, his gaze taking in the wet, scared hostages as the sprinkler system finally stopped.

"You're safe now. We're private security, hired by the Howard Underwriting Group. We were aboard *Imagine* in an undercover capacity from disembarkation. Authorities are now on the way. Please stay in your seats. We cannot allow you to leave this room until the entire ship is secure. Which it isn't. Yet."

Chapter Eighteen

2:44 a.m.

On Ace's way to the helipad, he found Leo on the floor in a narrow hallway that led away from the stage, flat on her back. He slid to his knees, eyeing the gash in her shirt. Once he made the decision to linger, he entered a dimension where time's passage became a reality upon which he was powerless to act.

Helmet off, her hair was wet and slicked to her scalp. With her gaze searching his, her eyes were large pools of color in a face that had gone pale. As the bronze flecks of light in her brown eyes seemed to fade, he started losing all the composure he'd tried so hard to harvest in the years since losing Kat.

"How bad?" he asked.

Her shallow breaths required effort. She'd managed to apply a one-handed tourniquet to her upper right arm. With her left hand, she was pressing clotting gauze to her wound. The gauze, standard issue in every field agent's first aid kit, wasn't doing its clotting job. The white mesh was red, saturated and dripping.

"Ribs. Must be broken. Hard to...breathe. Plate mostly did its job. One hit my arm." Her words were off mic. Normal protocols meant that when an agent was fighting for his or her life, their comms were silenced so job stress wouldn't agitate them. He guessed that Ragno had realized that Leo's situation was dire, from the lack of comms from Leo and the ASAP nature of the order he'd given to Marks. Now, Leo's gaze held his. She gave him a weak smile. "A bit of blood. Go."

A bit of blood? My ass.

Streams of red fluid oozed between the fingers of her left hand. The floor was carpeted, with a creamy swirl running through a bluish-black background. All around her, the light-colored swirl had turned red.

Fuck. She's bleeding out.

There was too much blood for a mere nick. Brachial artery? Maybe. He guesstimated what the volume of blood meant for bleed rate and mortal danger. The end result made him want to yell, punch a hole in the wall, and start bargaining with God for a different outcome than the one that looked inevitable.

"I'm sorry. Please don't be pissed," she barely whispered the words.

Breathe.

Yet he couldn't, because his worst nightmare was coming true. The sorry truth was that he was afraid. For her, and for him. Crystal clear clarity, the same sort that had struck him the evening before as he'd been standing next to her at the craps table, the moment when he'd finally realized he was in love with his best friend, hit him.

I won't survive if I lose her.

As Branch slid into position next to him, Ace tried to fight the slippery slope into hell's black hole. After a quick assessment, the team medic glanced at Ace. Marks didn't need to voice his worry.

Mortal concern for Leo was immediately obvious, in the grim set of his jaw and the depth of his frown.

Branch opened his backpack and started pulling out hemostatic granules, clotting gauze, syringes, and a field transfusion kit. "Ace. Move over."

Ace shifted to Leo's left, realizing that the knees of his pants were now saturated with her blood. She lifted her right arm so that Branch could maneuver the tourniquet. A river of crimson flowed down her arm, through her fingers, and onto Branch's hands as he adjusted the tourniquet.

"Brachial's in play?" Leo asked, her voice weak.

Branch's eyes again searched out Ace's gaze as he ripped open a packet containing an applicator full of clotting granules. While his grim gaze told Ace *'definitely,'* the medic answered Leo with, "Maybe."

If it's blown, she'd already be gone. If it's only nicked, she's got a chance.

"Ragno?" Ace barely managed to speak. "You hearing this?"

"Yes." Ragno's terse answer conveyed bucket loads of worry for her good friend. "I've confirmed that emergency medical support is on the way, but Chinese authorities are still not communicating clearly with us. We believe the advance team is in fighter jets, and we estimate they're twenty-five minutes out. Medics are about twenty minutes behind that. Roger?"

"Copy," Ace said, glancing at Marks, whose eyes looked even more worried. Forty-five minutes for medics was too long.

"Crap," Marks muttered. Louder, he asked, "Ragno. Does the medical unit have blood transfusion capability?"

"Determining now," Ragno answered.

If the answer was no, Leo's situation was even more grim. There was only so much that Branch could do with an in-field blood transfusion. She'd need lots of blood, fast, and none of it would do the trick if he didn't manage to stop her bleeding.

"I'm O-negative," Leo whispered.

"We're aware," Branch said.

Branch's quick glance sent even more concern Ace's way. Of course she was O-negative. Most people, no matter their blood type, could receive O-negative blood, but people with O-negative could only receive O-negative blood. Which meant that the trauma unit needed to be carrying that type of blood. For Branch to do a field transfusion, someone on board the ship had to be O-negative.

"Ace," Leo whispered, as Branch inserted clotting granules into her arm. He leaned towards her again. "Go."

Yeah. Need to get my ass in gear. But I can't.

Ace's veins pumped ice-cold dread as he gave himself the luxury of leaning forward on his knees, bending so that he was close to her but not crowding her. Unable to get his mind past the moment, he shut his eyes. Sluicing pain, deep in his chest, overcame him as the glass house his imagination had built for the two of them shattered. Searing hurt travelled through him, as jagged shards of all that beautiful hope pierced his mind and heart. He took a breath, trying to fight the resulting paralysis.

Please, God. Let her live. I'll do anything. Please. Help her. Help me. Help us.

He swallowed, fighting the throat constriction that came with his baggage of post-traumatic stress. He waited a beat, trying to compose himself while hoping like hell God was listening.

The familiar pulsing of anger started warming his fingers. Hands. Legs. Anger—at Skylar, and whoever else was behind him. At himself, for falling in love with Leo, when, after Kat, he'd sworn repeatedly that he'd never again love anyone who strapped on a weapon for a living. Sparks of fury gave him the strength to open his eyes and gaze into hers.

Anger and fury.

Not quite what he was asking God for, but he wasn't about to argue.

"Trauma unit has blood transfusion capability." Relief in Ragno's tone was palpable. "Again, we're having some communication difficulties. Not with signal strength, but with Chinese superpower attitude. We believe that O-negative is forty minutes out. Fifty minutes, max."

"Copy that," Branch said, throwing the granule applicator down and reaching for more clotting sponges and gauze.

"Tell them to fucking hurry," Ace muttered as he watched the pink fade from her lips. Her eyelids were heavy, but each time she forced them open she focused on his eyes.

"I'm fine," she whispered. "Whether I live or die. Go."

Her words hit him with the force of a tsunami. All Black Raven agents in the field had to have that attitude, but it shouldn't be the attitude of the woman he loved. He didn't drop his voice, not giving a damn that every agent now working the clusterfuck heard him and could possibly read between the lines. "Well, that isn't fine with me. You're going to live. That's a goddamn order. You understand that, Leo?"

Gritting her teeth and clenching her jaw, she held his gaze and was silent as Branch worked on her arm. Doubt in her eyes ripped his soul to shreds.

"Kamin," Branch said.

"Copy."

"Ask the hostages if anyone has O-negative blood," Branch said. "Send them here if they do. If I'm able to stop this bleeding, I'll lay the groundwork for a field transfusion. Just in case something delays the medics."

"Copy that," Kamin said. "Stand by."

When the wave of pain caused by Branch's maneuvering eased a bit, Leo's expression had changed to the slightest smirk of a cocky smile. "Can't wait to meet my Christmas present...hacked your phone...cutest puppy ever."

His chuckle caught in his throat. He'd bought a new phone just for the month of December, in an effort to keep her from guessing her gift. He'd established what he thought was a secure account. He'd even encrypted his communications with the breeder. "One day I'll figure out how to keep a secret from you."

"Name's now Trick. As in Trick or Treat. I can't stand Noelle." A glimmer of light in her eyes conveyed the complexity of emotions that came with their unresolved feelings for each other.

As he struggled with the urge to tell her that he loved her, the world faded away, until all he heard was her effort to breathe. Telling her he loved her wouldn't be the right move, especially not when he'd wasted the last two years by being her buddy. Like the finest of red wines, the depths of what could ultimately define them as a couple would need to be reached slowly. *If we get to couple-dom. A big IF. Because had I realized I was going to fall in love with a field agent, I'd have driven away from Black Raven...and her...on day one.*

Yeah—they loved each other as friends. They'd now entered a realm of something very different, and he'd never tell her until she was ready. Plus, her current predicament provided a gut-twisting reality check that made him keenly aware of his own limited capacity for any chance at the ideal version of a happily-ever-after with someone like her. They had a hell of a lot to work through before he could even think of saying that. Right now, it would scare the crap out of her, because it would make her believe she was dying. Plus, he was starting to believe that she'd been right, when she was trying to zip her dress in their suite, almost eight hours earlier.

It's never going to work.

Which meant he had no business saying *I love you.* But that didn't make the suck-ass reality of the here and now any easier. He drew a ragged breath, reminding himself to be the guy he'd been when they'd fallen into bed together. That guy had been sure that things would work. Positive he and Leo would find a way to be together. Confident they could transition to being the greatest of lovers as easily as they'd been the best of friends. He cleared his throat, but couldn't do a damn thing about his hoarseness as he mustered the courage for what could be his final words to her. "Let's do the same thing next Halloween. Deal?"

She nodded and tried to speak. Her reply was so faint, he couldn't hear it. Her lips were turning blue.

Fuck.

He needed to irritate her, to keep her fighting for her life instead of giving in and dying. "Something I've never told you before. You know that motorcycle race when we first met?"

She was struggling to keep her eyes, now glassy from pain and weakness, open. Each blink shut seemed slower and longer than the one before. Yet she whispered, "I left you in my dust."

"I pulled back and let you win. After you almost killed yourself by passing that truck, I figured anyone who needed to win that badly...should."

At that, Ace thought he saw a faint smile play across her lips. He chalked it up to wishful thinking, until she gave a chuckle that was so weak it sounded like a faint exhale. "I know what you're doing."

He leaned closer to her ear, gently moving some hair that had gotten in her eyes. "Now's the time for you to earn the nickname your father gave you. Win this fight. Stay with us."

With her left hand she squeezed his with a grip that was so weak it barely caught his attention. "Don't...let Skylar kill...those hostages. *Go!*"

Ace stood, watching as Branch worked furiously to stem the blood that was now pulsing through the bandage. It was fucking impossible to suck air into his restricted lungs. All he could do was stand there and watch the dull white of her skin turn gray.

Help her, Goddammit.

“I am helping her,” Branch said, his hands covered with blood as he pulled more bandages out of his backpack.

“Sorry, man. Didn’t realize I said that out loud. I’m—”

Scared.

“Distracting,” Branch finished for him. “Let me do my job. Go do yours.”

Chapter Nineteen

2:45 a.m.

As they jogged along the Terpischore Deck, towards the helipad, he glanced at Skylar, who was half-lifting, half-dragging May Wen. She sporadically put up resistance, kicking, clawing, and screaming. In the distance, the helipad was empty. He slowed to a walk, pausing to catch his breath. "Why the fuck isn't the chopper waiting on us?"

"I told you," Skylar, also slowing, glanced at him, his dark eyes bright with worry, which he wasn't wearing well. As he fought to control May Wen, sweat glistened on the man's brow. Even in the fresh, nighttime air, he could smell the stink of fear on the man, whose confidence had disappeared with the debacle in the theater. "Comms are down."

"They don't even know that we lost the theater?"

"Correct." Skylar tightened his chokehold on May Wen, who stopped wriggling and was finally quiet. He gestured to one of his men and directed him to go forward and turn on the helipad's landing lights. "Comms have now been off for eight minutes. They'll be coming at ten."

He fought past the lump of balled up anxiety in the back of his throat, which had formed with the explosions in the theater and was now threatening to choke him. He remembered their contingency plan. Ten minutes without comms from Skylar—at any point in the operation—meant a chopper from their escape route would come to investigate.

Knowing how much he and Skylar had planned their own operation, he wondered how the team that had burst into the theater had managed to stay under their radar. Their operation hadn't been performed by one or two wayward guests. The takeover had been orchestrated, from multiple points in the theater, and it had occurred in a matter of seconds, with precision. "How, in the name of hell, did this happen?"

By the stunned look in Skylar's eyes, he could tell that the man was wondering the same thing. After a long pause, Skylar shook his head. "I don't know. But they're good."

"Yes," he said, with a grudging nod. "They are."

As he watched a bead of sweat drip from Skylar's brow, and May Wen let loose a fresh scream, he fought to stay calm while absorbing the reality of just how much their plan had unraveled. "We've got her, though. With what we've already accumulated, she's enough. Now let's get the fuck off this ship and blow it to goddamn hell."

Chapter Twenty

2:47 a.m.

His heart lay on the floor bleeding out, but that didn't mean the goddamn job was over. With great effort, Ace started moving down the hallway. As he ejected the magazine from his rifle and inserted a new one, he couldn't help remembering another time...in an arid desert...when the medics themselves were attacked, so there had been no help...

The walls of the narrow backstage hallway seemed to undulate, closing in ahead of him and creating the illusion that his only option was to return to Leo. The creamy swirls in the blue-carpeted floor wriggled and rippled into cords that crawled up his ankles and calves and pulled him back.

Despite the PTSD-driven hallucination, enough synapses in his gray matter fired sufficiently to tell him that if he turned around, he wouldn't be able to leave her side. If he failed under these circumstances, he'd never function properly again. To battle the pull of his past, he gritted his teeth and clenched his jaw, fighting the flashback's paralyzing effect. Bending forward, he put his hands on his knees, lowered his head, and sucked in air.

Please, God. Help. Leo needs it. I need it.

Straightening, he resumed walking. With each step, his mind started clicking. Now that Leo was down, Ragno had control of her communications. For Leo, silence was the wrong move. Without hearing the chatter of her fellow agents, she'd feel isolated. Not a good thing. No matter what happened between them, he never wanted her to feel that way again. "Ragno. Activate Leo's comm."

"Agree. Might keep her...with us." Emotion choked her for a second. "I'm turning her comm back on. Leo. Stay with us."

Hearing Leo's close friend, who was normally unflappable, pause to choke back a sob somehow helped him find strength to reassure her. "Don't worry. Our girl's too damn tough to leave us. Plus, she knows we damn well need her brain on this one."

The effort that it took to say that dose of bullshit with bravado was huge, and he almost walked out the nearest door before catching his mistake. At the last second, he yanked his hand from the door handle that he'd been pushing on.

Fuck!.

He needed to get his goddamn act together. Stepping out of that door would have put him on the starboard side of the ship. If he walked out there, he'd be exposed to *Follower*. By now, the occupants of it had to be on the lookout for anyone who wasn't identifiable as a Quan operative. His near mistake could have been fatal for him and could have jeopardized the job. The potential severity of his error jolted him into focusing on the variables of what he had to do to save *Imagine* and its occupants. He turned from the doorway.

"Scott." He called the agent with the leg wound who was in the Compass Rose Bar. "Any sight of Skylar on the helipad?"

"Negative, sir."

"They've got to be there, in the shadows, waiting for the chopper."

"*Imagine*'s helipad landing lights are now on."

"I'm on my way up." The helipad was two decks above him, on the opposite side and end of the 440-foot ship. Saying that he was on his way helped him keep going. Plus, now that the theater was secure, it was damn well time for him to talk to the leader of the PLA Advance team. "Ragno. Put me on the line with Commissar Ming."

"Zeus is handling that. He's in the war room, across from me...giving me a headshake."

"Tell Zeus I said it would be damn nice to strategize with Ming what needs to happen when they get here. It seems like that's my duty as the lead agent on *Imagine*. Or, should I just not worry about Skylar's two hostages?" Ace reached the door that would lead to the port side of the Clio deck and opened it. Sucking in cool, head-clearing ocean air, he glanced right towards the bow, then left towards the stern. No Quans in sight. The night was dark, but stars twinkled. Moonlight was reflected on the ocean's rippling waters. Ace took the nearest set of stairs, two at a time. "Maybe I'll recline in a deck chair, sip a piña colada, and wait for the fucking rescue as I—"

"Understood, Evans." Zeus' words were heavy with a no-nonsense, humorless tone. "I'll add you to my line with the Commissar ASAP. The delay has nothing to do with you. Ming's using an interpreter to make sure there's no misunderstanding. Comms are a bit stilted, and he's an egotistical prick."

"Firepower of advance team?" Ace asked, reaching the top of the stairs, and running to the next set of exterior stairs, at midship.

"According to Ming, there's enough to destroy the following ship. Our intel tells me China's got plenty in the near vicinity of *Imagine*. We're catching the hot yellow spray of an international pissing match. China is secretive regarding military assets with everyone, especially the United States. Since we're an American private security firm, widely known to have contracts with our government, he considers us one and the same as our government. And, because *Imagine*'s still in what China considers to be its territorial waters, and bearing a Chinese flag, there's not a goddamn thing I can persuade the United States to do."

As he neared the top of the stairs, he heard heavy footsteps on the deck above him. He pressed himself against the wall, and glanced up to see two men, wearing camo gear, passing him. They saw him as he saw them. One turned, lifting his rifle. Ace fired before him. Two more Quans, down. "Will Ming fire at *Follower* upon arrival?"

"Working on that now."

Stepping over the dead guys, Ace glanced left and right, then headed down the deck. "What the fuck does Ming need to know before he blows that goddamn ship out of the water?

"He's concerned about the identity of *Follower*, which is unknown at this time," Zeus said. "He's being secretive about strategy—"

Frustration pulsed through Ace's veins. "How has Ming not comprehended what's at stake? I'll gladly tell him the facts, in simple, easily translatable terms. Here goes. Whoever is in charge is responsible for more than 100 deaths. The lives of two hostages now hang on our immediate actions. Ming can do a Google search and figure out that May Wen and Randy Howell are pretty important. Plus, a who's who of the world's wealthiest people will die when the missiles that are pointed at us are fired."

"Zeus disconnected midway through your diatribe," Ragno said. "He's talking to Ming. He'll be back with you...now. Here he is. Zeus only. Not Ming."

"I'm sharing your frustration." Zeus' tone remained steady and cool. "Urgency doesn't change that we're an American private security firm operating on a vessel that originated out of a city-state that a Communist country considers to be its own. Officials are in a bit of shock that we staged the operation as we did, and I'm sure as hell not explaining how we did it. Leo reestablished comms with us not even an hour ago. It's taken me a while to work up the bureaucratic food chain. Ming's first words to me, translated loosely, were, *'your motherless fucking American mercenaries deserve to die for creating this mess in my country.'*"

"He'll change his tune when he learns the details of what Quan Security is doing aboard this ship."

"Agreed," Zeus said. "But he's come a long way from his original perspective in a short time. Like it or not, he's in charge. In this case, diplomacy means we have to appear not to be the ones giving orders."

"Understood." Yet the only diplomacy he cared about was having Ming do what the fuck needed to happen, when Ace thought it damn well needed to happen. He thought for a second about the problem, and came up with an idea that might be a solution. Yet there was that niggling doubt that Ragno had created about his faith in Wen, and the doubt provided a caution signal.

"Ragno? Any more info on Wen? Any concrete reason why I should doubt my hunch that he's a good guy?" Unlike Leo, once comms had been restored, Ace hadn't been privy to the endless text streams of the agents working in Denver.

"Nothing concrete," Ragno answered. "Skylar is working closely with someone. Before we shut down Quan's comms, agents here, and Leo, suspected that Skylar was working with someone on the ship. Their hunch was based on Skylar listening to someone on *Imagine* on the encrypted line and the frequency of those comms, which we weren't able to decipher. We haven't ruled out Wen. Plus, whoever is doing this had access to the ship's schematics and systems, and they did for some time. Wen certainly had access. His shipyard built the ship."

He understood Ragno's concerns, yet his gut compelled him to believe that Wen was a good guy. "We managed to get access to the ship's schematics and systems, without building the ship," he said. "Plus, as security, Quan had access. And it could be that Skylar was in communication with the helm. Raznick's a likely candidate. At this point, we don't know who the hell is in there. Securing hostages was more of a priority."

"Leo gave us Raznick's name as a person of interest," Ragno said. "I'm clicking over to that team's analysis now. Yes. Agents here detected sizable monetary deposits into his accounts within the last three months. They're trying now to figure out the source of those wire transfers."

“So, Raznick’s more of a candidate to be Skylar’s partner than Wen,” Ace said. “I’m sticking with my hunch. Skylar and Wen are not working together. Let’s return to the idea of Wen helping us, because we’ve got a more immediate problem looming than who the ultimate players are. We’ve got to keep them from blowing up this ship and it doesn’t sound like Ming’s operating fast enough. Wen hasn’t gotten to be the wealthiest man in China by being ignorant on how to play political games. Agreed?”

“Agreed,” Zeus said.

“Agreed,” Ragno echoed.

“I’m almost to the helipad, where Wen was last seen. Give me a few seconds to get him on the line. If China’s wealthiest man can’t persuade Ming to listen to us, we don’t have a shot.”

“Great idea,” Zeus said. “Assuming your hunch is correct.”

It better be.

“Evans,” Branch said, through the com system.

“Go ahead, Branch,” Ace tried to brace himself for the bad news the medic might be delivering, while his mind raced across the distance he’d just travelled, over hundreds of yards of teak decks, down two stairwells, to the hallway where Leo lay with Branch at her side.

Please, God. No. Not dead.

Fuck it.

Can’t.

Can’t think like that.

"Leo's holding on. She can barely whisper," Branch continued. "She's trying to tell me something about a...prostitute. Got no idea why, but she's insistent that I need to tell you guys."

Keeping his eyes peeled for Wen, Ace felt a glimmer of hope for Leo's condition. Trying to communicate facts had to be a positive sign. "Ragno? Mean anything?"

"That was a thread earlier. I'm clicking over to that group's analyses, to see where they ended up. But first, rotors are spinning on *Follower*'s chopper. I'll let you know when they lift off. Copy?"

"Copy."

"Okay," Ragno said. "I'm back to the prostitute issue. Before you entered the theater, the group analyzing facial recognition had a ping on Miranda Lake, Howell's fiancée. Facial rec pegged her as a window worker in Amsterdam, from one of the more exclusive brothels."

"That would mean that Howell had brought a prostitute aboard, passed her off as his fiancée, then gave a pretty convincing act of grief-stricken horror as Skylar executed her." Ace thought about the show Howell had put on when Miranda had been shot. "Heartless. And clever. No one who witnessed that would think of him as a suspect."

"Yes, but the group determined that the facial recognition, prostitute identity was inconsistent with what our pre-cruise background analysis proved for her, which was that Miranda Lake was solidly American, from Iowa, trying to make her way in New York as a fashion model."

"But it now highlights questions about Howell, right?" Thinking aloud, Ace said, "He created a new genre of violent video games when he was a kid. Our pre-cruise due diligence on passengers brought up fluctuations in his finances—"

"Correct. Yet the Miranda Lake profile is flawless," Ragno said. "And the group dismissed the prostitute identification as an anomaly in the new facial recognition program, which is still in the testing phases."

"You're talking about Leo's program?"

"Yes."

"She's been working on redesigning it pretty steadily over the last two months. Given what I know about her work, I wouldn't dismiss anything it produces."

Chapter Twenty-One

2:50 a.m.

When Ace was twenty feet from the stern of the ship and the helipad, he slowed. He envisioned the deck plan as he edged toward the bright lights of the helipad. The rear portion of the interior space on the Terpsichore Deck housed the ship's salon, spa, and workout rooms. The helipad was between those rooms and the back end of the ship. He assumed Skylar and his gang of operatives, with Randy Howell and May Wen, were on the opposite side of the ship from where he stood. He'd bet his last dollar that they were also edging forward, ready to run for the helicopter as soon as it touched down.

A few feet in front of him, Wen stepped out of the shadows. He'd removed his tuxedo jacket. His white dress shirt clung to his skin. Dark circles under his eyes showed fatigue and worry. He kept his rifle at his side. Ace continued to trust his gut.

"Please," Wen said. "Help me rescue my wife. I'll do anything..."

Yep. A good guy. Not a bad one.

"I'm doing everything in my power to make that happen." Ace touched his watch, adjusting the audio line to pull in his conversation with Wen. "My comm system will pick up what you say. I'm connected to Black Raven HQ in Denver. They'll hear you. You'll hear them."

He quickly brought Wen up to speed about their difficulties communicating with the Chinese officials. He underscored the need to act quickly. Two sentences summed it up. "We're getting slow played by your country. We'll all die if they don't blow up that fucking ship now."

"Who's leading the operation?"

"Commissar Ming," Zeus answered, his voice as clear as if he stood next to them.

"Know him?" Ace asked.

"Too well. He's a petty bureaucrat with little man syndrome. In recent years he's struggled to gain control within the Central Military Commission. Currently, he's on the outs with our President. Not a good place to be."

"Friend or foe to you?" Ace asked.

"An old enemy dating back to college days. I know what kind of weapon power exists in our near proximity." The dark night mingled with *Imagine*'s lights, casting shadows on Wen's face that did nothing to hide the grimness and hard resolve in his eyes. "If Ming wanted to destroy *Follower*, it would already be gone. Which makes me wonder about his motivation. And just how much the man dislikes me."

"We need your highest-ranking friend on the line. Now. Someone with pull over Ming. Someone you trust to be damn concerned about your life, who will blow *Follower* out the water within a few minutes of talking to you."

"President Hu Jinmen." He rattled off numbers. "Private line."

Powerful friends in China couldn't get any higher than Jinmen, the General Secretary of the Communist Party of China and the Chairman of China's Central Military. "Ragno. Copy?"

"Yes. Securing a connection now," Ragno said. "Ace, the chopper on *Follower* lifted off. They'll descend upon *Imagine* within three minutes."

"Scott," Ace said, calling the agent who was in position in the picture windows of the Compass Rose. "Any Quans on the helipad?"

"None yet," Scott said.

"They'll all be there soon. Start picking them off. We can't let them get on that chopper. The second it lifts off from this ship, we'll be blown to pieces. And we cannot, under any circumstances, let them put May Wen and Randy Howell on the chopper." Whatever unfolded in the next few minutes, he knew damn well there'd be no good ending for May Wen or Randy Howell if Skylar was able to pull them into the chopper.

"Copy that. Take out the chopper?"

"On my signal. I'll be working on that as well. With Wen."

"Copy."

Wen nodded. "Got it."

Ace edged towards the stern, with Wen at his side, as they waited for President Jinmen to get on the phone. And, those weren't his only worries.

"Branch?"

"Yes, sir."

"How is she?"

The medic hesitated.

"Goddammit. Tell me."

"Fading." Branch continued. "Field transfusion ongoing, but she's still bleeding. She needs full-fledged trauma services, Ace. Soon."

Ace was looking into Ling Wen's dark brown eyes as he absorbed the news, which Wen heard. Wen gave Ace a slow nod, his eyes conveying grim understanding.

President Jinmen interrupted the downward spiral, deep in his gut, that Branch's news brought. Jinmen spoke in flawless English. "Hello, Ling. Something has to be seriously wrong if you're calling at this time of the morning."

After Wen quickly brought the President up to speed on the circumstances aboard *Imagine*, Zeus left the matter in Ace's hands. "A mass hijacking is turning into a mass murder, Mr. President, and we need you to stop it," Ace said. "Ragno, does the President have the video feed of the theater and the weapons on board *Follower*?"

"Working on that...now he does."

The line exploded with a conversation in heated, rapid-fire Mandarin, between Wen, Jinmen, and Ming. With a few seconds delay, Ragno translated and paraphrased what they were saying. "Ming's slow-playing is now over. The advance team will now take out *Follower* within five minutes. They'll use precision firing, but given the proximity, there will be wave action and repercussions on *Imagine*. Chinese military is aware of how close the two ships are. Now that the President is in charge, no one would dare screw this up.

"Just the kind of progress we needed. Thank you, Mr. President," Zeus said.

"Still longer than optimal," Ace muttered. "But I can work with it."

"Copy that, Ace," Ragno said.

The interior rooms of the Terpischore Deck blocked Ace's view of the other ship. "What's *Follower* doing?"

"Repositioning. Pulling slightly ahead, and turning slightly. Prepping for firing. I'm starting a countdown. Four and a half minutes to detonation by our advance team. Give or take a few seconds."

Before taking off at a run, he had to know what was happening with Leo. "Marks?"

"Yes, sir."

"How is she? No bullshit."

"Still with us. Fighting."

Ace breathed easier. He glanced at Wen. "Ready to take out a chopper?"

Wen nodded.

"Scott?"

"Yes, sir."

"We'll wait until it's almost landed. I want to draw Skylar's group onto the helipad. When I start firing at the tail rotor, you both will fire at the pilot in the cockpit. I'll try to herd Skylar's group to the port side. Wen will flank them from the rear. You'll cover all action from above."

Wen said, "Understood. My wife. Please. Be careful."

"Nothing but. You too. Scott?"

"Copy. Understood. And ready."

"Wen and I are advancing to the helipad. Now." He glanced at Wen, and said, "Go."

As they ran towards the helipad's bright lights, Ace heard the sound of chopper blades cutting through the dark night. He glanced into the sky; saw the dark outline of the helicopter as it approached *Imagine*.

"Three and a half minutes to zero," Ragno said.

Ace took off at a run across the helipad.

"Sir," Scott said. "Your six o'clock. Three Quans."

As Scott warned, Ace spun around, aimed, and squeezed off a few shots. He heard Scott's gunfire from the Compass Rose, above. Two men went down, as glass rained down from the picture windows that Scott's gunfire had destroyed. The third Quan, still standing, returned fire in Ace's direction.

Ace made it to the edge of the ship. He slid into position, flat on his belly, and semi-protected from Skylar's group by an equipment box that was built into the deck. He was ready to fire at the third Quan operative, but he didn't have to. Scott's gunfire had killed the man.

"Three minutes to zero," Ragno said.

Ace's view encompassed the full beam of the ship, from port side railing, to port deck, to the walls that framed the interior spa rooms, to the starboard deck, and starboard railing. Wen leaned against the port sidewall, about fifty feet from Ace's position, rifle hoisted, with a bead on the chopper's cockpit. The bright lights of the helipad indicated that Wen's eyes were on Ace, waiting for the signal to fire.

Skylar was one of three camo-clad men, observing the descent of the chopper, their hair blowing wildly around their heads. With them was a guy in officer's whites.

Raznick.

Skylar had a one-armed chokehold around a struggling May Wen, who he was using as a human shield. Beside them, Randy Howell didn't look to be under duress. No one was having to restrain him. The Quans didn't have a hand on Howell. No one had a weapon to his head or body. He was moving of his own free will, walking next to Skylar, and looking up at the sky as though anxiously awaiting the chopper ride.

"Ragno. Anything new on the Howell prostitute thing?"

"We ran the facial recognition analysis again," Ragno said. Given the noise from the chopper, he had to strain to hear what she was saying, but he had an advantage with the embedded mic system. "It's still pinging with the same result. Amsterdam prostitute. The weird thing is that we can't find a hole in her Miranda Lake identity. Whoever created it is damn good. Though Howell's history raises questions, we're throwing everything we've got at him and can't find anything that suggests complicity."

"Keep looking," he said, as the chopper hovered in landing position before dropping. "I know there's no conclusive link between video games and psychopathic behavior, but there are flags. Look for anything tying Howell to anyone at Quan Security. Or Commissar

Ming, given that Ming was slow playing us and Wen raised questions about him. Phone calls. Emails—"

"I'm not telling you how to shoot the chopper's tail rotor, am I?"

He chuckled as he aimed his rifle at the tail rotor, as the chopper descended. "I know, but you could. I wouldn't be offended. I'm just saying that what my eyes are seeing now, of Howell with the other Quans, is a far different image than what I saw when Miranda Lake was executed when the other hostages needed to be persuaded to pay up."

"Copy that. We'll keep looking on our end. Two and a half minutes to zero," Ragno said.

Ace squeezed off shots at the tail rotor. The screeching clang of bullets hitting metal filled the air. The front windshield of the chopper exploded simultaneously as Ling fired. The chopper's whir stalled. It choked to life again, and instead of a controlled descent, the tail rotor spun around. The chopper turned sideways, its blades grinding the deck with a chainsaw effect. Chunks of teak and fiberglass decking jettisoned through the air, before the chopper righted itself and slid further sideways. The chopper gained a bit of lift, resting on the railing, before tumbling into the ocean.

Taking off at a run towards the group, and flanking them from the side, Ace aimed and fired at a Quan who walked on the edge of the group. From above, Scott took out another one. Ace herded Skylar, Raznick, one Quan operative, and a hysterical, fighting-for-her-life May Wen in the direction of Ling Wen, who was waiting and ready to fire. May Wen screamed and struggled harder.

"Two minutes to zero," Ragno said. "Radar images show that *Follower* is closing in."

Either to get into a better firing position or for protection against incoming missiles. And there's nothing I can do about it.

"Ragno. Zeus. Tell Ming to hurry."

"The President just did," Zeus answered.

"Scott. Spray deterring gunfire in front of Skylar's group."

The *pop-pop-pop* of Scott's gunfire persuaded Skylar's group to stop in their tracks.

"Skylar," Ace called.

The group turned at the sound of his voice. "In less than two minutes the People's Liberation Army of China will blow up your escape route. You have nowhere left to run. I have men above you and behind you. Let May Wen go. Let Howell go."

Skylar's eyes darted with the wild look of a trapped animal. When he focused on Ace, he sneered as he tightened his arm around May Wen's neck. She lifted her hands to his arms as she struggled to breathe. "She'll die when I die."

Ace had a clear shot at Raznick, standing to Skylar's left. From the Compass Rose, above, Scott had a clear line on the camo-wearing Quan who stood to Skylar's right.

"Scott," he muttered so that his audio would pick it up, as he started squeezing the trigger to shoot Raznick. "Guy on Skylar's right. Now."

As Raznick went down, and the camo-wearing Quan operative to Skylar's right went down, gunfire sounded behind the small group. Ling Wen had fired. Evidently, Skylar hadn't seen Ling Wen, and hadn't realized that when he turned with May Wen, using her as a shield from Ace's gunfire, he was exposing his back to Ling Wen, who was more than ready for the siege to be over.

Skylar's head exploded into a rain of gray and red. When he fell, he took May Wen down with him. Skylar's rifle clattered to the deck, landing just inches from Howell's feet. May Wen's screams filled the night as she clawed and crawled away from underneath Skylar.

Ace kept his attention locked on Howell, waiting for him to reach for Skylar's weapon. He didn't. Which made him seem innocent. Or, at least too smart to show guilt.

Which is it?

Meanwhile, May Wen had fallen a foot or two away from Skylar's body. As she tried to stand, her husband ran forward and caught her in his arms. Howell once again remembered to wear the mask of a man who'd been afraid for his life. The contrast with how he looked now, with wide eyes, hands shaking as he wrung them together, and shoulders slumped, and how he'd looked just moments ago as he anticipated the chopper's arrival, was marked. He looked like a defeated, bewildered man now, while before he'd looked like a man whose only concern was how fast the damn chopper would arrive.

"Branch," Ace said, his eyes on Howell, but having to know. "How's Leo?"

"Still with us."

"One minute to zero," Ragno said.

In his peripheral vision, Ace saw May Wen clinging to her husband. She said something only her husband could hear. Stone-cold rage formed on Ling Wen's face as he looked up from his wife's shoulder and stared at Randy Howell. Before Ling Wen could remove his arms from his wife, Ace stepped forward, reaching for Ling Wen's rifle and pulling it from the man's hand.

"No," Ace mumbled to Ling, as he moved to stand between Ling Wen and Howell. Lowering his voice to the barest whisper, he said, "He's ours. No threat now. We can't kill him."

"If you don't kill him," Wen said, "I will."

Ace's gut also said, *kill him*, but it wasn't so simple. While Wen might have the stature of a man who was best friends with the President of his country, and perhaps had the leeway to be a judge, jury, and executioner, Ace didn't have such freedom. From his last mission as a Marine, Ace had a reputation as a loose cannon. Howell was a guest aboard *Imagine* and a client of HUG. Until facts conclusively proved otherwise, and Howell gave him a reason to kill him, Ace had to stand down.

"I cannot let you do that." Ace kept his voice low enough so that only Wen could hear him. Not Howell. "I've got this."

"Thank God you're here," Howell said to Ace, keeping up the pretense.

"Yeah," Ace said, watching for any sign that the man would hang himself by reaching for Skylar's rifle. It was a test. The same sort of test he'd employed in an Afghanistan village, four years earlier, on the men he'd felt responsible for Kat's death. "I've had a few conversations with God myself tonight."

"They killed my fiancée. They wanted..."

As Howell tried not to be pegged as a perpetrator of the heinous crime that had occurred aboard *Imagine*, fury pumped through Ace's veins. His vision became blurred and red at the edges. His mind flashed to the people who lay dead on the casino floor, as the air vibrated with the distant sound of fighter jets. He thought of Agent Amy Ryan, lying dead. The other agents on their team. The security personnel who he didn't know. Leo, fighting for her life. "You mean the hooker you picked up in Amsterdam last week?"

"How dare you!"

"He's one of them. One. Of. Them." Proving that she was stronger than she looked, May Wen hadn't devolved into tears. Her voice was strong and full of certainty. "He told the others I was enough. They'd get all the money they needed from you if they only managed to take me off the ship. He's one of them."

"Thirty seconds to zero," Ragno said.

Ace heard the rumble and hum of the approaching jets. His understanding of the strength and capabilities of the PLA's Air Force gave him faith that they'd hit their target. Before the night sky became alight with the sound of fury and wrath, Ace gridlocked his gaze on Howell. He remembered his pledge to Leo, a little more than two hours earlier, in the crawl space above the casino, that they'd kill the perpetrator of the massacre.

Reach for that rifle, you fucker. Just. Reach. For. It.

"You've got to believe me." Despite his words, Howell's eyes had hardened with the look of a man who was cornered. His eyes flashed with the realization that he'd made an enormous mistake by dropping the pretense of being a hostage in front of May Wen.

Howell bent fast, reaching for Skylar's rifle. The action made him a threat that sealed his fate. Before Howell managed to fully lift the rifle and take aim, Ace lifted his weapon and fired. As Howell fell to the ground, Ace took off at a run.

Leo. Alive. Please, God.

Chapter Twenty-Two

Denver, Colorado
One week later

The ding of a text message awakened Leo. She shifted on the couch, where she'd been dozing for most of the afternoon, and lifted her phone to read the text. Trick, who'd snuggled up to her under the blanket, protested the change in position with a yawn. The text was from Ace. She'd been expecting it.

'Just landed. Be there for kickoff. Wheels up again at 2300.'

The evening football game was starting in twenty minutes. Her team, the Giants, were playing the Cowboys. Both were fighting for a playoff spot.

She replied with, *'Hungry?'*

'Starving. Your appetite back?'

'Getting there.'

Truth was, she wasn't hungry at all, because she didn't know where their conversation would go. She'd been worried about it ever since she'd awakened a few days earlier.

'Want me to pick up something?'

Nice of him to offer. She thought about what he might feel like eating, and replied, *'I'll order in. Luigi's?'*

Even without a fast reply, she knew his answer would be yes. With the exception of spending the day at Last Resort, in Georgia, Ace had been in China since the *Imagine* job, dealing with after-action reports from Macau. God knew he had to be craving some familiar food.

Unexpectedly, new work had come out of the job for Ace. Ling Wen wanted to transfer a large chunk of security work to Ace and Black Raven. Ace had spent the day at Last Resort, personally selecting twenty agents who would head security teams for the Wens at their Beijing and Macau residences. The twenty agents were just the tip of the iceberg for the enormity of the projects that Wen had in mind. In the corporate world of Black Raven, where the monetary value of work that an agent brought into the firm was a large factor in the agent's overall value to the firm, Ace had scored the motherlode. If the jobs from Ling Wen Enterprises panned out, Ace would join the ranks of Black Raven partners before long. The company had many agents, but very few partners.

In a lightning-fast move, Trick stole her attention when she leapt from the couch, flying over the stepstool Leo had placed there for the clumsy, six-pound, long-legged puppy. She sprawled with all four paws spread out, then stood and shook off the after-effects of the fall. "You should use the stepstool, silly."

Mostly snow-white, with coal black ears, the dog was adorable. Black patches, not quite round, surrounded her coal-black eyes, giving her a baby panda look and making her irresistible.

Trick gave her an over-the-shoulder glance, as if to say, *'but that's not fun.'*

It had been hard for her not to tell Ace that she knew about the puppy. The cava-poo had stolen Leo's heart the minute she'd seen her in the photos the breeder had sent to Ace, and that had been early December when she'd hacked his new phone. In those godawful moments when she'd been worried she was dying, those last few minutes in the side stage area before she'd lost consciousness, Leo had worried about Ace as much as she was worried about herself. Telling Ace she knew about Trick, and mentioning Halloween, had been her way of saying, *'I love you, too,'* without explicitly using the three words that she doubted they'd ever actually allow themselves to say to each other. Which was yet another issue they'd have to confront if they went down the path of being anything more than platonic friends.

Trick, walking around the room, and wagging her tail with her nose down, gave Leo a solid clue to stop letting her mind drift and get her ass off the couch. She sat up, wincing with the effort. Searing pain emanated from where the bullet had entered her right upper arm, nicking her brachial artery. Her arm was bandaged and in a sling. Two of her ribs had cracked, where bullets had hit the body armor. Her chest was black and blue. Even regular breathing hurt. Coughing was pure torture.

As if on cue, her phone rang with a call from Ragno, who'd been monitoring the puppy's walking schedule. It had been four hours since she'd last been out. "Should I send someone up to walk her?"

"I'll just let her out on the balcony." Tucking the cell phone between her shoulder and her left ear, Leo stood slowly, giving herself a few seconds to gain her equilibrium. "Ace is coming over. He'll take her later, and I'll let him feed her. He'll get a kick out of seeing how fast she eats."

"His jet landed fifteen minutes ago. Nice of him to detour to see you from Last Resort before returning to China, right?"

A flutter of keystrokes filled in Ragno's expectant pause. There'd been more than a few of those pauses since the *Imagine* job. It was as though Ragno was waiting for Leo to say something about what had been made obvious to everyone who had listened to her and Ace's conversation in the off-stage hallway. Leo had no intention of doing any such thing. She focused on taking the few steps across the room, to the sliding door. "What's going on in the war room?"

"You and I are having no discussions about work. I've given Ace strict instructions on that as well."

"I'm dying here. Bored out of my mind."

"Dying? No. That ship sailed. Bored? Probably. Maybe watch Netflix. Surely there's something you haven't binge-watched. Or football."

"But I can't stay awake." She looked longingly across the room at her computer monitors and laptop. She knew not even to try. Her mind wasn't there. Doctors said her strength and mental energy would return quickly within a few days of stopping the painkillers.

Upon her arrival at home, two days earlier, Leo had given herself one more day with drugs. Her final painkiller had been last night. She wasn't so worried about the pain. What bothered her was that she still felt flat-out exhausted and, worse, it was hard for her to put her thoughts in a logical order.

"I don't think that boredom is making you sleepy. Losing most of the blood in your body, hours of surgery, broken ribs and jet lag on top of it all might have something to do with it, though. Call if you need anything. The entire cyber department is looking for an excuse to run up there and see you and Trick."

Leo opened the sliding glass door that led to her rooftop terrace. The top two floors of Black Raven's high-rise headquarters consisted of small, private residences for the partners to stay in when they were in Denver. The residence had been part of Leo's recruitment package, and Leo was the only non-partner with a residence on Black Raven's top two floors. She lived there when she wasn't working in the field or training at Last Resort. She loved that the cyber division, with its hum of activity, was only a short elevator ride away. Loved even more that Ragno, who also lived at HQ full time, lived next door to her.

As she tried to breathe in crisp, cold air, pain forced Leo to stop. She tried again, more slowly, while watching Trick squat and use the patch of grass that Ace, with Ragno's help, had arranged to have placed there.

With a little fresh air in her lungs, she started to feel better, until she turned around, walked back in the house and saw her Christmas gift for Ace. The box, wrapped in simple brown paper and tied with a bow, sat on the dining room table, where she'd left it. She'd been debating about whether or not to give it to him. She thought about the letter that was enclosed with it.

Decision made.

She took the box, which she thought of as gift option A, and brought it into her bedroom, then stashed it in a drawer in her clothes closet. From the same drawer, she pulled out the backup gift, option B, that she'd ordered for him even before the *Imagine* job. It was a generic gift, with a generic card. Both were store bought. Nothing special. She'd wrapped option B and put a bow on it, just in case she chickened out of giving him the more meaningful option A, which, with the letter that went with it, had the potential to be the most meaningful gift she'd ever given anyone.

Not going there. What was I thinking!?

As she placed gift option B on the dining room table, she heard the ding of Ace's reply text, no doubt replying to whether Luigi's sounded good. After going to the bathroom, she walked to the door and unlocked it for him. She'd been up for a full four minutes. There was no need to have to get up again in fifteen when he arrived. It was just too painful of a process. So she went to the couch and settled there with Trick on her lap.

Her heart twisted a bit as she read Ace's text. *'Luigi's – great. But do you feel like that? Really?'*

His words reflected the essence of how he'd always treated her. Unfailingly considerate. Caring. Even when he was teasing. He'd been right, of course, in their suite on *Imagine*, before they'd fallen into bed. They'd always acted like two people who loved each other—from the very beginning of their friendship, until now.

Her eyes blurred. Shaking her head, she blamed her emotions on the after-effects of the drugs that she'd been on since the shooting and typed her reply. *'Can handle chicken picatta and plain angel hair. Odd thing to crave, right?'*

'Nah. Not for you. As usual, going from 0 to 60 in a matter of seconds. I'll take my usual.'

After placing an order at Luigi's, she sent a text to the agents who were manning the first floor, then put the phone down. At least on text, Ace had seemed perfectly normal, in a good friend sort of way. She hadn't been alone with him since getting shot. Or, to be more accurate, if she'd been alone with him, she didn't remember it.

From *Imagine*, she'd been airlifted to a hospital in Hong Kong where, in the Ling Wen wing of the hospital, she'd received blood transfusions and surgeons had repaired her arm. Nurses had told her about the good-looking man who'd been at her bedside for hours.

She'd been drugged and asleep, dead to the world, for the first three days. After that, she'd been well enough to travel home with medical assistance. Ling Wen's appreciation for Ace and all things Black Raven extended to making sure that she and Agent Scott had top-quality medical attention on their intercontinental flight home, on one of his private jets. Wen also made sure the bodies of the Black Raven agents who had died made it home to their loved ones, without any red tape.

Lying down, she yawned, and didn't awaken again until she heard Ace's soft knock at the door. "Come in. It's unlocked."

Trick leapt off the couch when the door opened. Ace shrugged out of his leather jacket, hung it in the coat closet, then lifted the puppy. While his words were mumbled, sweet nothings for Trick, his gaze was all for Leo.

The blackness of his turtleneck set off the blue in his eyes. He watched how slowly she sat up, as he walked over to her and sat in the chair next to the couch. The ease with which he kicked off his shoes, lifted one jean-clad leg, crossed it over the other, and settled into a sitting position made her envious. “I never realized how important ribs are.”

“Hurts that badly?”

“The arm’s not so bad, but it feels like there are knives in my chest.”

He shifted the dog to the side, tucking the puppy between his thigh and the arm of the chair. He reached for the remote control that she’d left poised on the arm of the couch. “What are you taking?”

“Nothing. I threw away the pain pills last night.”

“Yeah. I can’t stand pain meds either.” He turned up the volume on the television. “Too bad the Giants are already behind.”

She gasped, turning from him and staring at the television. Wincing from the pain that came from the sudden movement, she realized she’d slept through kick off and... She narrowed her eyes, looking for the score on the bottom of the screen. Zero to zero. She started laughing, then wanted to scream with the pain. She inhaled sharply, which caused her ribs to hurt even more.

When he started chuckling, she threw a pillow at him, which was definitely the wrong move. She pressed a hand to her aching ribs. “Not fair. You can’t make me laugh for the next four weeks.”

“Making a friend with broken ribs laugh is something friends are supposed to do. It helps the healing process—”

“That’s total bullshit—”

“Nope.” He flashed his beautiful, easy smile, the one that she was sure was going to make him look like a perpetually youthful California surfer, no matter his age. It was the smile guaranteed to steal her heart, every time she ever saw it.

"Can't be bullshit," he added. "I learned that in the Marines. Ask your doctor."

The football game grabbed her attention. The quarterback for the Giants fired the ball in the air, straight for the tight end, who was open on the five. Leo held her breath in excitement until the tight end caught it and ran into the end zone. "Score!"

Capturing her excitement, Trick barked, then jumped off of Ace's chair, to the floor, and back onto the couch, licking her face. Moving carefully, so that managing the dog's affection didn't send ripples of pain down her ribcage, Leo said, "Funny. Before having her here, I never realized how quiet my place was."

"I did." His gaze had turned serious, as serious as she'd ever seen him. "I guess I thought you needed a little noise in your home life. She's an okay gift? Cause if you don't want her, I'll take her. Any one of my sisters would love her. I made sure of that before I risked it. Even Ragno would take her—"

"She's one of the best Christmas gifts ever," Leo said. "And she's mine. Thank you."

Feeding Trick, walking Trick, Italian food, and the football game provided both of them with perfect excuses not to talk about the elephant in the room. At nine forty-five, when he returned from taking Trick on a second walk around the block, she figured she was off the hook, if she wanted to be. He'd have to leave a little after ten to go to the private airstrip where Wen's jet would go wheels up at eleven.

I'm not going to wimp out. Never have, never will.

Even though the Giants were down by seven, she muted the television. She gingerly twisted herself up, and into a sitting position. Her dad had taught her that doses of medicine went down faster when you were sitting rather than lying down. Standing was actually better, but given the circumstances, there was no need to be too ambitious. He glanced at the television, then gave her a quizzical look as he unhooked Trick's harness.

"Ready to talk?" she asked.

He shrugged. "We've been talking."

"You're doing what you told me you always do with your family. Am I right? You're pretending that everything is fine."

He shrugged, but she thought his eyes darkened in an acknowledgment that storm clouds were on their horizon. "Not sure what you mean."

"Yeah," she whispered, making room for Trick to snuggle into the blanket next to her. "You do. You did it after Kat died. After you left the Marines, when you went back to California. Last summer, we talked about a lot of things when we were driving from California to Georgia. You told me that you never really wanted your family to know how hard that first year was for you. So, you hid your true feelings from them."

He returned to the chair he'd been sitting in. His eyes lingered on the television for a few seconds, taking in a commercial about fresh ingredients on pizza. He glanced at his watch, then turned his gaze back to the couch. He finally looked into her eyes. "Okay."

"Okay? That's all you've got?"

"Not sure what else to say." His words were calm and cool, but the glance at his watch had spoken volumes.

"You're hiding your feelings now. Acting like everything's fine."

His expression was flat, but in his eyes she saw a simmering brew of hurt, pain, worry, and anger. "I probably should get going."

"The airport's only fifteen minutes away, and you're flying privately. We've got plenty of time. So stop faking that everything's okay and talk to me."

Chapter Twenty-Three

Leo was right. Of course, she was. He'd been faking. He'd actually paced the hallway, giving himself a pep talk, before bracing himself and knocking on the door of the apartment. Truth was, the contradictions were so acute, his emotions so raw, he didn't know what to feel, except as miserable as he'd ever been.

And that was saying a lot.

"I was going to wait till you were better, and—"

"No way. You warned me you'd be pissed if I got hurt. Go on. Get it off your chest."

Her eyes, burning with a fiery light as she focused one hundred percent of her attention on him, looked the same as they'd always looked. The slight flush in her cheeks seemed healthy, yet he couldn't look at her without remembering what she'd looked like in that off-stage hallway, on the floor, with pale skin and blue lips. "Aw, hell, Leo. Pissed doesn't quite describe it. I haven't yet sorted through my feelings or the things I need to say. I don't want to make the same mistake I made on the ship, when I blurted out half-baked thoughts and persuaded you to fall into bed with me."

She gave a short, sarcastic laugh, then winced with pain. He watched her visibly shake it off, then keep her arms folded around her chest. "What are you talking about? You might have the power of persuasion, but you're not that good at it. Do you think I would have had sex—or whatever you want to call what we did—without wanting to?"

"Good to know." He stood, wishing he felt more relief over her statement. Then again, he knew, deep inside, that she wouldn't have gotten into bed with him unless she wanted to. Which only highlighted one aspect of their problem even more. If they were both attracted to one another, how the hell were they going to keep up the charade of being just friends?

He walked over to the sliding glass door, stared at the snow that had started to fall on the terrace, then turned back to her. She was sitting cross-legged on the couch, the only obvious sign of her injury was the bandage on her arm and the sling. Aside from that, with black leggings, and a black tank top, she looked just like she had on any other evening when they'd watched football together.

The problem was all his. He crossed a line somewhere by falling in love with her. On *Imagine*, in that hallway where the cream-colored swirls in the carpet had absorbed her blood, he'd crossed another line. One from which he wasn't sure there could be a return. "You were right, of course. A real relationship between us would never work."

He thought he saw her flinch. When the coral-pink flush in her cheeks deepened, he realized she wasn't hurt. When she answered, her angry tone confirmed that she was pissed. "Are you saying that our friendship isn't real? I sure wish I'd have realized it was a figment of my imagination."

"Of course our friendship's real. But we're so much more than friends that I don't see how we can ever unravel all the things that we are. I don't know how we can salvage anything, once we start tearing it apart. The truth is—," He drew a breath, not knowing whether he could say it. He didn't want to admit how afraid he'd been. How the fear...*Fuck it.* She deserved at least part of the truth. The part that he felt he could articulate. "I was so afraid for your life that I almost screwed up the whole damn job. I couldn't breathe. I almost didn't walk away from your side. Almost couldn't—"

When the puppy yelped, moved closer to Leo, he realized he was yelling. He didn't care. He continued, "You never should've been on that stage. And you stayed there longer than you should have. I can't believe you put yourself in harm's way like that. I'm so damn furious with you that..."

He let his words trail.

"That what?" Sarcasm weighed heavy in her tone. "Go on. Finish your thoughts."

"Fuck it. Forget about it."

"I was doing my job." There was anger in her voice, and he didn't blame her.

Yeah. Bingo. You hit the nail on the head, with a sledgehammer. That's the problem. The job.

He clenched his jaw and kept his mouth shut. His gut instinct told him that going down that path, now, wouldn't be productive. Her tenacity and fearlessness were some of the things he loved most about her. Yelling at her because she'd been doing her job would be pointless. Her fearlessness was part of who she was. The truth was, it had been a brilliant move on her part to get out of the crawl space and drop into the props booth. If he, or any Black Raven agent with a desire to do the job the damn correct way had been in her position, on the stage, they'd have tried for a better shot at Skylar.

She spoke again, with a simple statement that echoed his thoughts and underscored the true nature of the problem. "I was doing what any agent should have done."

"Yeah. I get it. I'm fully aware that I'm faulting you for my own limitations. Blaming you for the fact that I don't want you to put yourself in situations where you can get killed, when our jobs require us to do just that." He shook his head and ran his fingers through his hair, realized his chest had tightened in a way that couldn't be healthy.

For a second, he wished there was a physical reason why he felt so damn miserable. A heart attack, one that was mild, survivable, and of limited duration, would have to be better than the chest-squeezing heartache he was feeling. "The more field jobs you undertake, the higher the probability you'll be injured again. Or worse."

"That applies to any agent. Even, I might add, you."

He glanced around her apartment, which, in Black Raven style, was sleek and ultra-modern. A bank of computer equipment was built into the far wall of her living room. In a matter of seconds, she could be in real time with the cyber division and the constant hum of activity that existed there, a few floors below. Next to the computer monitors, a locked gun cabinet contained her private arsenal of weapons.

Black Raven was more than her home. It was her world. She lived it, breathed it, and thrived in it. He couldn't imagine that she'd be willing to give it up, for anything or anyone. "I know there's a part of you that's always going to be that thirteen-year-old who the NYPD had to hold back from running into the towers to save her dad."

The flush in her cheeks deepened. "Is there a point here that's relevant to today?"

He drew another breath. He worried, for the thousandth time in the last few days, that the feeling of impending doom that he'd had while sitting in her hospital room, vowing to himself that he was going to pull back from her, was never going to leave him. Not until they resolved their issues. Which meant plenty of talking. About feelings. Something neither of them liked to do. Which was, perhaps, yet another reason they'd pretended to be just friends for so long. "Given your clear enjoyment of fieldwork, the odds are minus zero you'll ever quit. Which means I have no business being so close to you, because the worry I felt for you on that damn ship taught me a valuable lesson..." And *fuck*, this was leading to one of the points he didn't want to get into. At least not now.

He knew the words he needed to say. One day, hopefully soon, he had to tell her that in order for him to breathe, for him to have any hope of a normal life where he wasn't crippled with fear for her safety, he needed her to stop fieldwork. He'd do the same for her, if she asked.

But he also knew her well enough to know that she'd only consider the idea of quitting if she loved him more than she loved fieldwork. At least for now, that wasn't a question he was prepared to ask.

Or, rather than her quitting, he'd have to learn to live with his worry over her. Given the last few days of hell, he wasn't sure it was a possibility. Couldn't imagine that he could ever do it.

Amidst all of his uncertainty, the only thing he knew for sure was that they weren't ready for that discussion. Given the rawness of their feelings over what had happened to her on the *Imagine* job, they'd both end up really angry.

So he stayed silent, while in his best friend's eyes, he saw understanding of the depth of his struggle. Her eyes weren't simply mirroring his pain, though. He also saw a bit of a struggle of her own. Underlying the compassion, he also saw a firmness that told him she wasn't going to give him any slack.

And while he was almost hobbled by emotional pain, she wasn't hesitating. "Words, Ace. Use them. You said you learned a lesson. What is it?"

My worry for you will cripple me. It's going to infect all aspects of my life. When we're on jobs together, and even when we're not, as long as you're throwing yourself into mortal danger, I won't be able to breathe. And here's the real problem. I'm not sure that matters enough to you. Not sure I matter enough to you. I'm not sure if you'd be having this sort of pain if I had been the one laying in that damn hallway, bleeding out. Fuck it all, but the real point here is that if I'm going down this road alone, maybe the best thing...is to just let me go.

"A lesson that I haven't quite embraced yet," he said instead of the truth. "It kills me to believe that you were right while we were talking about...the possibility of us being a couple...on *Imagine*. The truth is I don't know how we could possibly make anything other than a friendship work. So, let's be friends. Best friends." He tried to give her a casual smile. "But no more pedicab rides."

And let me take the time that I need to figure out how to—if I can—separate love from friendship like one sorts precious gold nuggets from river silt. I'm thinking even our silt is better than nothing. Maybe.

She stood, slowly. Trick jumped off the couch, and sat at her feet, while she straightened herself. Once she was upright, she shot him a look that was pure Leo. Open, honest, mocking, and furious.

She strode into her bedroom, came out with a box, and shoved it at him. "Here's your Christmas gift. As much as I love Trick, I think I'm going to win the best-Christmas-gift-ever prize. Go. Fly off to China. While you're there, think. Because next time we have this conversation, I want one hundred percent honesty. No holding back."

***

Twenty minutes later, he was on the jet. He settled into a leather seat and snapped his seatbelt. He gave the pilots a thumbs-up.

The co-captain nodded. "A half hour, sir."

Ace reclined and shut his eyes, wishing that sleep would come, but knowing the idea was laughable. Evidently, restful sleep was a thing of his past. Anytime his eyes were closed, like now, he was back in the off-stage hallway. Walls were undulating. Cream swirls in the blue-carpeted floor had wriggled and rippled into cords that were strangling him. Leo's body was there, but she was gone. The hallucination didn't stop with her death. In his sleep-deprived world, his mind created a scenario where Howell made it into the helicopter, with Skylar and Raznick and May Wen. The chopper had flown to *Follower*, and *Imagine* had been blown to pieces by *Follower*'s missiles. Innocent people had died a fiery death, and, as the dark ocean became awash with their blood, they sank to the ocean floor with the ship. It was all his fault, all because he'd frozen when Leo was injured and dying, and hadn't been able to prevent danger that was damn well preventable.

With a start, he opened his eyes.

And was damn glad to see that he was on the jet.

He forced himself to think about how Leo would look now, half-dozing on the couch with Trick snuggled next to her. The flickering lights of the television would be casting shadows in the room. He glanced at his watch and checked the score. The Giants were winning. More than anything in the world, now that he'd managed to escape, he wanted to be back in that room with her.

A sure sign that I'm screwed.

He decided to work. He stood and reached into the compartment where he'd stowed his things. Instead of finding his laptop, his fingers ran across Leo's gift for him.

He grabbed the box. She'd taped an envelope to the bottom, tying the box and envelope together with a red bow. He turned the overhead light on, sat, and opened the box. It was a watch, but not an ordinary watch. Not one driven by modern technology. He studied the breath-taking beauty of the gold and silver face of the watch, made all the more stunning by the intricately crafted complications.

He knew Leo well enough to know the gift meant far more to her than whatever the monetary value might be. The meaning behind the watch tugged at him, adding to the raw, tumultuous feelings that wreaked havoc in his chest as he opened the letter.

December 17th

Ace,

Forgive me—this is a re-gift, of sorts. I first thought about giving this to you last summer, when we were driving across the country in your Airstream, staring at the night sky in the Arizona desert and arguing over whose playlist was more likely to keep us awake. The stars that night reminded me of this watch. I even told you a bit about it then.

The more I thought about gifting it to you, the more it seemed like something I needed to do, so you'd understand the value I place on our friendship. After Halloween night, and our pedicab ride, I knew I'd chicken out of giving it to you in person, so I decided to write this letter to go with it.

Please accept one of Dad's favorite watches. As a kid (and even now), I was mesmerized by the beauty of this watch, with its ever-changing dials showing the stars, moon, and sun. When the dials reflect the nighttime, the blue background reminds me of your eyes.

Of all the watches in his collection, I remember him wearing this watch the most in the years before he died. He wasn't wearing it on 9/11, because the horologist was working on a glitch in the perpetual calendar.

Dad always taught me lessons. With this watch, he taught me about complications—the special functions that exist on a watch in addition to telling time. He'd analogize watch complications to life. He'd say that, if handled correctly, with proper attention to the details presented and meticulous care, complications in life, like on a watch, can be beautiful enhancements.

Which gets me to the point of this letter. After our pedicab ride on Halloween, I have the feeling our friendship may soon be facing some complications. Because if you don't bring up our kiss again, I think I'll have to, even though I've avoided the topic each time you've tried to raise it. I know I told you not to talk about it, but maybe it's time to talk about it.

Here's the catch. Dad taught me that complications aren't effortless. They don't just work themselves out. Intricate complications worthy of the finest watches (and lives) take careful engineering, attention to detail, and meticulous care. As a kid, I didn't quite understand his point with the analogy.

I think I do now.

To be honest, I've thought about the paths we can take from our pedicab ride. Even now, as I write this, almost two months later, I'm just as torn as I was when I let the elevator door close, with you on the other side. At that moment, I wanted to run into your arms. But I also wanted to pretend that our kiss never happened. I feel the same way now—torn as to which path we should take.

As much as I know we shouldn't go there...that it'll never work...there was something magical in our kiss that I can't forget. As a matter of fact, there's something so magical about the two of us, together, I'm starting to think that no matter what complications we'll need to resolve...we should try.

For some odd reason that I can't fathom...I can't seem to think my way through this.

I hope you treasure the watch. The horologist fixed the calendar after 9/11. I had him re-tune the watch in November. Patek Phillippe watches take tending, but nothing too tricky. I'll explain later.

Whatever happens between us, let's try to be friends (at least) for as long as the perpetual calendar on this watch is intended to run.

No matter what.

Leo

On his second read, it occurred to him that the date of the letter was before the *Imagine* job—before he had tried telling her how he felt for her as she was zipping her dress. Before the circumstances of their recent job had crystallized, for him, his own limitations, forcing him to admit that being in love with her would bring a crippling fear for her well-being that he might never overcome.

As he gripped the letter, a glimmer of hope pulsed through his veins. She was the smartest person he'd ever met, and he'd be a fool not to see the hints that provided a way to claw his way out of the rut in which he found himself. By giving him a glimpse of where her thoughts had been prior to the ill-timed conversation that he'd instigated on *Imagine*, she'd given him hope that somehow they'd navigate the turbulent waters ahead, and make it to the other side with a future together. By handing him the letter after the lame, half-truthful conversation he'd just had with her at her place, she'd placed them firmly back at square one, where they should've been on the morning of November 1, before the elevator doors closed.

When he read the letter a third time, the words that stood out the most were, *'As a matter of fact, there's something so magical about the two of us, together, I'm starting to think that...no matter what complications we'll need to resolve...we should try.'*

Hope surged through him, waking his body from the heavy lethargy of depression. As the pilots fired the engines, he unhooked his seat belt, then stood and went to the cockpit.

"Change of plans."

Chapter Twenty-Four

"I have until six a.m. I thought maybe we could hang out a little longer." Ace stood in the doorway of Leo's apartment. She'd answered as he knocked, having been alerted by the front desk that he was on his way up.

She opened the door all the way so that he could enter. Before he could step over the threshold, Trick stood on her hind legs and scratched at his calves. "I thought the jet was scheduled to depart."

"It was. Wen won't mind. I have some time before I need to meet with him." Standing still, on the threshold, he lifted his wrist so that Leo could see he was wearing the watch. "I thought I should thank you in person."

She smiled, with a twinge of uncertainty that stole his heart. "It looks great on you. My father would be glad you have it."

"I'm...awed by this gift. Your letter's even better."

And I damn well wish I knew what to say in reply.

"I'm just not good with emotional things," she said. "I usually think that feelings just get in the way..."

As her words trailed, she bit her lower lip. He wasn't used to seeing the woman he knew as a decisive powerhouse struggle with uncertainty. It made him love her more, and he became fixated on how she was chewing on that lip. Which was sort of what he wanted to do, himself. First, he needed to find some more of the right words. Otherwise, he was going to miss an opportunity to tell her how much she meant to him, the way she'd managed to do, so eloquently.

He cleared his throat, knowing she wasn't ready to hear that he loved her. Besides, there were ways of saying *'I love you,'* without using the three words that normally expressed the sentiment. After all, if he was interpreting her letter correctly, she'd just done that exact thing.

Right? Maybe. Shit. Assume it's so.

No words came to mind.

So instead of starting the conversation where the *Imagine* job had left them, which would only lead to issues he doubted that either of them had the know-how or the fortitude to resolve at the present moment, he went to a different point in time. One that had issues that were equally unresolved, but which were far more pleasant. "I never should've let those elevator doors at The Roosevelt shut on you, after our kiss," he said. "And I never should've stayed quiet about our kiss for so long."

She gave an eye roll, with an understanding smile. "I get it. Even tonight, I almost wimped out with handing you the letter. I had a backup gift. A cashmere sweater that's the color of your eyes. There's even a Hallmark card with it. This is better, I think, because..."

As her words trailed, he stayed silent for a minute, almost drowning, once again, in the uncertainty that came with the conflicting feelings she inspired.

Man up, idiot. Tell her.

"You said you want one hundred percent honesty when we next talked. There are a lot of details I can't seem to sort out, but my bottom line is that I can't imagine my life without you." He cleared his throat again, almost choking. "I want your friendship. Want your laughter. Want...all of you. Without you, I'd forever be incomplete."

"Wow," she whispered, with something akin to tears glittering in her eyes. "It took me two pages and multiple rewrites to say something close to that."

The chokehold on his chest finally started easing. Trick, at his feet, gave a mewling yelp that helped him keep his mind where it needed to be—in the present. Knowing it was time to get out of the doorway, he scooped Trick off the floor, held the warm, wriggling puppy in the crook of his arm, and nodded in the direction of the living room. "Maybe we should just sit together for a while. Talk."

She nodded and walked over to the couch. He sat as she did, pushing the blanket she'd been using away. Aware of her injuries, he made sure not to move too much. The remote control fell to his side, on the pillow where her head had been resting. The blankets smelled like her. The pillow smelled like her. Even better, she smelled like her.

He lifted the remote control, and turned off the television, leaving only soft lamplight in the room, and silence. Just the two of them, breathing softly. His arm was on the back of the couch, lightly touching her shoulders. Trick was nestled next to her.

"This feels good," she whispered. "Almost like we should've always been doing this. So close to each other. It's also weird, though. There are so many reasons why not..."

With her nestled into the corner where his shoulder met his chest, he leaned back into the couch, giving her a few inches of breathing space. "I know what you mean by feeling torn, like you said in the letter. To be honest, I feel like I'm facing the most important battle of my life."

She gave a low chuckle. "A battle?"

"Yeah. I don't think I've won you over, at least not yet. I do think, however, that there's going to be a moment in your life, in our lives, when the complications—," he snapped his fingers. "Fizzle away to nothingness."

She gave a headshake. "I'm not sure how that could happen. Are you there, now?"

He thought about the turmoil he'd experienced ever since the job. The honest answer to her question was no. He could think of quite a few reasons why they shouldn't love one another. Reality was, he bet he was a lot closer than she was to ignoring all the 'why not' reasons. Which simply reaffirmed his instinct to take it slow.

"What do you say we just enjoy this night, before we confront the issues."

She shifted, slowly, so that more of her weight was leaning into him. "That's not much of a plan. I think we should try to sort a few things out."

Now?

Like hell.

Reminding himself that she was the same woman who'd disappeared from New Orleans without a goodbye, he decided to start slowly. "Okay. We'll try. Eventually."

He was so damn happy to inhale the essence of rose that lingered on her skin and all around her, to feel the warmth of her body, and have his forearm resting lightly on the back of her neck, that the hurt in his chest finally started easing. Touching his lips to the smooth skin of her forehead, he immediately felt better than he had in days.

"But let's not jump too far ahead of ourselves,' he added, pulling his face from hers, and looking into her eyes. He ran his fingers along the back of her neck, lightly tracing lines and making circles where her hair met her nape. "For now, I just want to sit with you. Hold you. That's it."

With a slight smile, she let her head fall against his hand, forcing a little more pressure where he was rubbing. She gave him the sexiest smile he'd ever seen—just a slight tilt of her full lips, with her eyes half closed. That gorgeous peachy-pink color had returned to her cheeks. "Maybe we can do a little more..."

As warmth started pumping through his veins, his brain sent flashing, slow-down signals. "You're injured—"

"But I could handle another kiss. Like our kiss in the pedicab." Before her lips touched his, she added, "Well, this one needs to be gentler."

"I can do gentle," he said.

"Really?" She gave a slow head shake. "I'm looking forward to seeing your gentle side."

He kept the finger-thing going at her neck, definitely not bending to kiss her yet. "My kisses can be whisper soft, actually. Kind of like a butterfly's wing rippling through the wind. You know, gentle stimuli in one area can have...explosive effects elsewhere. Chaos theory."

She started laughing, then stopped in mid-chuckle. She bent forward, reached for her side and winced. She leaned her forehead against his shoulder. “Ouch!”

He shifted, pulling one leg up and turning, so that he was almost facing her. He bent so that his nose was in her hair, at the crown of her head, as she snuggled into him. He inhaled more freshness. More of her. “You’ve heard of chaos theory, haven’t you?”

“Of course, but never in the context of kissing. And, if you keep making me laugh—.” She looked up, with a gleam of light in her eyes. “—You’ll have to go sit in the chair.”

Behind her, he glanced at Trick. The puppy cast a sleepy eye up at him, then rolled over and fell asleep again.

He refocused on Leo. “Once I get going, you won’t laugh. I promise.”

While his words were light, she searched his eyes. He didn’t think he needed to say anything more. At least not now.

We’ll sort through the complications. I’m going to win you over. Persuade you that we’re better off as a couple, no matter what we have to go through to get there.

Her nod gave him hope that she didn’t need more words. Their kiss was so gentle at first it was almost chaste. For the impact that it had on him, it was the most important kiss in his life. With the touch of their lips, the unbearable weight that came with knowing how close he’d been to falling apart and jeopardizing the *Imagine* job lifted. The vice-like tightness that had squeezed his heart at knowing how close she’d come to death, made worse by feeling that the moment was subject to perpetual repetition as long as she continued to do field work, loosened. As he leaned into her, and tasted the woman he loved most in the world, his spirit lightened and all became right in his world.

With her first delicate sigh, he pulled her in closer, certain of one thing. *This battle's just beginning, but I'm going to win.*

Or I'll die trying.

Unfortunately, further complications are coming Leo and Ace's way.

Catch up with them on their next Black Raven job, in *Insertion, A Black Raven Novel.* Available in 2019.

Imagine Book Club Discussion Questions

Since the publication of my first book, one of my greatest thrills has been to talk to readers after they've read my stories. I love the unpredictability of the individual reader's experience with my stories, and I'm often surprised when a reader tells me which elements and themes resonated. Because talking to readers provides such a thrill, I feel extremely fortunate that I've been invited to attend various book club meetings as a guest author while the group discusses one of my novels.

After the first few book club events that I attended, I decided to create discussion questions for the novels. You can find questions related to all the Black Raven books at stellabarcelona.com, on the individual book pages and on the book club questions page. If you select *Imagine* for your book club, you might enjoy these questions with your group:

1) Black Raven agents Sylvia Leon (Leo) and Adam Evans (Ace), the lead characters in *Imagine*, were best friends for two years before their first kiss. Do you believe that one kiss between two friends can dramatically alter a friendship? Was Leo's reaction to their kiss understandable? How about Ace's?
2) Could you envision the cruise ship based upon the author's description? Which scene in the story provided the most memorable images of setting, and why?
3) If you could go on a cruise anywhere in the world, where would it be? Why would you select that location for a cruise, rather than a non-cruising trip?
4) When strategizing how to regain control of the cruise ship, Ace and Leo discuss "Entebbe." Are you familiar with the 1976

hijacking of the Air France flight that was en route from Tel Aviv to Paris, and the rescue mission that followed in Entebbe, Uganda? Does your knowledge of the hijacking come through contemporaneous news reports, historical accounts, movies, or another source? What did you think of the author's use of this real-life event in *Imagine*?

5) What did you think of the story pacing? Discuss the parts of the story that flowed fastest, and slowest, for you.
6) The defining moment in Leo's life that provided motivation for her to become a Black Raven agent involves September 11, 2001. Do you believe that Leo's reaction to the events that occurred on that day was plausible? Where were you on that day? How old were you? How did it affect your life?
7) In one scene in *Imagine*, Leo hears the "Dance of the Sugarplum Fairy" and is almost overcome with emotion. In another scene, she becomes happy when she hears "When the Saints Go Marching In." Do certain songs inspire visceral reactions in you? Which songs, and why?
8) Ace and Leo have a running joke where they limit their eating for a day to foods that start with a certain letter. If you had to choose one letter, and could only eat foods that start with that letter for an entire day, which letter would it be? How long could you go without eating any of those foods? *(A note from the author – I would choose P (pasta, popcorn, potatoes, pizza, etc.) and wouldn't (couldn't!) go more than a couple of days without P foods).*
9) (a) What did you think of Ace and Leo's Christmas gifts to one another? In Leo's letter to Ace, she explains her motivation

behind her gift for Ace; Ace's motivation for the gift that he gives Leo is explained more subtly. Why do you believe Ace gave Leo the gift that he did?

(b) What is the most meaningful gift that you have ever received? On what occasion did you receive it? What made it so meaningful?

10) In terms of Ace and Leo's relationship, did you find the end of *Imagine* satisfying? Did you believe the ending was plausible within the context of their relationship?

11) (a) Have you read other novels in the Black Raven series? If not, did you feel that you understood the world of Black Raven sufficiently to enjoy *Imagine*? If you've read other novels in the series, was your prior knowledge beneficial to your enjoyment of *Imagine*?

(b) Do you read other fiction series? Describe what you enjoy about the series–are there recurring characters, similar plot elements, and/or plots that span several books?

12) If *Imagine* were made into a movie, who do you think would best play Ace? Leo? Which scene(s) provided the most memorable images of the characters and would best translate to film?

Hi there —

Thank you for reading *Imagine*. I hope you enjoyed it. Please help spread the word about *Imagine* by posting a review and by telling your friends about it. If you do take the time to write a review, thank you!

I love to hear from readers. You can find me on Facebook and Instagram, or email me at stella@stellabarcelona.com. You can also reach me through my website, stellabarcelona.com, which has blogs that I update from time to time, some book-related, some not. Book pages on my site have extra information on my novels, including excerpts and book club questions. There is also an "Ask Stella" blog series, where (almost) any question is fair game.

If you'd like to keep up with news from me, you can join my mailing list. Don't worry—I'm too busy to send frequent newsletters, and I promise I won't share your email address. If you'd prefer to use the U.S. mail, I can be reached at P.O. Box 70332, New Orleans, Louisiana, 70172-0332.

Thank you again, and stay in touch!

Stella

p.s. I've lived in and around New Orleans my entire life, and I love to share my city with others. If you're planning a trip here, and looking for ideas of what to do, visit my website for a list of essential things to do in the city and my ten favorite things to do in the French Quarter.

ABOUT THE AUTHOR

In day-to-day life, award-winning author Stella Barcelona is a lawyer and works for a court in New Orleans, Louisiana. Yet she's always had an active imagination, a tendency to daydream, and a passion for reading romance, mysteries, and thrillers. She's found an outlet for all these aspects of herself by writing romantic thrillers. She lives minutes from the French Quarter, with her husband and two adorable papillons who believe they are princesses.

Deceived, Stella's first novel, was inspired by New Orleans, its unique citizens, and the city's World War II-era history. The continuing character of Black Raven Private Security Contractors was first introduced in *Deceived*. Black Raven takes flight in *Shadows*, *Jigsaw*, and *Concierge*–romantic thrillers inspired by current events. Stella is working on the next installation in the Black Raven series, *Insertion*, which will be released in 2019.

Stella loves to hear from readers, and can be reached through Facebook and Instagram. She can also be reached through stellabarcelona.com, which has information about her books, book club questions, release day news, giveaways, and more.